THE CAT AND THE CITY

THE CAT AND THE CITY

NICK BRADLEY

atlantic *fiction*

First published in hardback in Great Britain in 2020 by Atlantic Books, an imprint of Atlantic Books Ltd.

10 9 8 7 6 5 4 3 2 1

A CIP catalogue record for this book is available from the British Library.

Hardback ISBN: 978 1 78649 988 2
Trade paperback ISBN: 978 1 78649 989 9
E-book ISBN: 978 1 78649 990 5

Printed in Great Britain by TJ International Ltd, Padstow, Cornwall

Atlantic Books
An imprint of Atlantic Books Ltd
Ormond House
26–27 Boswell Street
London WC1N 3JZ
www.atlantic-books.co.uk

To my parents, for everything . . .

. . . and my brothers, for the rest

Contents

青猫

萩原朔太郎（大正12年）

この美しい都會を愛するのはよいことだ
この美しい都會の建築を愛するのはよいことだ
すべてのやさしい女性をもとめるために
すべての高貴な生活をもとめるために
この都にきて賑やかな街路を通るのはよいことだ
街路にそうて立つ櫻の竝木
そこにも無數の雀がさへづつてゐるではないか。

ああ　このおほきな都會の夜にねむれるものは
ただ一疋の青い猫のかげだ
かなしい人類の歴史を語る猫のかげだ
われの求めてやまざる幸福の青い影だ。
いかならん影をもとめて
みぞれふる日にもわれは東京を戀しと思ひしに
そこの裏町の壁にさむくもたれてゐる
このひとのごとき乞食はなにの夢を夢みて居るのか。

A Blue Cat

by Hagiwara Sakutaro (1923)
Translation by Nick Bradley

To be in love with this city is a good thing
To love the city's buildings, a good thing
And all those kind women
All those noble lives
Passing through these busy streets
Lined with cherry trees on either side
From whose branches countless sparrows chirp.

Ah! The only thing that can sleep in this vast city night
Is the shadow of a single blue cat
The shadow of a cat that tells the sad history of humanity
The blue shade of happiness I long for.
Forever I chase any shadow,
I thought I wanted Tokyo even on a snowy day
But look there – that cold ragged beggar in the alleyway
Leaning against a wall – what dream is he dreaming?

Tattoo

Kentaro held the hot cup of coffee to his lips and blew at the rising steam. The back office of his tattoo parlour was dimly lit, and the light from his laptop screen gave his dirty white stubble a blueish hue. Reflected in his glasses, a long list of links on an open webpage scrolled up slowly. His hand gripped a Bluetooth mouse, the buttons covered with greasy finger marks. His coffee was still too hot to drink. He put it down, just to the right of a coaster on his desk, and idly scratched his crotch.

He clicked on a link and was faced with a loading bar.

A short pause, then a webcam live stream loaded. The screen showed the interior of someone's bedroom. A small apartment, with lots of legal textbooks on a shelf – perhaps a university student. On the bed a couple was kissing. Naked. Oblivious.

Kentaro sat and watched. Then he unzipped his trousers and reached inside.

The shop's doorbell sounded. Kentaro froze.

'Hello?' a girl's voice called out from the waiting area.

'Sorry, just a minute.' He shut the laptop quickly, composed himself and walked out to greet the customer.

Standing at the doorway was a high-school girl. At first glance there was nothing remarkable about her. She was wearing the typical sailor-style uniform with the standard bobbed haircut and baggy socks. She'd dyed her hair blonde to stand out, but that's what they all did these days. She looked to be in her final year. Probably made some kind of mistake coming in here.

'How may I help you, miss?' Kentaro did his best to put on his customer-care voice.

'I'd like a tattoo, please,' she said, her chin raised high.

'Ah, miss. Excuse me, but how did you find this parlour?'

'A friend recommended it.'

'And your friend is . . . ?'

'That doesn't matter. I want a tattoo.' She made to walk into the rear of the parlour.

Kentaro placed a hand on the wall to stop her. 'Miss, don't be silly. You're too young.'

She looked at his arm. 'I'm eighteen. And don't call me *miss*.'

He lowered his arm awkwardly. 'Have you thought about this properly?'

'Yes, I have.' She looked him in the eye. 'I want a tattoo.'

'Maybe you should go away and give it a few days' thought.'

'I've already thought long and hard about it. I want a tattoo.'

'But maybe there are some things you haven't thought about. You won't be able to go to *onsen*.'

'I don't like hot springs.'

'People will think you're yakuza. Could be a bit scary for a nice young girl like you.'

She rolled her eyes. 'I don't care what people think. I want a tattoo.'

'It's expensive – can cost as much as three million yen.'

'I have money.'

'Listen, I do it the traditional way here – *tebori* – all of it's done by hand. I'm not one of these upstarts you find in Shibuya with their cheating methods. Even the gangsters I tattoo can't handle this kind of pain.'

'Pain, I can handle.' She looked directly at Kentaro, and he saw then something in her eyes, a soft brightness, a light green colour – almost transparent – that he had never seen before in a Japanese person.

'I wonder.' He flipped the sign on the front door over to CLOSED, then gestured for the girl to follow him. 'Come through to the back room and we'll have a chat.'

He flicked on the top lights as they entered the back room, and now the bed-like table his customers lay on was visible, as well as the photos of the various clients he'd had over the years – hissing dragons, gawping koi carp, topless women, Shinto gods and elaborate *kanji* sprawling across the naked backs, buttocks and arms of his customers. Most of whom were yakuza.

Kentaro had learnt his trade from one of the old masters of Asakusa, and was famous for his skill and dedication to his art. He loved nothing better than to tattoo a fresh piece of skin, elaborating scenes from ink onto small spaces of bare flesh. The only thing that came close to the satisfaction of creating a masterpiece on another human was the feeling of dominance over the gangsters he worked on.

'This might hurt a bit,' he'd tell them.

'I can take it,' they would reply.

That's what they all say.

And then he would begin work on them, and he'd feel the pain in their movements, in the subtle shift of their muscles and bodies, in the sound of their gritted teeth, as he gouged away gently at their bodies with his metal needles in the traditional style he had learnt from his old master, leaving his mark on them indefinitely. It gave him great pleasure to think of his mastery over these kings of men, these lords of the criminal underworld. His creative control was supreme; he alone decided the images and stories that would be a part of his client forever – sometimes even after death. If the client donated their skin to the Museum of Pathology it would be cut from their cadaver before cremation, then treated correctly and stored. Many pieces of Kentaro's work were on display behind glass at the museum.

He knew he was the best – as did the yakuza who respected him greatly as an artist. But he'd never had many female customers – not even the female yakuza came to him for their tattoos. They all went elsewhere.

But here was a female customer now, standing right in front of him.

'Where shall I sit?' she asked.

'Oh! Hold on.' He pulled a chair from the corner closer to his own. 'Here, take a seat.'

She sat down gingerly and put her hands in her lap.

'So, what would you like a tattoo of?'

'The city.'

'The city?'

'Tokyo.'

'That's not very . . . *conventional.*'

'So what?' Her eyes flashed again.

'Where do you want it?'

'My back.'

'That's going to be tricky . . .'

'Look, mister. Can you do it or not?'

'Sure. I can. No need to be sassy. I just need to figure out how.' He put his chin on his hand, looked at his closed laptop, then it hit him. 'Oh! Just a minute.'

He opened his laptop and tapped his fingers on the keyboard, impatient for it to come to life again. It did, just in time to depict a girl facing the webcam, bent over, getting pounded hard from behind. The speakers of his laptop let out a low moaning sound.

He closed the browser window as fast as he could.

Kentaro's face was red as hell. He shot a furtive glance at the girl sitting next to him, but she was looking at the photos of his previous customers on the walls. Maybe he'd got away with it. Close shave.

He opened up a new browser and clicked on a saved bookmark that took him to Google Maps. The software loaded up and he typed 'Tokyo' into the search bar. The map zoomed in, and then the city filled the browser window. He clicked on satellite view, then zoomed in further, the detail getting larger and larger. Gridlines of buildings divided by roads, canals winding along thin alleyways, the sprawling bay, and the veins and capillaries of train tracks pumping people throughout the city.

'That's amazing,' she said. 'I want that on my back.'

'No, *that* is impossible,' he said.

'I came to you because you're supposed to be the best.' She sighed. 'I guess they were wrong.'

'No one could do this.'

'I'm sure I could find someone for the right price.'

'It's not about price, it's about skill. I'm one of the few true *horishi* left in Tokyo.'

'So what's stopping you?'

'It'll take time. Could be a year, could be four.' He took off his glasses and rubbed his face with a sweaty palm.

'I've got time.'

'It'll be painful too.' He fought back a smirk.

'I told you already: pain is not an issue.'

'You'll have to get naked and lie face down on the table.'

'Sure.' She began to unbutton her shirt straight away with no hint of shyness.

Kentaro felt a hot twist in his stomach and quickly looked down at the floor. He ran to the bathroom to get some baby oil. It definitely wasn't necessary, but he'd had an idea that he would use it as an excuse to touch her body. He imagined his master who'd trained him when he was an apprentice – he'd be turning in his grave seeing him pulling this baby-oil trick. When he came back into the main room she was already naked, lying face down on the table. Kentaro couldn't quite believe his eyes. Her skin was perfection, unblemished. The muscles of her lower back led perfectly down to her round buttocks, swelling briefly into powerful thighs. He swallowed as he walked towards her.

'Uh, I just need to rub your back with oil.'

'Whatever.' She shifted slightly.

He squeezed out a glob of the oil onto his right hand – the bottle made a farting sound, which he almost apologized for, then thought better of it. He snapped the cap back on and began to rub the oil into her skin. It glistened under the lights, and the heat he'd felt in his stomach earlier began to spread downwards.

'So . . . what's your name?'

'Naomi.'

'Mmm . . . Naomi . . . Pretty name. And . . . do you have a boyfriend?'

She rolled over slightly to face Kentaro and looked straight at him again, her eyes a soft flash of green. He could see her breasts.

'Look, mister. I'm not gonna put up with any funny stuff. I came here for a tattoo, and that's all I want. I saw you looking at some weird stuff on your laptop earlier, and I'm fine with that – each to their own – you know. I don't know how that couple would feel about you spying on them through their webcam though. Maybe that's something you should have a think about. But I'm not gonna have you perving on me. I'm paying you for a service, so be a professional. Okay?'

Kentaro held his oily hands limply in the air. 'Spying? Webcams? I don't know what you're—'

'Save the bullshit. I don't want to hear it.' She lay back down. 'And by the way, your flies are undone.'

Kentaro looked down at his trousers, did up his flies, then got to work.

⁂

Work was something Kentaro had always been good at. He could concentrate for hours at a time – the client usually asking for a break before he himself ever grew tired. When he was tattooing a customer, he threw everything he had into the task, and his work had always been highly praised by fellow artists.

Naomi came to visit him over the course of several months, whenever she had the time. And he was always glad to see her. He had some superfine needles especially made by the best knife-seller in Asakusa.

He began inking out the entire city all over her back, shoulders, arms, buttocks and thighs. He started with the roads, the outlines of buildings, the rivers – tracing the outline before he even started thinking about the colouring of the tattoo. He had to complete the ghostly shell-like skeleton of Tokyo, and only once this was finished could he begin shading and colouring. The entire tattoo would take a couple of years to complete and would require regular visits over that period, in which he would work on a portion each time – there was also the small matter of how much pain the customer could take in a single session.

He jumped straight into the task of inking the city, which he always did in the traditional *tebori* manner, carving and inking lines deeply into Naomi's skin with his metal needles. She was truly one of the toughest customers he'd ever had. She didn't even blink at the pain. He used a pair of loupes attached to his glasses to draw the finest of detail in the tattoo and created microscopic features of the city, which retained its overall structure when viewed from afar.

Kentaro struggled only in one matter: it was impossible for him to hold the entire city in his mind while he worked. He would have to work on small levels and refer to a zoomed-in portion on his laptop. Unlike all his previous designs, which he had been able to visualize fully while working, the size and scale of the macroscopic city was just too much to retain in any human brain.

It took several visits to ink the outline. The last part he finished was his very own parlour in Asakusa. He planned on leaving the roof of his parlour blank as the final space to sign his name – keeping to tradition.

Once he had completed the outline of the city in black ink, he then faced colouring, the shading and the detail. He decided to start with Shibuya.

'Hmmm.' He paused in thought.

'What's wrong?' Naomi asked, lifting her head.

'Oh, I'm just trying to decide whether to have people actually *crossing* the intersection at the Shibuya scramble crossing, or whether to have them waiting for the green light.'

'I don't want any people.'

'What do you mean?'

She lowered her head back to the table and closed her eyes. 'I just want the city. I don't want any people.'

'But it won't be a city without people.'

'I don't care. It's my back, it's my tattoo. I'm paying.'

'Hmmm.'

Kentaro felt a twinge of pride. It was true that Naomi had paid regularly, and was a good customer. But he was one of the finest tattooists in Tokyo. His customers agreed to *his* designs. They never told him what to do. His inner artist flared, but as the Japanese saying went: *kyaku-sama wa kami-sama desu* – the customer is a god.

Well. She had said no *people*. Animals weren't people, were they?

He smiled to himself and shaded in a small cat – two blobs of colour, like a calico – just opposite the statue of Hachiko the dog in Shibuya. And then he went about his work.

⁂

It was during the shading of the tattoo that Kentaro really began to lose his mind.

Naomi would talk during their sessions, asking him to describe the parts of the city he was working on. She would tell him the season she wanted for each location, and he would then colour the maple trees red for autumn, or the bright yellow of the gingko trees, or shade in the soft pinkish white of the sakura in Ueno Park in spring.

'Where are you now?' she'd ask.

'Ginza. I've just done the Nakagin building.'

'Good. It's winter in Ginza.'

'I see.' And he would begin shading and colouring the fine white snow that had fallen overnight. The city was becoming like a patchwork quilt of the seasons.

Often when Kentaro had been working on a part of Tokyo and talking to Naomi about that place, she would come back for her next session having visited that part of the city. She would bring a small present or souvenir for him – sweets from Harajuku, gyoza from Ikebukuro – and he would feel his face going red in embarrassment.

They'd sometimes drink green tea together and she would tell him stories of things that had happened, or things she'd seen – how the building of the new Olympic stadium was progressing each time she walked past it – she told Kentaro stories of all the people she saw going about their lives in the city, and he would listen quietly without interrupting.

One time, during a break in a session that had gone on for hours, as Kentaro was cleaning his instruments, Naomi had pointed at a large art book of Utagawa Kuniyoshi ukiyo-e prints and asked about it. Kentaro had got it down from the shelf and let her take it to an armchair and sit down with it. Utagawa had always been an artistic inspiration for Kentaro – his master had introduced his work to him and had made him practise for months copying Utagawa's paintings before he was allowed to even touch a piece of skin. Naomi sat with the book on her lap, turning the pages slowly.

'These are so great,' said Naomi, examining each painting in detail, her finger on the page sometimes tracing the lines of numerous cats and skeleton demons.

'He was a legend.' Kentaro sighed.

'I love this one.' She tapped her finger on the page, and Kentaro looked across to see the courtly scene with a ghostly cat head floating in the background. Cats stood on their hindlegs and danced like humans with handkerchiefs on their heads and arms flung wide.

'Yeah.' Kentaro swallowed a chuckle at the thought of the trick he had played on Naomi by tattooing the cat on her back.

'And look at these ones.' She held up the book to him. 'He's turned these kabuki actors into cats!'

'Now that's an interesting story,' said Kentaro, pausing while putting away his tools and coming over to look at the book over Naomi's shoulder.

'Go on.' She looked up at him with her strange eyes.

'Well, back then, kabuki had become a raucous and decadent affair – almost like an orgy.'

'Fun,' she said, grinning cheekily.

'Well, the government didn't think so. They outlawed any artistic depictions of kabuki actors.'

'That's crazy!'

'It is. Anyway, Utagawa replaced the human actors with cats. That was his way of sidestepping the censorship.'

'Clever guy.' She glanced back down at the image of three cats dressed in kimono, sitting around a low table playing shamisen.

'My old master was obsessed with him.'

'Where is your master now?'

'He passed on.' Kentaro pointed at a photo on the wall. 'That's him.'

Naomi looked at the photo of the gruff-looking man standing with a younger Kentaro in front of the same tattoo parlour they were both in now. 'Looks kind of serious.'

'He was. So strict. Had me waking up at 4 a.m. and sweeping and cleaning the parlour all day. Wouldn't let me so much as touch a needle or a bit of skin until I'd done that for two years. Mad old bastard.' He shook his head and smiled.

Naomi gazed at Kentaro thoughtfully. 'How come you don't have a disciple?'

He sighed, softly, without the usual condescension. 'Where to begin . . .'

'At the beginning?' She shrugged.

'Well, the government did another great job of giving *irezumi* a bad name – just like the old kabuki censorship. They've associated the practice with criminals, so fewer people want to get into the trade. You know, it was once an honourable thing to get a tattoo in the old days – it was the mark of a fireman. The public loved and respected firemen – not like these crude gangsters who show off their tattoos these days. Anyway, I'm getting off the point . . . what was I saying?'

'You were saying why no one wants to be a *horishi* anymore.'

'Oh, yes. Now, of course you've got your amateurs in Shibuya who use all this new-fangled technology to tattoo. No one wants to learn the old *tebori* method. No one wants to do hard work. Everyone wants to do things the easy way. But none of them are true artists.'

'Like you.' She smiled at him.

Kentaro blushed and looked at the floor. 'Come on, Naomi,' he said, finishing his tea. 'We'd best continue.'

And that was the day it first happened.

When Kentaro was halfway through colouring the tattoo, his eyes happened to pass over the Shibuya section of the city that he had already completed. He saw the statue of Hachiko the dog, his eyes carried on to the shopping streets of Harajuku, but then something clicked in his mind. He flicked his eyes back to the statue.

The cat was gone.

He blinked and shook his head. Maybe tiredness was finally getting to him. But he looked again: no, the cat was not there anymore.

Perhaps he had imagined drawing the cat on her body? Yes, that was the simplest explanation for its absence. He had probably dreamt of drawing the little cat in, and it had seemed so vivid he had imagined it to be reality. Yes. Everything was surely fine. Dreams could sometimes invade reality, couldn't they?

But that very same day, when he was about to shade the area around Tokyo Tower, he caught sight of something that gave him a cold shiver. He was making his way with his eyes up the street from Hamamatsucho Station towards the area around Tokyo Tower. And just down a side street branching off the main road, he saw the cat.

'What the . . .'

'Is everything all right?' Naomi stirred.

'Oh, yes,' he replied. The needle in his hand was shaking a bit, but he steadied himself. Perhaps he had misremembered the location he had originally put the cat in. Surely that was the explanation. He ignored the cat and began to work again, colouring the red and white pattern of Tokyo Tower.

But the next session, before working, he searched for the cat in the side streets near Hamamatsucho Station again, and could not find it. And then when he was colouring in the trees of Inokashira Park in Kichijoji, he saw the cat lurking by the lake in the middle of the park.

It was definitely moving.

Kentaro began to dread his regular sessions with Naomi. He couldn't begin work until he had first found the cat, and he would sometimes spend an hour scouring the city in search of it before he could get to work with his needles and ink. This, in turn, was delaying the overall progress of the tattoo, which had begun to take longer than he had planned. Naomi never commented on how much time he took, and gradually their sessions grew exhausting as he became haunted by the spectre of the cat. He would dream about it roaming the city, and he would spend most of the night in a waking nightmare, sweating in dread at the scramble to find the elusive cat. *Can't catch me*, the cat taunted, blinking its steady green eyes at him. *Stupid old man. Can't can't can't.* He wanted to grab it by the scruff of the neck and shake it, carve it out, pluck it clean away from his work – *his* art, *his* Tokyo and *his* Naomi most of all.

Because she *was* his, wasn't she? Sprawled out before him day after day.

One session, he spent most of the afternoon looking for the cat, scanning the streets and alleyways, but it was nowhere to be found. The relief soaked over him like warm water – he must have been imagining the cat's existence from the beginning.

But as his eyes flickered through Roppongi his heart fell: the cat was there, emerging from a subway exit. Its tail raised high, as though taunting him.

He only managed thirty minutes of hurried work on the tattoo that day before Naomi had to leave.

▲
▲▲

It was when Kentaro was nearing the end of his work on her that he understood what he must do. He had black rings under his eyes; he had lost his appetite, was finding it hard to swallow food and had grown skeletally thin. His dirty stubble had grown out into a shaggy beard, and his eyes, like black inked dots sunken deeply into his skull, stared vacantly at the walls of his parlour. Even before, he'd rarely gone out much or been hugely social. He'd usually spent most of his time on the Internet, looking at art books or drawing and painting designs on paper. But now he made his way along the old streets of Asakusa, muttering to himself as he went. He walked quickly, bumping into a homeless man wearing a purple bandana. Kentaro lost his temper and shouted uncontrollably at the stranger, who apologized profusely until he continued on his way. He bought a knife from the famous blade master of Asakusa he always visited. The blade master looked at him a little strangely, but didn't comment on his haggard appearance or the fact that Kentaro usually bought only needles from him, never blades.

Kentaro took the knife home and sharpened it. He tested the blade against his finger and it drew a burst of blood from his skin with only the slightest pressure. He taped the knife to the underside of the table, where Naomi wouldn't see it. And he waited.

Naomi came for what they both knew would be her final session, undressing quickly as usual. Kentaro did his best to act naturally as she talked to him about a summer fireworks festival she had been to, showing him photos of the yukata she had picked out. He nodded and smiled, pretending to listen.

He worked well, in a kind of giddy contentment that this waking nightmare would soon be coming to an end. He finished a final section of shading Kita-Senju on her arm, then he cast his eyes around the Asakusa area, looking for that last blank space to fill – the roof of his very own tattoo parlour. He traced his way from the Kaminari gate at Sensoji Temple to his parlour. Here's what he would do: he'd sign his name on the roof of the building declaring the tattoo as finished. And then he would reach for his knife and begin.

But as soon as he went to sign his name, he saw the cat sitting outside his shop.

He knew then, with a terrible certainty, that if he were to glance up from the tattoo on Naomi's body and look outside the door, he would see the cat sitting there, its green eyes watching him.

He gulped and closed his eyes.

The city was still there though. Like he was seeing it from space. His mind's eye was a camera looking down on it. Then the camera began to zoom in, down onto the globe, onto Japan, onto Tokyo, all the way down to street level. It flew through the red roof of his tattoo parlour, and there he saw himself working on Naomi's perfect back, on the tattoo of the city. The camera didn't stop. He'd lost control. It flew once again into the tattoo, and kept going down: through Japan, through Tokyo, into Asakusa, through the roof of his parlour and into the tattoo once more. And on and on endlessly.

Unless he opened his eyes, he would be stuck like this. Looping round and round, zooming in on the city forever, trapped. But he kept them shut.

For when he opened them, he would see that there was no longer space for him to sign his name in the roof of his parlour. It would be filled with a real red roof. He'd be faced with a city, with the millions and millions of people moving in and around, through subway stations and buildings, parks and highways, living their lives. The city pumped their shit around in pipes, it transported their bodies around in metal containers, and it held their secrets, their hopes, their dreams. And he'd no longer be sitting on the other side watching through a screen. He'd be part of it too. He'd be one of those people.

With his eyes still shut, he reached under the table, hand scrambling desperately for the knife.

He trembled as he opened his eyes.

The muscles in Naomi's back flexed and came to life.

And so too, did the city.

Fallen Words

'There once was a shrewd antique dealer named Gozaemon.'

Ohashi paused, and his eyes gleamed in the low light. He had tied back his grey hair under a purple bandana, and wore his beard long and shaggy on his wrinkled face. A thin man, for his age, but with just a tiny paunch belly forming, he knelt on a cushion with his hands held in front of him, in the customary stance of the *rakugoka*.

'He was a sly and cunning man,' he continued, his voice echoing softly around the silent room, *'who thought nothing of disguising himself as a poor monk and visiting the houses of the elderly, on the hunt for treasures to sell in his antiques shop at hiked-up prices.'*

Ohashi had performed *rakugo* in crowded venues, to the rich and poor, and every time he treated each story as if it were his last – as though his words might be carried into the crowd on his dying breath. He had selected today's story specifically for his current audience. He cleared his throat and continued.

'One day, after swindling a woman of an expensive bookcase, this crooked man Gozaemon stopped by a sweet dumpling shop to eat. He sat on a stool outside the shop and waited for his food. As he was waiting, he spied a dirty old cat lapping milk from a bowl. But it was not the cat that interested him. The bowl, which the cat lapped greedily from, was an antique – one he was certain he could sell for 300 gold pieces. Gozaemon felt a cool sweat and the familiar sense of excitement at the prospect of a steal. He composed himself as the old woman who owned the shop came out with his food.'

When Ohashi took on the words of his characters, his voice and mannerisms transformed completely, so one would think the character he was portraying had possessed him. When he played Gozaemon, he shifted to face the right, clasped his hands together and spoke glibly. When he played the old woman he shifted to the left, hunched over and contorted his features, appearing to have aged thirty years in a split second. He faced the audience in between these snippets of dialogue to perform the jovial voice of the narrator.

'"What a lovely cat you have," said Gozaemon.

"What? That old mog?" replied the old woman in surprise.

"Yes. It's a darling cat." Gozaemon knelt down to pet the cat. It hissed at him, back arching. "Reminds me of my own, who sadly . . . no, it's too painful to even talk about . . . My children loved that old cat so . . ."

Gozaemon pretended to stifle a sob, and the old woman tilted her head to one side.

"Perhaps . . . Oh, it would be too much to ask." He looked up.

"What?" asked the old woman, jutting out her lower lip.

"Well, would you be willing to sell this cat?"

"That old flea bag?"

"Yes, this charming cat."

"I'm not sure. It keeps mice away from my shop."

"I would be willing to pay . . ." said Gozaemon, his voice wavering slightly.

"Oh yeah?" The woman raised an eyebrow.

"Three . . . no, two gold pieces?"

"You said three."

"All right, you drive a hard bargain, madam. Three it is."

"Done."

Gozaemon smiled. He handed the old woman three gold pieces, then knelt down to pick up the cat, who promptly bit him on the hand. But Gozaemon ignored the pain. He swooped down on his real target, the expensive bowl the cat had been drinking from.

"Oi," the woman said sharply. "What you doing?"

"Oh, just taking the cat's bowl."

"Why?"

"The cat will need it."

"I'll give you another one." And she went inside her shop, coming out with a cheap old thing. She wiped it on her apron, leaving a brown smear.

"But surely the cat will miss its own, ah, special bowl."

"That cat will drink from anything. Besides, you can't have that bowl. It's worth 300 gold pieces."

Gozaemon was shocked, but did his best to hide it.

"Three hundred gold pieces? That's an awfully expensive bowl to let a cat drink from."

"Yes, but it helps me sell mangy cats for three gold pieces a pop."

The old woman gave a sly grin.'

Ohashi let the end of his story fall perfectly. He bowed low to his audience and smiled. He wiped the perspiration from his brow. It had been a flawless rendition of 'Neko no sara' – 'The Cat's Dish'.

His audience let out a meow.

Ohashi got up from his filthy cushion and walked towards the calico cat. It had been sitting silently all the while. The only audience member today, watching upright with its paws down in front – the same stance as Ohashi's, when he had performed his tale. He gave the cat a little scratch behind the ear.

'Now, let's get you something to eat.'

They left the meeting room of the abandoned capsule hotel and walked through the decaying corridors to where Ohashi slept. It was dark in the old hotel, but Ohashi had been squatting here so long he could navigate through the place with his eyes closed. The cat, similarly, had no problems. The dark also helped hide some of the hotel's more disagreeable elements: the fungi that grew on the walls, the rotten floorboards, the peeling wallpaper and the ghoulish faces on the old Kirin beer advertisement posters, smiling faces torn to shreds, curling away slowly over time.

It had been the cat that first led Ohashi to the empty hotel ten months ago, when he'd been lost in the city, looking for somewhere to sleep. Ohashi had been shivering under a bridge on a freezing night when the little cat had licked him on the hand, looked him in the eye and then walked on a few paces before stopping to wait for the old man to follow. The hotel had closed many years ago, and no one had bothered with it since. Another victim of the burst bubble economy – too much supply and not enough demand. If he'd told the story to anyone, they wouldn't have believed him, but the cat had saved his life.

Now, the cat and Ohashi walked through rows of empty capsules: tiny sleeping pods stacked one on top of the other. Each was like a truncated coffin, with a small curtain to pull across at bedtime to cover the entrance. Drunk salarymen of more decadent times would've slept here after missing their last trains home. But now the capsules were unused – all except one.

Ohashi ducked inside his capsule to turn on a small battery-powered lamp. Surrounded by empty spaces, he'd decorated the inside of his little pod with old photos, carefully curated to remind him of better times. The photos depicted a younger, slimmer Ohashi, performing *rakugo* dressed in a stylish kimono, signing autographs, greeting fans, appearing on television, meeting famous people – from the days when he'd been able to fill theatres and hang out with movie stars and artists. From the days before.

He kept his old family photos in a copy of *No Longer Human* by Dazai Osamu, and rarely opened the book to look at them anymore. He'd never really liked Dazai Osamu much, anyway.

Kneeling on his futon, he reached inside the capsule and pulled out some canned fish from a shopping bag, popped the ring-pull open, and placed it on the floor for the cat. The cat meowed and nibbled at the fish while Ohashi stroked it idly and flicked through a newspaper.

After eating its fill, the cat watched Ohashi holding the newspaper and staring off into thin air. But the cat wanted his attention. It rubbed its head against Ohashi's baggy sleeves and trousers, marking him with its scent, a gesture Ohashi understood to mean *you're mine*. He dug out a salmon onigiri from the same bag, peeled off the wrapper and chomped at it slowly, washing it down with a cold bottle of wheat tea from the same bag.

'We'll go out for a wander in a minute, you and I,' he said to the cat, speaking between mouthfuls. 'And then I might meet some friends this evening.'

The cat licked its paw and blinked.

Ohashi slipped out quietly through the window into the back alley – the way he always came in and out of the capsule hotel, the same way the cat had first shown him. He never used the front door, so as not to arouse suspicion from the police, or the nosier inhabitants of the neighbourhood. He let the cat out too. It went roaming by itself during the day, on the hunt for better food than Ohashi could provide.

Ohashi also went out during the day to hunt.

He crossed the road, slipped down an alleyway and pulled the blue tarpaulin off the wooden cart he'd painstakingly made from bits of wood and two old bicycle wheels. He pushed it out onto the main streets, and the wheels made the familiar rattle that accompanied him when he went foraging.

He spent his days scouring the city for cans to recycle. He rummaged in small bins placed next to the hundreds of thousands of vending machines dotted throughout the streets of Tokyo. He would empty each bin, and flatten the aluminium cans with a heavy metal cudgel to fit more in his cart. It had become a mechanical routine, punctuated by the rattling wheels of his cart and the *clang clang* of the cudgel crushing cans against the pavement. When he'd collected as many as he could, he would smash them down even smaller, pack them up in bags and take them to a weighing station in exchange for money.

The streets had been a maze to him when he'd first begun this life. The endless convenience stores and chain restaurants all blended into one long street, which threaded its way in and out of the skyscrapers of Shinjuku, the clothes shops of Harajuku, through the department stores of Ginza, all the way out to the high-rise apartment blocks that lined Tokyo Bay. Walking the city wasn't something he'd ever had to do in his old life – he'd always taken taxis, or ridden the subway – but now he had to navigate the entire city on foot, and it had taken him a while to get his bearings.

Tokyo gyrated around him at such a high speed these days. The cars whisked by, the trains zoomed overhead, even the people swarming out of the subways zipped past him as he pushed his cart slowly through the streets. In his old life, he'd been one of those fast movers, unafraid of the pace and pulse of Tokyo. But now, he could no longer board the subways or ride the elevators to the tops of skyscrapers to admire the views. Now these skyscrapers served only as landmarks on the horizon to get his orientation. Those beautiful sunset views of the city from high were a fading memory. When he closed his eyes to picture the city these days, he could only see it from street level.

After a long day collecting cans, with bent back and tired feet, he stopped by a Lawson convenience store and approached the rear entrance. He sat down on the pavement by his cart and waited patiently. Right on time, the door opened and a boy in his late teens walked out. He was wearing the blue and white striped Lawson uniform.

'Ohashi-san!' the boy called out.

'Ah! Makoto-kun.' He stood to greet the boy. 'How are you today? How are your studies?'

'Oh, fine, fine.' The boy looked tired, and ran an awkward hand through his slightly unkempt hair. Ohashi liked that he didn't spike it with gel like most of the other kids his age. Makoto held a plastic bag slightly out of sight in his other hand.

'Excellent. And you'll graduate soon?' Ohashi stood very straight and still, hands held formally at his sides, his body positioned in front of his cart as if trying to hide it.

'Yes. Well, I just did.'

'So, what's next?'

'I've applied for an internship at a legal department in a big PR company that's dealing with the Olympics.' Makoto shrugged. 'My parents' idea.'

'They must be proud of you. And I am too.'

Makoto smiled, and then remembered the plastic bag hanging awkwardly from the fingers of his other hand. 'Oh, here you are.' The bag clinked as he handed it over. 'It's not much, but this is all I could get for you this week.'

'Makoto-kun! This is more than enough, thank you so much.'
Ohashi began rifling through the contents: tins of fish, bottles of
wheat tea and onigiri – all out of date and due to be thrown away. He
paused when his hand brushed against a bottle of alcohol. 'Ah . . .
Makoto-kun?'

'Yes?'

'This shochu . . . I'm afraid, I don't need it.' He took the bottle
from the bag.

'Sorry. I forgot you didn't . . . Well, you can take it anyway. Perhaps
one of your friends might like it?'

'I'd rather not, if it's all the same to you.' Ohashi held out the
bottle to Makoto. 'I'm sorry. I don't mean to be ungrateful. I can't . . .
Why don't you have it? You're a . . . good . . . um . . .'

There was an awkward silence as Ohashi looked at the wall,
avoiding Makoto's eyes.

'Well . . . if you're sure you don't want it.' Makoto took the bottle.

'Thank you so much, Makoto-kun. Have a lovely evening.'

'You too, Ohashi-san. Will I see you next week?'

'That sounds perfect, if it's not too much trouble.'

'Take care.'

'Goodbye.'

Ohashi hung the bag from a hook on his cart and pushed it down
the street away from the convenience store. Makoto looked on until
the older man had turned a corner out of view. He thought for a
moment about how sad it was to see a good man like that, down on
his luck. Always so polite and formal. He looked a bit like Gen from
the Street Fighter II series with his grey beard and hair.

He shook his head, and then went back into the shop.

▲▲

In the evenings, after a hard day of work, Ohashi would meet up with
his friends at the camp – a little village of blue tarpaulins and cardboard boxes nestled by the train tracks in a park only the homeless
visited. Those who lived there made an effort to keep the camp

orderly – anyone not tidy enough would likely be ejected. The smell in winter was not so overpowering, but in the height of summer, local residents complained about the odour of urine. The trains that rumbled by served as a kind of clock tower for the community, the clanks of the wheels on the tracks a constant reminder of time passing. Those who lived in the camp kept to themselves, living quietly, and, for the most part, the police left them alone.

Ohashi made his way along the neat rows of compact houses, looking for his buddies.

'Over here!' a voice called out to him.

He turned to see a group of three men huddled around a small fire beneath one of the few trees in the park. He strolled towards them, gait dignified.

'Evening, gentlemen,' said Ohashi. He took off his shoes, placed them with the others, and sat down on the blue tarpaulin they'd laid out. Four pairs of shoes were now neatly lined up on the grass.

Shimada greeted Ohashi with a little nod and his usual serious expression.

'Evening, Ohashi-san.' Taka's round face was set in its permanent warm smile.

'What have you been up to today?' asked Hori, thin and toothy.

'Same old. How have you fellows been?' Ohashi took a bottle of wheat tea from his bag and offered some to the group. They all declined, and knew Ohashi well enough by now not to offer any of their saké in return.

'Went to church,' said Shimada.

'Got some free food,' said Hori.

'Nourishment for the soul,' said Taka wistfully.

'Yeah . . . that, and soup.' Hori laughed.

A train clattered past, halting the conversation temporarily.

'You should come too, Ohashi. Get some free grub.'

'Yes, Ohashi-san. The Lord always has space in his heart for you.' Taka's eyes pleaded.

'Oh, I'm all right,' Ohashi replied, looking awkwardly at the dancing flames in the middle of the group as if there were something there that required urgent attention. He cast around, searching for anything, his eyes eventually falling on the cross Taka wore around his neck.

Ohashi allowed himself to recall the one time they'd convinced him to come to the church. Hori and Shimada just turned up and pretended to be good Christians, but Taka really believed it all, deep down. It had made Ohashi sad to see all these men, down on their luck, jumping through hoops to get some free food. Before getting fed they had to listen to a preacher with a cheap suit and slicked-back hair talk about how Jesus had died to save everyone. The preacher had said, without a trace of doubt, how the people of Hiroshima and Nagasaki had paid for their sins. Ohashi couldn't believe his ears for a second when he heard that. Could this man really be saying such a dreadful thing? Did he actually believe the words coming from his mouth? Ohashi had never gone back after that. It made him sick to think of Christians preying on the poor men while they were at their lowest, feeding them with slop food and even worse ideas. Buddhists would never do that. Then there were all those condescending women serving miso soup in the yard afterwards. Ohashi could tell from the way they wouldn't make eye contact, the way they wrinkled their noses, that they hated the smell and unkempt looks of the homeless men. They only served the soup to tell themselves they were good people – it was obvious.

'There were some rumours floating around,' said Shimada.

'Oh?' Ohashi looked at Shimada, whose serious face was cast down.

Shimada looked up. 'They're cracking down on the homeless in the city.'

'How so?' Ohashi shifted his weight to get comfortable and took a sip of wheat tea.

'Olympics,' said Hori. 'Go on, Shimada. You tell him.'

'Well . . .' Shimada drank some saké. 'People disappearing off the streets. Like, Tanimoto, remember? No one knows where he is. Gone. Haven't seen him in weeks. Disappeared. Something's going on, since they announced the Olympics. Knocking down old buildings, building new stadiums. They're cleaning the streets. Tidying the place up, you know. Getting rid of *undesirables*.' He snorted. 'The city's changing.'

The conversation paused again as another train clattered past, right on time.

'Maybe Tanimoto-san went back home to his family?' said Taka, continuing their conversation.

'People don't just go home after *this* life,' said Shimada. He raised his grubby palm. 'This dirt . . . it doesn't wash off. We're less than human now, even to our families.'

Ohashi looked blankly at the sky as the other three sipped on their drinks.

'I heard they're putting people in vans and taking them away,' said Hori.

'Who said that? Did they see the vans?' asked Ohashi.

'Dunno. But there are rumours, you know.'

'Where would they be taking them?'

'Who knows . . .' said Shimada.

'Fishy,' said Ohashi, looking off into the distance.

'Like Taka's breath.' Hori grinned toothily.

The four of them sat around the fire, sipping on their drinks, staring thoughtfully at the flames. Then a loud voice from the shadows snapped them from their collective meditations.

'Oi!'

'Oh shit,' muttered Shimada.

'Urgh.' Hori shook his head.

Ohashi felt his mood drop.

'What are you bastards doing?' A large, lumbering figure approached the fire, not quite visible yet, looming closer and closer.

'Nothing,' said Hori.

'Whaddya mean *nothing*? Looks like you're doing *something* to me. What's that you're drinking?'

'I've some wheat tea here, if you'd like, Keita-san,' said Ohashi.

'Pffftt. Wheat tea! Who needs that rubbish? Unless you've mixed it with something.' Keita's burly features were visible now, his pockmarked skin catching the faint light flickering from the fire. He peered at Ohashi, and Ohashi held his dull gaze.

'I'm afraid I don't drink alcohol,' said Ohashi, despite being certain Keita already knew this.

'Rubbish. I've seen you drunk as a skunk, pissing your pants,' said Keita.

'I think you must be mistaken,' said Ohashi coolly.

'Calling me a liar?' Keita had manoeuvred his way behind Shimada and found the large plastic bottle of cheap saké the group had been sharing. 'Here we are. That's what I'm talking about.'

He picked up the bottle, took off the top and began to glug down the alcohol in massive gulps. The hand that gripped the bottle was missing two fingers – the ring and pinky.

'Hey, steady on! That's to share,' said Hori.

Keita stopped and wiped saké from his mouth, staring back at Hori in irritation.

'Yeah, and I was just taking *my* share. Stingy bastard.'

Ohashi held up his hand. 'Come on, I'm sure there's enough for—'

'No one asked you.' Keita turned towards Ohashi. 'Who the hell do you think you are anyway?'

'I'm just trying to—'

'You don't even live here. I see you about, acting like you're better than everyone else. Coming and going like you're some kind of big shot.'

'I honestly—'

'You think you're better than us. And you slink off at night without telling anyone where you're going. Are you even homeless? I bet you've got somewhere to live, probably even got a girlfriend cooking you meals, and you just come down here to sponge off us poor buggers.'

Ohashi was shaking slightly.

Taka spoke up for him. 'Keita, Ohashi didn't mean to be rude. He was just—'

'I don't care what he was trying to do. He should watch himself.'

'Are you threatening me?' Ohashi fixed his eyes on Keita.

Keita replaced the cap on the saké and tossed it aside. He yanked up his sleeve, revealing his gang tattoo. Then he reached into his pocket and pulled out a huge mobile phone, which looked like a relic of the 1980s. There was an unsettling glint in Keita's eyes whenever he produced the phone. There was something decidedly convincing in his embracement of the role of yakuza thug.

'All I'm saying is, don't mess with me, okay?' said Keita. 'All it takes is one call to the family, and they'll come sort things out.'

Keita stared back at Ohashi, until Ohashi dropped his eyes, shaking his head.

'Gentlemen, I think I'll take my leave. Have a lovely evening.'

'Don't go, Ohashi,' said Shimada. 'It's still early.'

'Thank you, but I'm tired from work today.' Ohashi put on his shoes and picked up his shopping bag. 'Have a lovely evening.'

As he walked away he could still hear their voices slowly fading in the distance.

'Keita, why do you always have to act like that?'

'What? He started it! He's such a snob. He thinks he's better than everyone else.'

'He's a nice guy.'

'He gives me the creeps. I don't trust anyone who doesn't drink.'

'Oh come on.'

'And what's with that purple bandana? Looks like a tit.'

Ohashi felt relief only when he had made his way through the empty streets, crept back into the hotel and slumped down in his capsule. He covered himself up with his blankets and fell asleep.

▲▲

Ohashi fed the cat and ate his paltry breakfast of onigiri and wheat tea, then slipped out of the hotel to begin another day looking for cans.

Trudging time was a difficult part of the day for Ohashi. The act of walking, the rhythm of it always made his mind jump back and forth between memories. Scenes from his childhood would shift into his high-school days, which would bleed into his life as an apprentice *rakugoka*.

26

Performing had been his life; now it was gone. What would the old master who'd once trained him think of him now?

These were the kinds of thoughts Ohashi avoided. All those memories led to the same abyss. Instead, he tried to think about his friends at the camp.

They all had their histories, their secrets. But there was a mantra in the community: *the past is the past*. And none of them ever talked about it. They had already paid any debts they owed for what they had done. By living as outcasts, they paid every day. That was their punishment.

But there were certain things Ohashi could infer from his friends.

Christian Taka slept with a doll, and sometimes he let his Tokyo speech slip into Kyushu dialect. Ohashi had some theories about Taka's doll, but he tried not to dwell on them. Serious Shimada didn't talk much, unless he had something important to say, which Ohashi liked. Toothy Hori from Osaka always turned everything into a joke. But that was important to the group. If they couldn't laugh at life, what was the point?

And Keita . . . Well, Keita. Ohashi felt bad to admit this, but he would rather that Keita wasn't there at all. He had those tattoos, and he was missing fingers, so they all knew he'd been yakuza at some point. And that mobile phone he carried around and threatened everyone with was so clunky it was almost laughable. And why did he never use it, even when he was attacked by youths? Still, Keita was a fierce fighter and handled himself better than most of the other homeless men.

Because sometimes they got beaten up.

It was no big deal to them now. Young punks would come by for a bit of fun after drinking. The worst thing was to be caught alone. That was when the harshest beatings were dealt out. The youngsters would gang up on a single homeless guy and just keep kicking and punching. It would carry on until they ran out of energy. The first time Ohashi had been beaten, he'd noticed as the blows went on they started not to feel so bad. It was like weathering a storm – the wind and rain had to let up eventually. Something began to numb him from the pain, or the punks started to lose energy.

Either way, the pain lessened as the beating went on. It was better to relax the body and not resist, then there would be fewer broken bones. The worst was if they kicked a tooth out. That made eating harder. Ohashi did his best to protect his head from the attacks. But then a foot or a fist or an elbow would catch him in the testicles. And then that was a whole new pain that ate away at his stomach from the insides.

Whenever Ohashi went out collecting cans, he tried his best to look around the streets and take in his surroundings. To view the things in the scenery that he felt to be beautiful, the small things that gave him pleasure. The sun rising in the morning, edging its way through the gaps between the buildings, the hazy sky that obscured the tops of the skyscrapers in the distance, the clouds that formed patterns that looked like a clowder of cats chasing one another. Life still had some pleasure for him, no matter how small.

He'd watch the people walking past too. He did his best not to be noticed, and most turned their heads away from him whenever he passed by. There were the odd few who would stare, as if he'd done something wrong, or mutter under their breath, 'Get a job' . . . that kind of thing. But most of the people he passed on the street would be going about their solitary lives in the big city. There was something reassuring about that.

By 11 a.m., Ohashi was in the Shimbashi area and already tired. He bought a can of coffee from a vending machine, cracked it open and sat on the ground by his cart to watch the world go by. Two taxi drivers were standing near the vending machine drinking coffee and smoking. One of them was short and fat, the other tall and skinny, but they both smiled at Ohashi and said hello. Taxi drivers always reminded him of his brother, Taro. What was Taro up to now? Another memory that filled him with shame.

The chubby taxi driver came over and handed three empty cans to Ohashi, who thanked him. After his own little break, Ohashi crushed up all four cans including his own and tossed them in with the others, before heading on his way. When he got home he hid his cart in the alleyway for the night, then went to see his friends.

⠠⠠

He knew something was strange when he approached the camp, because he could hear shouting.

Crouched in a bush, hunched cat-like, he watched the tents from afar.

There was a man in uniform carrying Taka's doll at arm's length, by its leg. And there was someone in handcuffs now, being taken away. And the men in uniform were ripping up the tents, pulling up the blue tarpaulins and shoving them in the backs of pickup trucks. They were tearing the cardboard apart and piling it into stacks.

Some of the homeless were fighting back, but the men in uniform were stronger, better nourished, sober, and they had telescopic batons. Ohashi stifled a gasp as a uniformed man drew one, flicked his wrist casually to extend the baton to its full length, then advanced slowly towards a protesting man looking in the other direction. Thwack. With a sharp hit to the knee, the protester crumpled to the floor. One after another, the homeless were dragged across the remnants of the camp and shoved into the back of a vehicle. But, wait, hold on. That wasn't a police car. That was a van. And it didn't have a flashing light. Ohashi strained his eyes to make out the writing on the van. *Clean Sweep*, it said. In clear black letters.

Time to go.

⠠⠠

Ohashi ran. He could feel his tiny paunch bounce every time his feet hit the pavement, along with the jiggling of the loose flesh that had collected under his nipples with old age. His muscles temporarily forgot the pain of a hard day's work, and every cell in his body dedicated itself to putting as much distance between himself and the slow reverse blossoming of the blue tarpaulin city.

As he ran, a strange memory kept playing in his mind. A biology lesson from his high-school days. The teacher had told the class that if a man or woman were to jump on the spot, as long as they were in good shape, only their sexual organs would bounce. Any other form of bouncing on the human body indicated unwanted fat. Everything should be useful; everything should be muscle. He thought of the camp: was it unnecessary flab on the city? Did it need to be removed, like fatty tissue from a body by liposuction? Had it been cut and scraped away from muscle? Disposed of. Then all that came to his mind were words falling rhythmically between breaths: unwanted, unnecessary, unsightly, uninspired, unprepared, unknown, unsignificant – wait – that wasn't a word, but it seemed like it should be—

'Oi!'

A call from somewhere. He glanced over his shoulder but kept running.

'Ohashi!'

There it was again. But this time it was clearly his name. He spun around.

Peeking around the corner of an alleyway was a familiar toothy face. 'Over 'ere!'

Ohashi stumbled towards the toothiness. As he approached, a skinny arm yanked him into a back alley. Just in time, as a police car whisked past them, its siren shrieking a distorted laugh. Some kind of joke that these old men were not a part of, and never would be.

Ohashi caught his breath leaning against the grubby wall of the alleyway.

'Ohashi-san! Praise be to God you are safe.'

Taka's God was looking out for him.

'Are the others all right?' Ohashi straightened himself, having caught his breath.

'They took Shimada.' Hori looked grey-eyed and more gaunt than usual. 'Taka had been to church, and I'd gone to get a drink from the vendy. When we came back, they'd already started tearing the camp down and taking people away.'

Taka's God obviously hadn't deemed Shimada worthy. Perhaps he was too insignificant.

'What are we going to do?' asked Hori.

'Perhaps we could seek refuge at the church?' Taka looked at them both hopefully.

Ohashi hesitated. 'I've an idea,' he said slowly.

'What is it?' Hori smiled eagerly.

Ohashi swallowed. 'I know a place we can all stay. There's plenty of room.'

'Where?'

'But you'll have to promise to be quiet.'

'Of course, Ohashi. We'll be quiet. As quiet as mice.'

'All right. Follow me.'

Ohashi hoped his voice didn't betray his reluctance. Was this a mistake?

⚏

'Where on earth?'

Ohashi held the swing window open as Hori and Taka stepped inside.

'Be careful – just stand there, by the wall. I'll show you the way once I'm inside.'

'It's dark, Ohashi. Where are we?'

'Just a second.' He stepped down into the bathroom and pulled the window gently behind him, leaving a small gap. 'Hold on.'

'You don't shut it?' asked Hori.

'I have a friend who likes to visit me in the mornings. I'll introduce you tomorrow.'

'Is it a *girl*-friend?' Hori laughed.

'You'll see tomorrow.' Ohashi smiled.

He reached into his pocket and pulled out a small torch.

'This way.' He flicked on the torch and motioned towards the bathroom exit.

'Heavens above! Where are we?'

'It looks like a *sento* to me. Is that a bath, Ohashi?'

'It's an old capsule hotel.'

'Wow! You've been living in a hotel all along! You're like a king, Ohashi-sama!' Taka's voice was one of awed respect rather than jealousy.

'Hey! Why didn't you tell us about this place?' Hori's voice was raised in excitement. 'Do the baths still work? I'd love a dip.'

Ohashi flicked the light in Hori's direction, who blinked and squinted.

'Oi! Watch where you're shining that thing!'

'Oh, sorry!' Ohashi shone the torch around the bathhouse, illuminating the old grey tiles and the far wall with its mosaic depiction of an old crumbling Mount Fuji surrounded by forests, lakes and clouds. The tiles had fallen off in parts, leaving an unfinished jigsaw puzzle of a mountain.

'There's no running water here,' said Ohashi. 'So I'm afraid we can't use the baths. Follow me.'

The three of them made their way through the capsule hotel. It took longer than usual, having to stop for Hori and Taka's gasping at all the ghostly and interesting aspects of the abandoned hotel – the locker doors ripped off their hinges, the wallpaper peeling off the walls, the thick black layer of dust and dirt covering the floors of the hallways – all of which Ohashi now took for granted.

Once they reached the capsule room, Ohashi pointed out which one was his. Hori and Taka nodded respectfully before taking a capsule on either side. They both left one spare capsule's distance. They wanted to be close, but everyone needed a little privacy.

'Now, would you gentlemen like some supper?'

'Ooh, yes please! How very charitable of you.'

'I'd murder some grub!'

The three of them sat down to a simple dinner of onigiri and wheat tea, which Ohashi took from his personal supply and divided up fairly. As they sat in dim light, each man's face slowly became creased with deep pensive lines.

'So.' It was Ohashi who broke the silence. 'What's the plan?'

'Perhaps we should go to the church?'

'I feel like it might be a bit risky at this time,' said Hori.

'The Lord will provide for us—'

'I'm sorry, Taka-san. But I agree with Hori.' Ohashi spoke solemnly. 'We don't know whether we'd be safe at the church.

Perhaps they are co-operating with the police now. Who knows?'

'But where will we get our food?' Taka looked at the ceiling.

'I can get some,' said Ohashi.

'Enough for the three of us?' asked Hori.

'I think so.'

'*Man cannot live by bread alone*,' quoted Taka.

'But what does the Bible say about onigiri?' asked Hori. 'Imagine Jesus trying to open one of those.'

Even Taka allowed himself to laugh at this.

Ohashi made his excuses early that night. It had been a stressful day. They said goodnight to one another, and each man went to his own respective capsule of solitude. Alone with their thoughts, they eased slowly off to sleep, sharp lullabies of worry and fret tugging relentlessly at sweaty dreams.

▲▲

Small pools of light leaked through the hotel's high windows in the mornings. On a cloudy day, it was not much light at all, but on a day when the sun was out in full, the capsules were bathed in a warm glow. On these days, the cat would seek out patches of sunshine, spreading its belly across the floor.

Ohashi woke early and went to greet his furry companion, lying down on the floor so the cat could jump onto his stomach. The calico cat wobbled as it pressed its paws onto Ohashi's soft flab. He scratched it gently under the chin, and stroked its arched back with his other hand. The cat gave off purrs of pleasure, like a car engine idling at a red light. He studied the cat's face with its slightly red chin, drool collecting in the corner of its mouth. Those beautiful green eyes, what had they seen? As he often did, Ohashi thought of his father. His father had been obsessed with cats and had any number of them prowling around his writing study at any time. One of Ohashi's favourite things as a child had been to curl up with a *rakugo* collection in the corner of his father's study, stroke a cat, and keep quiet.

What had these green eyes seen? Where was this cat from? Imagine all the secrets and lies it had been privy to, the things that humans get up to when they think no one is looking.

'Is that your *friend*?'

The cat turned its head towards Hori, who was climbing out of his capsule. Ohashi felt the animal's claws dig in slightly, weighing up the situation. Should it flee from this toothy man, or was he a bringer of tuna, like his purple-headed friend?

'Don't be afraid. This is Hori-san. Say hello to Hori-san.'

'Clever little puss.' Hori scratched the cat between its ears, and Ohashi felt the claws retract. 'What a handsome little cat. Look at the lovely colourings on its back – the shape of it looks so familiar. Is it a boy, or a—'

A crashing sound came from the direction of the main entrance, followed by the mumble of two male voices coming down the corridor towards them. He never used that corridor. A great bulk pushed its way into the room, and Ohashi felt a heaviness in his stomach. Keita. Taka followed behind.

'You scoundrels. You've been hiding out here all along! Like rats in a hole!'

'Ohashi-san!' Taka was smiling uncomfortably. 'The Lord truly blessed us with a fortuitous meeting this morning!'

'Please, gentlemen,' said Ohashi, standing up and setting the cat down, 'in future, don't use the main entrance. Use the window, like I showed you.'

'All right, keep your pants on.' Keita swung himself into an empty capsule and lay down, making himself at home.

'I'm sorry, Ohashi-san,' whispered Taka. 'I did ask him to follow me to the back alley, but he just burst in through the front door.'

'It's all right.' Ohashi spoke quietly.

'What are you lot whispering about?' Keita bellowed from inside the capsule.

Ohashi brought his palm to his face.

'Any grub? I'm starving,' asked Keita, sticking his head out. He nodded at the cat. 'Whose mangy mog is that?'

Ohashi went and fished out food from his diminishing supply. He divided it between them all equally, and fed the cat. He would need to get more food from Makoto soon.

▲▲

That evening, Ohashi came home to a scene.

He knew something was wrong as he climbed in through the window. He could hear talking and laughing, even from outside the hotel. It grew louder and louder as he made his way towards them.

Someone had lit a small fire in the middle of the room, and a large group of men were standing around the sputtering flames. He could make out Keita, glugging from a big bottle of shochu, and then there were people Ohashi had never seen before. They were all standing around the fire talking loudly in excited voices. Taka and Hori were there too, laughing. When they looked up and saw Ohashi their wide smiles faded into awkward sheepishness.

'Look who it is.' Keita leered at Ohashi drunkenly.

'Gentlemen. May I ask what is going on here?' Ohashi addressed Taka and Hori.

'Just a little get together, that's all,' said Taka.

'What's it to you anyway?' Keita jeered.

'Well, this is my home too. It was my home first,' said Ohashi. 'It would be nice if you treated it with a little respect.'

'*Your home.*' Keita snorted. 'That's rich. You just came along and found an empty building. Anyone can do that. Look at him, with his poncey bandana. Acting like he's king of the castle, with only a stupid cat for a friend.'

The group roared with laughter. Even Hori and Taka joined in.

'Well, I'd appreciate it if you kept the noise down. It wouldn't be good if someone came and found us.' Ohashi made straight for his capsule.

'Come on, Ohashi. Come join us for a drink,' whispered Hori.

'No, thank you. I'm tired.'

Ohashi got inside and shut the curtain and settled himself down to re-read his well-thumbed copy of *The Makioka Sisters*, ignoring the noise.

'Hey, Ohashi.' It was Keita.

Ohashi lowered his book and scowled at the curtain. If he kept quiet, maybe the fool would go away.

'Ohashi.'

'What?'

Keita pulled back the curtain.

'Look. I'm sorry. Didn't mean to be rude. Here.'

Keita held out a chipped glass of transparent brown liquid.

'What is it?' Ohashi asked, eyeing Keita's face apprehensively.

'Your favourite. Wheat tea.' Keita smiled. 'You can have it here with your book, or you can come join us for a chat. Up to you. Just wanted to make peace.'

'Thank you, Keita. That's very kind of you. Perhaps I'll come join you.' Ohashi crawled out of the capsule and took the glass of tea from Keita, then they both went back to join the group.

Hori was in the middle of telling a funny joke about a samurai and a priest – he was nearing the end – so Ohashi sat silently and listened. The joke was a good one, but Hori's storytelling technique wasn't quite up to Ohashi's standards – his timing was all off, and he rambled too much. Hori finally laid out the punch line, and again everyone erupted in loud laughter. Ohashi felt his stomach clench in panic as the noise echoed, picturing the van with the black letters circling the nearby streets. He reached for his half-forgotten cup and took a sip of the wheat tea.

That taste.

He almost swallowed, but instead he spat. He threw the glass on the floor, where it smashed. His whole body shook. And then the rage bubbled up inside. The rage at what he had done, at what the taste had made him do. To his family, to himself, to his life. His own fault. He looked at Keita, who was laughing his terrible hiccupping laugh.

'I'll kill you,' Ohashi said in a low voice.

Keita kept laughing.

Ohashi made for Keita. Hori reached forward and tried to place a hand on Ohashi's wrist, but Ohashi shook him off. And then Ohashi's hands were around Keita's neck, and he was squeezing hard. And there were arms on him, pulling him away, but they did not have the strength to stop him. He squeezed and squeezed with all the hate and regret and despair that he'd hidden away deep inside. He watched Keita's face turning from red to blue, and he kept crushing and gripping.

And he would've kept going, if it weren't for an iron-like force yanking him away, and then his arms were pinned behind his back, and something was pulling him away from Keita, and he could see Keita gasping in gulps of air. And then he felt the cold hardness of metal slapped around his wrists, and when he looked around all he could see was blue. Blue uniforms, with faceless people inside them, huddled around him, towering over him, glaring and squinting. And when the faces of Ohashi's friends came into focus, there was fear – but was it the fear of the blue uniforms, or fear of Ohashi himself and what he had tried to do?

'He . . . he . . . tried to kill me!' Keita's lips were ringed purple and his nostrils flared wide.

'Book them all,' came a loud voice from the shadows. 'And put out that fire.'

And then they were bundled into the backs of vans, pushed and pulled and shoved. They bounced around in the dark, Ohashi staring into the blackness.

⚊

'Good morning.'

Ohashi opened his eyes and squinted at the blurry shape in front of him.

'Here.' A figure held out a steaming mug of coffee. 'Drink this.'

'Thank you.' Ohashi took the mug carefully, and rubbed his eyes with the other hand. His body ached from sleeping on the hard bench of the cell.

'I'll give you a minute to wake up, but I have to take you to the interview room.'

Ohashi looked up to see a young police officer standing at the open cell door. He appeared to be in his mid-twenties and had a kind face. He reminded him a little of Makoto. Ohashi held the steaming cup of coffee to his lips and blew lightly on it before sipping.

'Where am I?' asked Ohashi.

'Holding station. We just need to have a quick interview with you – a formality really – you should be free to go after that.'

'Thank you.'

'Let's get a move on, sir. We've got a ton of interviews to get through, and we want to keep to schedule. You can bring the coffee with you.' The policeman gestured to the open door.

Ohashi stood up and followed the policeman down the corridor with uncertain steps. The sounds of their footfalls echoed off the walls, like the clang of his cudgel smashing cans on the pavement. It resonated deep inside Ohashi's stomach and made him feel a little sick.

The interview room was plain: yellow walls, a table in the middle, a strip light overhead and two chairs either side of the table facing each other. The officer indicated for Ohashi to sit.

'Wait here. Someone'll be in to speak with you shortly.'

He sipped on his coffee and stared at the wall, wondering what would happen to him. The door opened, breaking his reverie, and an older officer entered carrying some sheets of paper.

'Hello there. No, don't get up. My name is Fukuyama, and I have a few questions to ask you.'

'Pleased to meet you, Fukuyama-san.' Ohashi gave a little bow.

The officer sat and held his pen above a form at the ready. 'Right, first things first. Do you have any kind of identification on you?'

Ohashi shook his head and looked at the floor.

'That's quite all right. Let's just fill out this form together shall we. Surname?'

'Ohashi.'

'First name?'

'Ichiro.'

The officer nodded and scribbled. 'Age?'

'Sixty-four.'

'Occupation?'

'Well . . . I suppose . . .'

The officer looked up. 'Do you have a job?'

'Well, I collect cans. But I don't suppose . . .'

'Hmm . . . maybe falls under waste control. Name of employer?'

'I don't really have an employer as such . . .'

'Hmm. Shall I just put *unemployed*? Maybe that's easier.'

'That's fine.'

'Address?'

'Umm. Well . . .'

'Sleeping rough?'

'You could say that.'

'Not a problem, Ohashi-san. If you can just provide us with an address of a family member – any relative will do. Oh, and their phone number. We'll need to call them so they can come pick you up.'

'Well . . .'

'Any relative will do, Ohashi-san.'

'I don't keep in contact with anyone.'

'Look.' The officer took off his glasses and rubbed his eyes. 'Ohashi-san. I really understand how difficult this might be for you. You might have fallen out with your relatives. You might not want to talk to them anymore. I understand completely. But it really is crucial that you give us this piece of information, otherwise . . . Well . . .'

'I have a younger brother.'

'Excellent!' The officer looked hopeful. 'And what's his address?'

'I haven't spoken to him in years.'

'Do you have his address?'

'I think so.'

'Brilliant. You can write it down here.' The officer slid him a pen and a scrap of paper.

Ohashi wrote down the address of the house in Nakano he had visited many years ago. He remembered family gatherings at the house, greeting his sister-in-law, playing with his young niece. His brother, Taro, was always so content. Not a lot of money, but so happy with his beautiful wife, his sunny daughter Ryoko and that old cherry tree in the garden. Taro could've achieved so much more than being a taxi driver. He'd always written such wonderful poetry, dream-like and rich with imagery. Father had been so proud of him.

Ohashi had performed private *rakugo* for the two families under that cherry tree. A tear formed in his eye as he thought about the audience: there'd been his brother Taro, his sister-in-law, his niece Ryoko and then Ohashi's wife and daughter. He remembered their smiling faces as he told his stories. But Father had stopped coming when his performances began to get more outrageous.

Taro would be so ashamed of him now.

He passed the scrap of paper back to the police officer, who looked at it and slid it back quickly. 'If you could just write his full name also.'

Ohashi wrote the characters, 大橋太郎 Ohashi Taro.

'You've lovely handwriting, if you don't mind my saying so. Right. I'll just go confirm this. Relax, everything will be fine.'

What a terrible way to get back in contact with his brother after all these years. He raised the cup of coffee absently, tilted it back against his lips, but was rewarded only with the cold powdery sludge at the bottom of the cup. It left a bitter taste in his mouth.

Ten minutes or so later, the officer returned to the room with a man wearing a suit. Ohashi found himself immediately disliking him. It was difficult to say exactly why, but there was something false about him, despite his efforts to appear affable. For one thing, he spiked his hair with gel in the way Ohashi didn't approve of. His smarmy appearance reminded him a little of the church preacher who had said such terrible things about Hiroshima and Nagasaki.

'Ohashi-san. Bad news, I'm afraid. I telephoned the address you provided me with, and I'm sorry to say that your brother no longer lives there. The current owner could not say where he has moved to, and we have no means of obtaining records to indicate his new residence.'

'Oh . . .'

40

'Now, Ohashi-san. If you could just think hard about any other relative, anyone will do. A distant uncle, a cousin. Anyone.'

'I don't have anyone.'

'Think, Ohashi-san. It's important.'

'I'm sorry. I don't have anyone else.'

The officer sighed. 'Well, I have no choice but to declare you "of no fixed abode" and pass you on to this man here, Tanaka-san.'

'Pleased to meet you, Ohashi-san. Have no fear, we'll take care of you.' The smarmy man gave a condescending smile, looking back and forth from Ohashi to the police officer, like a man watching a tennis game between two incompetent children.

'I'm sorry, Ohashi-san. There's nothing we can do.' The police officer got up and left.

Ohashi was left with the man in the suit, who sat down in the chair the officer had vacated.

'Now, Ohashi-san. We will be taking you to our facility not far from here. It's a wonderful new home for you . . .'

Ohashi listened to the long and winding explanation, designed to deceive. But he saw it for what it was – the theft of his last worldly possession: his freedom.

▲
▲▲

The cat padded lightly along the alleyway towards the hotel window. Then it slowed its pace. There was something different in the air, a smell – smoke? Something was wrong. The bathroom window was still open, so the cat slunk inside.

It was quiet in the corridors, and the strange smell grew stronger as the cat clipped steadily along. As it approached the capsules, it saw the remains of a put-out fire, and then the emptiness. Silence, broken by a nervous mew.

The purple-headed man was not in his bed. His things were gone, but his scent remained.

The cat whined.

Where had the purple-headed man gone?

Where was breakfast?

The cat waited for a few minutes, yawned wide, then slowly went back the way it had come.

It sauntered down the alleyway, tummy grumbling, seeking food. There was an unease in its gait, a subtle indication of a broken routine. It would miss the purple-headed man. But it knew somehow it would be fine. The city was its friend. The city would provide.

⁂

The purple-headed man was purple-headed no more.

They took his bandana from him, dressed him in orange overalls and showed him to his new home. As the door shut behind him he noticed this cell was somewhat larger than the capsule he had grown used to. The floors were tatami matting, and there were two futon laid out. One of them was already occupied by a large sleeping figure covered in blankets and snoring loudly. The capsule was certainly cleaner and bigger than the one he was used to, but this one had bars on the windows, and locks on the doors.

Ohashi slumped down on the vacant futon and let out a sigh. As he did so, the snoring coming from under the blankets stopped. When Ohashi glanced over, the blankets pulled back to reveal a lazy eye, which widened as Ohashi reeled back in shock.

'Oh, it's you,' said a low voice from under the blankets.

'Hello, Keita.' Ohashi sighed.

'Still haven't forgiven you.' Keita pulled the blanket down and sat up.

'Nor I you.' Ohashi spoke through tight lips.

'Anyway, where the hell are we? Prison?' Keita yawned and rubbed his eyes.

'I don't think it's a prison. Didn't the police discharge you?'

'Seems like a prison to me.'

'Well, it's not.'

'All right. Keep your hair on.'

Ohashi put a hand to his hair. With the bandana gone, his bald patch was exposed.

'If you're going to talk to me like that, Keita-san, I would rather not talk at all.'

'Coming from the man who tried to kill me.'

'I didn't try to kill you, Keita.'

'Did.'

'Well, you shouldn't have done what you did. Should you?'

'It was just a joke. Wouldn't have done it if I'd known you'd flip out like that.'

'Look, Keita. I don't want to be here in this room with you, and I presume you don't either. But we have no choice in the matter. Shall we just forget it and move on?'

'Suits me.'

Ohashi closed his eyes.

'I could murder some saké,' mumbled Keita.

Ohashi thought about this. He didn't tell Keita that he was pretty sure there wouldn't be any saké. The two of them lay in silence, taking in their strange and sterile new home.

▲
▲▲

'Argh.'

Ohashi looked at the bundle of covers on the other futon. Keita was writhing around uncomfortably, his sheets visibly moist with sweat.

It was night-time, just before lights out, and Ohashi could hear the squeak of the guard's leather boots in the hallway. This wasn't a prison – family members could come and pick up the residents at any time – but as the prim-voiced Warden Tanaka would announce in his suit every evening before they sat down to a cafeteria dinner, 'This is a better place for you chaps than out there on the streets. You're safer here.'

It had only been a few days, but the food was awful, worse than the slop they'd served at the church. If the Warden caught you stirring it around your plate you might get a glare, or worse, a demerit, which lost you privileges like access to the facility's pebble-filled yard. Ohashi had looked around for Taka and Hori at meals and yard time, but there was no sign of them. Perhaps they were on a different floor – there seemed to be a rotation for use of facilities. Every window was barred, which only made Ohashi think of playing with the cat in the soft pools of sunlight, shining through the grimy windows of the old hotel. Where was his cat now? He missed her. Night-time always came as a relief because he could forget about where he was, even if only for a moment. But now Keita had started with his moaning again.

'Are you all right?' asked Ohashi.

'Leave me alone!'

'What's wrong?'

'How can they not have any alcohol in this shithole?'

'Here, drink this.' Ohashi took a glass of water to Keita.

'Fuck off. I don't need your help.'

'Drink it. You'll feel better soon.'

'How would you know? Mr *I-Don't-Drink-Thank-You-Very-Much.*'

'I used to drink, Keita. A lot more than you do. And I got through it.'

Keita pulled the covers down and eyed Ohashi suspiciously. Beads of sweat were forming on his brow.

'You sure it'll get better?'

'I'm certain. It just takes a few days, and it's terrible, I know. But you'll be feeling much better soon. You have to keep hydrated though.'

Keita extended a shaking hand and tried to take the glass from Ohashi.

'Shit.' He almost dropped it.

'Here, let me help.' Ohashi brought the glass carefully to his lips.

Keita looked like a small child, glugging away pitifully on the water.

'Get some sleep.'

They turned out the lights, leaving a faint glow.

Ohashi was almost drifting off when Keita woke him again.

'Hey.'

'What?'

'Are you awake?'

'What do you think?'

'Sorry. Did I wake you up?'

'Go to sleep, Keita.'

'Can't.'

'What's wrong?'

'I just can't stop thinking about things.'

Ohashi grunted. 'Well, stop.'

'I can't.'

'Can't you just think quietly?'

'Sorry.' Keita was quiet for a few seconds. 'But don't you ever get like that?'

'Like what?' Ohashi sat up and threw off his covers.

'Where you can't stop thinking. You look back at every choice you ever made in life, and all you can see are the mistakes. The things you did that brought you to where you are.' Keita stared into space, as if he were looking at something Ohashi couldn't see. 'And how if you'd just done a few things differently, if you'd just made better choices, then you'd be in a better place right now.'

Ohashi slumped back down, rolled over to face the other way, but didn't speak.

'Or maybe,' said Keita, 'we were just unlucky.'

'I know I wasn't.'

'Why?'

'I was the luckiest man alive, once.'

'How so?' Keita sat up slightly.

'I had a good upbringing, a loving mother and an inspiring father.' Ohashi swallowed. 'Then I had a beautiful wife, a lovely daughter and my dream job.'

'What happened?'

'Doesn't matter.'

'Was it the drink?'

'I don't want to talk about it.'

'Suit yourself.' Keita paused, but then continued. 'I know I made mistakes. My parents told me not to join the yakuza. But I was young and stupid then. All I could think about was looking cool and getting laid. I remember going to Asakusa to get my tattoo done. Was just trying to impress a girl. Thought if I joined the yakuza I'd get the money and the status. She ended up going off with some other guy anyway. Said he was more *respectable*. You can never win.' Keita sighed. 'Should've listened to my parents. The yakuza didn't look after me like they said they would. All it took was a couple of mistakes. Two fingers. They kicked me out. No one ever wanted me in their family.'

'That's not true, Keita.'

'Yes it is. I know I'm rude and annoying. People don't like having me around.'

Ohashi shifted in his futon, and looked over to where he could see the dark outline of Keita's hulking body. 'You're one of us, Keita. Me, Shimada, Taka and Hori. We're your family now.'

The outline of Keita's head turned to face Ohashi. 'Really? You really mean that?'

'Of course.' Not true, but Ohashi would've said anything to get some sleep.

'Thanks.'

'It's okay, Keita. Let's get some rest.'

There was a short pause, then Keita spoke softly, half asleep.

'I'm sure your wife and daughter still love you, Ohashi-san.'

Ohashi swallowed an unexpected lump in his throat.

'Goodnight, Keita.'

▲
▲▲

That night, like many other nights, he dreamt of Tokyo.

But it was different. He was walking along with his cart, but the sky was purple and orange. The streets were empty, not a person in sight. He walked amongst the crumbling skyscrapers covered in patina, and he could see the buildings sinking into the ground in the distance, near the bay. The earth shook, and the buildings crumbled and disappeared. Liquefaction. That's what it was called. Then the quaking stopped and everything was still again.

The trains were empty and rusted to their tracks. The convenience stores looked like they had been raided. Food spilled out from the shelves, out into the streets, but it was all rotten and inedible. Empty coffee cans were piled up like mountains, waste and debris everywhere. But no people.

He kept walking until he came face to face with his old friend, the cat.

'Follow me,' said the cat, jumping onto a high wall. 'Come on.'

'I can't.'

'Yes you can. Try four legs instead of two. Works better that way.'

He dropped onto his hands and knees, and sure enough, he was lighter on his feet and more agile. He jumped up onto the wall next to the cat, and the cat looked smug. He caught the reflection of himself in the other cat's eyes. He was a cat too now, and they didn't need to talk to communicate.

They climbed across rooftops together, up to the highest points on the decaying skyscrapers. They climbed trees, they snuck into small spaces, they chased mice, and they raced through the empty streets.

The city was theirs.

⚇

'So what happened to them?'

'Who?'

'Your wife and kid?'

Ohashi ignored the question.

'It was a daughter you had, wasn't it?' Keita persisted.

Ohashi glanced at Keita quickly. He detected no malice in the question, but that didn't stop it from being an unwanted one.

'Can we talk about something else?'

'Why do you always avoid it?'

'Avoid what?'

'Talking about your past.'

'Because it's none of your business, Keita.'

'No wonder they left you.'

'What did you say?'

'I said, no wonder they left you.'

'How dare you.'

'What? You never talk about anything. You're just this stuck-up old man who thinks he's better than everyone. I can't take it anymore, locked in a cell with a pompous old twat.'

'And here I am, stuck with a crybaby yakuza reject.'

'Go to hell, old man.'

There was a bang at the door, and it was opened at precisely the same time.

'What's the point in knocking if you're just going to barge in anyway?' Keita complained.

'Keita, be quiet!' said Ohashi.

A grim-looking man stood at the door scowling. 'Which one of you said that?'

'Him.' Keita pointed at Ohashi.

The guard turned his eyes on Ohashi. 'Watch it. Smartarse.'

'I didn't—'

'Don't wanna hear it. You're both on demerits. No leaving your room tomorrow.' He slammed the door and it was silent again.

'Asshole,' Keita whispered.

Ohashi rolled over but was too angry to sleep.

After a short while, he sat up and adopted that familiar stance. 'All right, Keita. You want to hear a story? I'll tell you a story. There once was a man named Ohashi, who had everything and lost it all . . .'

Ohashi sat neatly on his bed, with his knees tucked beneath him and his hands held out in front, in the proud manner of the *rakugoka* that he was, and always would be.

That, at least, was something that could never be taken away from him.

Street Fighter II (Turbo)

Guile's Stage / Sonic Boom / Tiger Uppercut / Yoga Flame / Yoga Fire / Spinning Bird Kick / Hadoken / Dragon Punch / Round One / Start

'Don't you think he looks *just* like Dhalsim?' Kyoko leant over towards me as she whispered conspiratorially into my ear.

I felt her hot breath on my neck and caught a whiff of her perfume over the tobacco and cheap booze filling the karaoke booth. It was the first thing she'd ever said to me. We'd worked in the same office at the PR company for a while now, but hadn't spoken so much as a word to one another all that time. She'd always just looked straight through me at work, and I'd never given her a second thought either. It was as if we'd been invisible to each other until that moment.

I turned my head in the direction of the man she was referring to. He was holding a glass of shochu in one skeletal hand and a microphone in the other.

'Excuse me?' I'd heard her well enough, but couldn't quite believe she'd said it.

'Oh come on, Makoto-kun! Dhalsim! You know, from Street—'

'Street Fighter II. I thought that's what you said.'

'Don't you think?' she asked, this time giggling.

I looked at him again. He was lolling his bald head around as he slurred the words of the song, occasionally spilling shochu on the girl sleeping next to him. Now that she'd pointed it out, yes, he did. His facial expression was exactly like one Dhalsim would pull. The spitting image. It was the face he pulls after you uppercut and knock him backwards, before he gets stunned.

'Yoga flame,' I said.

She snorted her drink through her nose. 'Stop!'

'I didn't know you were a gamer.' It didn't come out how I meant it to. I'd hoped to sound surprised, in a convivial way, but what I sounded like was a jerk.

'Oh, I'm not.' She sipped her drink and looked at the lyrics playing their way out on the karaoke TV screen. 'Well, except Street Fighter II.' She turned up the corner of her mouth in a crooked smile. 'Guilty pleasure.'

'Which one? They made a few.' I sat up straighter.

'Turbo.'

I leant in closer. 'When did you play that?'

'My older brother had a Super Famicon. We used to play when we were kids.' Her eyes caught the light from the TV and glistened moistly.

'Hey! You two! What are you nattering about?' Ryu, the Line Manager, ducked past Dhalsim and came to sit between us. He smelt like he'd been sleeping in his suit for a week, and had a soya sauce stain on his shirt as he often did. He turned to me and slurred, 'Makoto, are you bothering her?' before putting his arm around Kyoko. 'Kyoko-chan! Put a song on. You haven't sung all night. A good-looking girl like you must have the voice of an angel.'

'Oh, Ryu-kun. You know I don't like to sing.' She poured more beer from a big frosty bottle of Kirin into his empty glass. She wiped the condensation carefully from her hands with a small towel she took from her handbag. 'Your voice is so . . . manly. Why don't you sing another song for us?'

I lit a cigarette and looked the other way.

These work nights out were such a drag. It would've been great if I could get out of them like Flo, that American translator girl. She just said she wasn't feeling well, and everyone let her off. Why couldn't I do that? Sad fact: because I'm Japanese. And the nail that sticks out will be hammered in.

But on these work nights out, no one ever got a chance to talk or get to know one another. All we did was get wasted and sing karaoke. Then we had to listen to the bosses drone on about how great they were, and how things were a lot harder in the days when they first joined the company. How we all had it easy, yada yada yada. Last time I checked, they were the ones who had it easy in the bubble. My generation was fucked from the start.

Big Boss was on the microphone now. He was screaming out a bad version of The Clash's 'London Calling' – really murdering it. He looked like an oversized baby, little wisps of hair flapping and flopping on his bald pate. It didn't even sound like English. I sat there nodding, smiling and laughing when I was supposed to. Drinking myself into a stupor. What I really wanted was to get the hell out of that booth and go home to bed. But now I couldn't stop thinking about what Kyoko had said. How she played Street Fighter II as a kid.

Turbo, no less.

Now I really, really wanted to play a game of Street Fighter II Turbo.

▲▲

The night slipped on like a convoluted sentence, punctuated with chicken wings, potato fries, onigiri, beer and kimchi. Shochu mixed with ice, shochu mixed with oolong tea, shochu mixed with water, shochu mixed with shochu mixed with shochu. Some annoying fucker took off his trousers, got on a tambourine and battered it so loud next to my ear during 'Hey Jude' I could feel my tinnitus crescendoing in time to the music.

I couldn't help but sneak looks at Kyoko. She was wearing a pink Polo sweater, cream trousers and wore her long hair down. Did she normally wear it in a ponytail? What was it that had changed? Was I getting drunk? I mean, she was a beautiful girl. Too beautiful for someone like me. I'd always just thought of her as this typical Office Lady, getting together with all the other OLs at lunch times to talk about shopping, or make up, or whatever it is that girls talk about.

Don't get me wrong, guys talk about inane stuff too – like baseball and *kyabakura*. I can't stand that shit – people talking about things they think they *should* talk about, so as not to be socially awkward.

It must've been the Street Fighter II comment, because now all I could think about was playing against her.

And beating her to a pulp – in the game, of course.

As I watched her sipping on her drink, quietly bobbing her head to Big Boss singing 'With or Without You' by U2, I started to fantasize about playing a game against her.

Maybe she'd pick Chun Li as her character. I'd pick Ken, of course. We'd go to Guile's stage in the US because it has the coolest music, the fighter jet in the background, and the spectator guy who looks like he's wanking himself off. The music would kick in (that tune goes with anything), the commentator would say, 'Round one. Fight!' and the timer would start to count down.

Maybe she'd throw the first move, quick as lightning, a fireball straight at me, and I'd just keep firing the *hadoken* back at her. I'm a patient player. I'd be happy throwing fireballs, waiting for her to make that fatal mistake that everyone does after a while. She'd grow restless, and decide it was time to make an attack. She'd jump into the air, aiming a hard kick straight for my head. And anyone who was watching would probably think, 'Right, this is it for Ken. Game over. His head is going flying.'

And they wouldn't be too wrong in thinking that. Even a Street Fighter aficionada might worry I'd left it too long, that I should've countered, blocked, or avoided the attack. But that's because I've always been really good at one thing (and everyone's got to have their one thing, right?). I've always been able to pull off Ken's strongest move quicker than anyone I've ever played against. Maybe if I'd been born in the old days, I would've been famous as some kind of quick-draw samurai (like Toshiro Mifune in the film *Yojimbo*), or if I'd been born in the States in the old west, I would've been like Butch Cassidy (or was the Sundance Kid faster . . . ?).

So, there she'd be, flying straight for my head, and then my thumbs would move so quickly you'd hear the flicking sound of the keypad (your eyes wouldn't register any movement) but here's what would happen:

→ ↘ ↓ ↘ → + Hard Punch

Then Ken would launch himself in the air (he travels slightly further sideways than Ryu, and that's why I pick him), his fist a ball of flame. The punch would connect right in her thigh, and she'd go flying backwards, knocked on her ass. Then I'd jump in with a hard flying kick, knock her to the ground, then throw a hard leg sweep (just as she was getting to her feet), which would knock her to the ground again. She'd stand up stunned, all dizzy with the stars (or birds) circling her head, then I'd do Ken's rolling throw, launching her into the air. Chun Li would hit the deck skidding along, kicking up dust till she came to rest, and the whole screen would shake as time slowed down. Then Ken would raise his fist in triumph, and my points would ring up on the screen – all 30,000 of them – the commentator's American accent would chime in, 'You win! Perfect!'

I don't know what it would achieve. She wouldn't be impressed or anything. That's not exactly how you make friends, I know that.

I snuck another look at her again. She'd really got my interest now.

What kind of loser would she be? Would she be the kind who gets angry, throws the controller at the floor and gets in a sulk? Would she try to distract me in the next bout to win? Maybe she'd be a good-natured loser. Maybe she'd end up annoying me by staying cool, just taking everything in her stride.

I was pretty sure of one thing though: she'd never win. Unless I let her.

Well, however it turned out, I knew I had to play her.

▲▲

The end of one of these karaoke parties is almost worse than the party itself.

The night was still young, but we were too old for Shibuya. Standing outside the Manekineko karaoke complex in a ring, we all waited awkwardly to see what would happen. It was that moment when no one is being honest about what they want to do next. Some people want to slip off home, but they don't want others to know that's what they want. Other people are trying as hard as they can not to show how much they want to keep drinking, to go on to the second party *nijikai*; maybe they think if they show how much they want it, and the prevailing winds don't coincide, it's a reflection of their popularity in the group. Who knows.

I had other things on my mind. I'd positioned myself next to Kyoko, and was trying to pick the perfect moment to get her attention, without being noticed. The *tejime* handclap was drawing near, and I needed to chat to her somehow.

'Thank you, everyone, for coming out tonight,' Dhalsim had the role of party organizer today, and his bald head was reflecting the neon of Shibuya as he flailed his limbs around enthusiastically, 'and I'm sure we can all agree that tonight was a great success. Now if you'll all join me together in bringing a close to the night—'

'Aaaaaaaaagggggghhhhh!' We all turned to see Big Boss, arms spread wide, screaming a terrible primal yowl into the night sky. 'Aaaaaaaggggghhhhhh!' He beat his chest like Donkey Kong.

'Big Boss, are you all right?' Dhalsim extended an arm, resting a hand on his shoulder.

Big Boss shrugged it off. '*Baka yaro!*'

'Big Boss!' voices cried out, and all eyes were cast on the unfolding scene.

I took my chance. 'Kyoko!' I whispered.

She turned her head slowly away from the action and looked at me dully.

'Kyoko, I was just wondering . . .' I loosened my collar. 'If you want to, and I completely understand if you don't . . .'

'Yes?' She eyed me suspiciously.

I had to hurry. Big Boss had grabbed one of the new girls by the shoulders and was kneeing her softly on the bum, pretending to beat her up. Everyone was scrambling around trying to stop him (without usurping his authority). Concerned cries of 'Big Boss! Please stop!' rang out intermittently, while the new girl looked aghast as the head of the company kneed her in the backside repeatedly while he screamed out unintelligibly to the heavens.

'Kyoko, would you like to go play Street Fighter II with me?'

'Where?' She raised an eyebrow.

'At a game centre. I'm sure there's one nearby.'

There was a coughing sound, and she looked away from me, and nodded in the direction of Dhalsim, who'd managed to break up the ruckus. Big Boss had miraculously calmed down, and now everyone was standing in a ring again with their hands held out. They were all looking expectantly at me.

'Oh, sorry.' I held my hands out, and we all did the *tejime* clap.

So that was that then.

No Street Fighter II tonight.

▲▲

I wanted to go home after the circle broke, but when I saw Kyoko sticking around for the *nijikai* I decided to stay too. We were on the way to some bar our *senpai* was raving about. I was walking by myself smoking a cigarette when I felt a tug on my shoulder and was pulled bodily into the alcove of a doorway.

'What the—' I turned to see Kyoko with her finger to her lips, then she wrapped a hand over my mouth.

The two of us watched from the alcove as the rest of them filed past, gossiping and chatting excitedly, on their way to the bar. When the last of them had gone, Kyoko took her hand from my mouth.

'Come on.'

'Where?'

'In here.' She walked towards the double doors behind us, and they slid open automatically.

As the doors opened I could suddenly hear the loud sounds of zombies exploding, power-ups, mega jumps, hyper-dashes and blaster attacks. I followed Kyoko inside, into the overpowering bright strip lights of the game centre. A rainbow of multicoloured pixels flashed around us, bathing us in greens and reds and blues. Over the loud sound effects was a louder constant soundtrack of Kyary Pamyu Pamyu blasting out over huge speakers high up on the walls. We walked along the aisles of taiko drummers and the guitar strummers who beat out a solid rhythm for all the dancing mayhem and the mad uzi shoot-'em-ups we passed on our way. It looked like Kyoko had been here before. She headed with purpose straight for an old-looking coin op on the farthest wall.

She stopped in front of it. 'Here.'

'Wow! Vintage,' I said. Reaching for my coin purse, I took out two 100-yen coins.

'No.' She raised her hand. 'You need to get tokens from over there.' She pointed to a machine on the wall.

'No problemo.' I strutted over like a big shot, whacked a 1,000-yen note in, and collected a fistful of tokens. 'This should be enough, right?' I handed them to her.

'More than.' She put the tokens down on the edge of the machine, took two in her hand, crouched down and slipped them one by one into the slot.

The machine let out that familiar triumphant sound and indicated two credits. I let her go on the left. I took the right-hand side. We were standing so close together, and I wasn't sure if I was imagining it or not, but I felt like parts of our body were almost touching. I had a strange sense of excitement, almost as if electricity was jumping between the two of us.

'Ready?' She looked at me, her hand hovering over the player one start button.

'Sure.' I placed mine over the player two button; it was slightly sticky.

'On three.' She exhaled deeply. 'One, two, three!'

We both pressed down on the buttons at the same time.

The screen froze, went white, then displayed two words.

GAME OVER

'What the hell!' I beat the side of the machine with my fist. 'Come on!'

'It's okay,' she said softly. 'Must be broken.'

'Shit. Is there somebody we can complain to?'

'Not that I know of.'

'Damn. I was looking forward to that.'

'Never mind.'

'What are we going to do with all these tokens now?'

'We could play some other games?' she said sunnily.

'But I wanted to play Street Fighter . . .' I sounded like a whining brat.

She lifted her pink jumper sleeve and looked at a small silver wristwatch. 'It's getting late.'

'Yeah. Maybe we should call it a night.' I felt defeated.

The sound of the game centre and the whoops and shouts of the players filled my ears, and I suddenly felt sick. The bright flashing lights and grating music were too much.

'Can we go outside for a second?' I started to walk away.

'What about all these tokens?' she asked.

'Just leave them.' I waved my hand and carried on walking.

Outside, I leant against the wall and breathed fresh air in gulps.

'Are you okay?' The sliding doors shut behind Kyoko. She stood there with her coat folded neatly over her arm.

'Yeah, I'm all right. Just needed to catch my breath.' I tried to mask my disappointment.

'So . . .' she said.

'So . . .' I replied.

'Are you tired?' she asked.

'Not exactly.' I lit a cigarette.

'Because, well, I know it's crazy, and it might be a little far, but . . .' She bit her lip.

'Yeah?' I took a drag on my cigarette and blew a cloud of smoke away from her, towards the bustling neon streets.

'I know this bar. Well, actually it's my friend's bar.'

'Yeah?'

'It's a Street Fighter-themed bar.'

'No way!'

'Yeah, it's called Yoga Flame. It's decorated with all these Street

Fighter II figurines and memorabilia. He has a giant TV with a Super Famicon hooked up to it, and the customers can play as much as they like – as long as they pay for their drinks.'

'Awesome. Let's go!'

'I'm glad you like the sound of it. But the only problem is . . .' She scratched her head.

'Yes?'

'It's in Chiba.'

'Chiba?'

'Yeah, too far, right? Let's forget it. Maybe another time.'

'No. We can go tonight. Chiba's not *that* far.'

'Really?' Her eyes lit up. 'You don't mind?'

'Of course not. As long as they have Street Fighter II.'

'Brilliant.' She clapped her hands. 'Well, the last train leaves pretty soon. Let's go to the *konbini*. We can get some beer and snacks for the journey.'

▲▲

We sat on the train with a polythene bag from the convenience store filled with icy cold cans of beer, kimchi pork onigiri (with the limited edition salty *nori* seaweed) for me, and a packet of soft white sandwiches (with the crusts cut off, filled with smooth peanut butter) for her.

We'd had to change trains in the city a couple of times, but I just followed Kyoko. Judging by the speed at which she caught the connections, it was obvious she must take this route a lot. In the stations and on the platforms, she cut a path straight through the drunkards reeling around in search of their last trains. When we were finally sitting on the *kaisoku* train that took us directly to Chiba, we could relax and crack open some beers. I held the bag from the convenience store in my hand. I coughed nervously, and told Kyoko about the part-time job in Lawson I did while I was finishing Law School.

Her eyes lit up, and she said in English, 'Don't you know that's against the *Law* . . . son?' then switched back to Japanese. 'Get it? Against the *Law* . . . son!'

There was an awkward silence, and her face went red. I should've been laughing. Why wasn't I laughing? It was a good joke – but I was more taken aback at how good her English pronunciation was. Her accent was perfect. My English was okay – I'd passed the *eiken* and TOEIC; I knew lots of tricky grammar and vocabulary – but heavily accented. I'd never been able to lose that *katakana* pronunciation I'd learnt in school. Still, why was I leaving her hanging? I should've been laughing at her joke.

'That's funny,' I said, lamely.

She punched my arm. 'You don't have to pretend.'

'No, I mean it.' God, I sounded like an asshole.

'So you worked in a convenience store, too, eh?' She giggled. 'I still have nightmares about stocking shelves.'

'I hated opening these.' I held up the bag I was holding, then tied it into a neat knot and put it in my pocket. I tried to make her laugh with weary stories of my days as a convenience store clerk, stories about all the funny and weird people who came into the shop every day – all those lives: the girl with the strange green eyes and the scary tattoo, the taxi driver who always bought a bento for lunch. Did any of those customers notice when I quit and moved on? Did they notice me, or was I just a worker robot to them? And whatever happened to the nice old guy with the purple bandana? I used to meet him outside the shop and give him the food we were going to throw away. Poor old guy. But he'd just stopped coming, even before I quit the job.

'*Kanpai*,' she said, clinking her Asahi tin against mine, bringing me back to the present. She made a point of putting her can lower than mine, which slightly annoyed me. It was almost like she'd beat me to it.

'*Kanpai*.' I glugged down on my beer and smacked my lips.

'So . . .' she said.

'So . . .' I said.

'I suppose we never really said it before but *yoroshiku onegai shimasu*.' She bowed her head.

'*Kochira koso, yoroshiku onegai itashimasu*.' I bowed lower, and spoke more formally. Hopefully that would make up for losing on the *kanpai* front.

'You're so formal.' She took out the hand towel from her handbag and wrapped it around the can.

'So, how come you know so much about trains to Chiba?' I jumped in with my flying-kick attack.

'Because I live there.' She blocked.

'Why do you live so far out in the sticks?' I did a leg sweep with a low kick.

'Rent's cheaper.' She jumped over my leg. 'Where do you live?' She kicked me in the face.

'Ummm . . .' I was stunned.

'Sorry, I'm being nosey.' She jumped nimbly back into her part of the screen with a full health bar. 'When did you start playing Street Fighter?'

I felt a little more confident dealing with this kind of question. 'When I was a kid. I used to play with my brothers.'

'Older or younger?'

'Both. I was the middle.'

'Middle, eh? Me too. And who was the best at Street Fighter?'

'Well . . . That's a difficult one to answer.'

'How so?' She sipped on her beer and took little bites from her sandwich.

'When we were kids, it was my older brother. He used to whoop us all the time.'

'Then what happened?'

'I don't know, but one day, I beat him.'

'Oh wow. Well done.'

'No . . . It wasn't a good day.' I thought back to what happened the day I'd beaten him. The way my younger brother had been so happy to see me win, he'd let out a laugh. Older brother had been livid. He was shaking with anger, but instead of attacking me, he grabbed younger brother and started to punch him in the face. I looked on, horrified, unsure what to do. 'Anyway, what about you and your older brother? You said earlier you played against him. Who was better?'

'I was, of course.'

'So where's your older brother now?'

60

'He's dead.' She looked out of the window.

'Oh . . . I'm sorry to hear that. That's terrible.'

She looked down at her sandwich and screwed up her face. 'No. I'm sorry.'

'What do you mean?'

'Urgh.' She shook her head, then beat her hand against her forehead. 'He's not really dead. I have no idea why I said that. I'm sorry. That was a really fucked-up thing to say.'

'Oh . . .' I took a long glug on my beer. Was she mental?

She put her hand on my arm. 'Look. I don't know why I said that. Can you just forget I said it?'

I swallowed my beer. 'Sure.'

'My older brother isn't dead. And we haven't fallen out or anything. We get along fine. He lives in Gunma. He's married. His wife is lovely. He has two beautiful kids. I go see them regularly. But . . .' She looked out the window again into the darkness. Somewhere out there, the waves were rolling across the horizon slowly, but we couldn't see them. Perhaps we could all feel their movement from the rocking train.

'But?'

'But . . . I don't know. It's stupid. Don't you ever just feel like things change? Like, even if something dramatic or terrible in your life *doesn't* happen, just the act of growing older is like a massive trauma anyway. When I think of sitting on the tatami with my older brother when we were kids, there's just something overwhelmingly painful about the thought of having lost that moment. This wave of nostalgia which constantly reminds us that we can never go home again. That those kids sitting on the floor, so young and so happy, are dead and gone now. They're never coming back. And don't get me started on my younger brother, who is *so much* younger . . . he's stopped going to elementary school, and he won't talk to anyone. And there's nothing I can do to help him. He used to be such a happy kid, but it's like the very act of growing old is slowly killing him . . .'

I didn't know what to say, so I just kept quiet. I couldn't believe she was being so candid.

'I'm sorry. I'm talking rubbish.' She sighed.

'No, I don't think so. I get it. Family is tough.' Ugh. There I go again, sounding like a douchebag.

'Thanks.' She turned and smiled at me, reaching into the bag for a kimchi pork onigiri which she handed to me. 'You're a good listener, you know.'

'Cheers.' As I took the onigiri, our fingers brushed slightly, and her eyes flicked up to mine. I blurted out something quickly. 'So, who's your favourite Street Fighter character?'

She didn't even blink. 'Ken. You?'

Why did I assume Chun Li? God I'm sexist. 'Ken.'

'The true player's choice.' She smiled.

'Do you put in the speed cheat when you play?' I tested her.

'Of course.'

'Do you remember how to do it, because sometimes I forget—'

'Down, R, Up, L, Y, B. You have to do it on controller two.'

Wow. She knew her shit. 'Hey, did you hear the story about M. Bison—'

'About how Balrog the boxer was originally going to be called M. Bison in America because he was modelled after Mike Tyson, but then Capcom worried Tyson might sue, so they switched the names around?'

'Is there anything you *don't* know about Street Fighter?' I was impressed.

'How would I know whether there was or wasn't?' She giggled.

'Can I make a confession?' I said.

'Shoot.'

'There were always two moves I could never do in the game.'

'Really?'

'Yeah. I could never do Dhalsim's Yoga Teleport or Zangief's Spinning Piledriver. I'm kind of afraid to ask, but, can you do them?'

'It took me a lot of practice. They're tough moves.'

I'd underestimated this girl.

'Do you mind if I take a nap?' she asked.

'Go for it,' I said.

'Would it be rude if I rested my head on your shoulder?'

'No, please do.'

She laid her head on my shoulder, and I felt the softness of her hair as it brushed against my collar.

'Wake me up when we get there.'

'Sure.'

⚠

The passengers thinned out the further from Tokyo we got. Now the carriage was almost empty. We sat side by side facing the dark windows, the bright light making it impossible to see outside. I sat there thinking. I knew I was never going to beat Kyoko at Street Fighter II. As sure as this train would arrive at Chiba Station, I was going to get my butt kicked.

As I was thinking about this, we stopped at another station where no passengers got on. The familiar beeping sounded, indicating the doors were about to shut, then a small calico cat jumped through the narrowing gap of the train doors, and sprang up onto the seat opposite.

'Whoa!' I said, unable to stop myself. Kyoko stirred a bit but didn't wake up. My left hand immediately crept towards my pocket, as carefully as I could, to get my smartphone and snap a photo of this commuting cat.

Sitting upright, the cat looked directly at me.

In its luminous eyes I saw something. Something chaotic. A city reflected in its irises. It was like the cat saw us all moving around, and just as the image of the city bounced off its eyeballs, so too did the cat reject any idea of human form or control. This cat had no master, and I envied it for that.

Kyoko was leaning her head on my shoulder still, her soft breathing making her chest rise and fall rhythmically. My fingers were still snug inside my pocket, touching my phone, but just as I got it out, the train pulled in at the next station. The doors opened, and just like that, as though it knew exactly where it was going, the cat jumped up and left the train. I looked at the photo I'd taken: blurred and shaky rubbish. The cat was an indistinct ball of colour leaving the train. I tapped the trash can image on my phone and the scene sucked away into nothing. I looked up from my phone, and out of the train window I saw the cat strolling away down the platform, its tail held high. As the train began to rock again, I settled back and closed my eyes.

Sometimes I feel like this whole city is one vast organism. It's like a human being that we're all part of. But we're restricted by the roads, by the waterways, by the tunnels, the trains. It's like our paths are all laid out for us, and there's no way of deviating from them. That's what makes that cat different from us. It can jump on and off trains randomly. But we humans are bound up in the fate of the city. No one can escape its clutches. I'd love to pack up and leave for the countryside, but I can't get away. I'm stuck here. Kindergarten, Elementary School, Junior High, High School, University, Internship, Internship to Job, Job to Retirement, Retirement to Death. That's my life, already laid out before me. Me, and all those other millions of people I brush up against every day. The city needs us, and we need the city. Symbiotic fuck tonnage.

⁂

Let me just press pause for a second.

So, up until now, you might have noticed I've been talking about everything in the past tense. Some of you might have been wondering, 'What happened in the end?' Well, the truth is, I'm telling my story *now*. And *now* is on this train with Kyoko. The cat has just come onto the train and jumped off, and it's got me mulling over the events of this evening in my mind.

I wonder if any of you have ever felt this kind of sinking feeling, like you just know what's going to happen. It's like this train I'm on – there's no deviating from the tracks. As I sit here, I think I know exactly how the evening is going to play out. In fact, I'm sure of it. This is what's going to happen:

We'll get to Chiba. Kyoko and I will be excited to arrive.

We'll head to her friend's bar and we'll be chattering about how much we want to play.

We'll be deciding how many stars we should have each, which stage we should fight at and all that stuff.

Then we'll draw closer to the bar, and we'll see the sign in big letters above the door saying YOGA FLAME. But then our eyes will fall on the white piece of paper stuck to the door, and we'll both go silent.

We'll know before we even read it that it says something like:

CLOSED TODAY DUE TO FAMILY EMERGENCY. APOLOGIES.

And then we'll kick around trying to think of ideas. Maybe we'll go to a bar and have a drink while we decide what to do next. And then maybe I'll say something silly without thinking like:

'Hey! We could go to a love hotel!'

And she'll look at me with disgust and say, 'What kind of girl do you think I am?'

And I'll realize I didn't preface that statement properly, and I'll say, 'No, no. I mean sometimes there are love hotels that have game consoles. We could search online for one in Chiba that has a Super Famicon. That way we could still play Street Fighter.'

She will still be put out by the comment and will say something like, 'I'm not just some kind of slut, you know.'

And then I'll get awkward and sullen, because it wasn't what I meant.

We'll have an argument, where she will realize I didn't mean it the way it came out. Then I'll be looking sorry and dejected. She'll say sorry too. Then she'll say something like, 'My place isn't far from here. You can stay the night if you like.'

And I'll say, 'Do you have Street Fighter II?'

And she'll say, 'No, but . . .'

And I'll say, 'It's okay. I'll just go home.'

She'll say, 'But the trains aren't running till the morning.'

I'll say, 'I don't mind waiting.'

She'll say, 'Well, let me keep you company.'

I'll say, 'No, it's fine. You just go home.'

65

We'll pause.

She'll say, 'Okay. Goodbye.'

I'll say. 'Goodbye.'

We'll turn and walk in different directions.

And when I see her on Monday morning, she'll just look through me as if I'm invisible.

⁂

None of this has happened yet. I'm still sitting on the train imagining the future. But why is it that it seems like it's already happened? Like it's happened thousands of times before, that it always will happen, like a piece of CCTV footage of the city, stuck on a loop. She's still resting her head on my shoulder, and all I can think about is whether we have any control over our lives. How can I change the future? Because what is fate, but that moment when you're playing the computer on the hardest difficulty setting, you've run out of life force and you make that one mistake. It's those excruciating moments that pass by like an eternity before that final hit comes. You know you've fucked up, and there's no way of going back. You can press pause as much as you like, but it won't stop what's going to happen.

Time to press start again; to un-pause this game and let it play out to the end.

She lifts her head and opens her eyes.

'Are we there yet?'

Sakura

'Ueno, please,' she says, ducking her head as she gets into the back seat.

I nod and pull the lever beneath my steering wheel, which automatically closes the rear doors. We set off in silence. She's wearing a pink kimono with a sakura blossom pattern, ever so subtle. From the looks of her traditional hairstyle, I'd say she's from out of town. Women in Tokyo don't wear their hair like that anymore. Reckon she's from a town with a bit of history – somewhere like Kyoto maybe. Rich, very well-to-do. Wouldn't like to guess her age – that wouldn't be very gentlemanly. Sometimes if I'm bored and the day is dragging on, I try to work out what kind of person a passenger is. It's good to weigh someone up when they get in, try to guess who they are, what they do and where they're going. I don't make a habit of prying into their lives though. Most of the time I just focus on the road. Try not to be nosey. People's business is their own.

'Lovely spring day, isn't it?' she says.

'Most certainly is,' I reply.

'Years since I've seen the blossoms in Tokyo.' She sighs.

'Come far, have you?'

'Kanazawa. I don't come to Tokyo often. It's a treat for me.'

'Well, I hope you enjoy your stay.'

'Thank you.' In the rear-view mirror, I catch her smile. 'I'm here to see my American friend, from Portland, Oregon. She used to live in Kanazawa, but she moved here to be a translator.'

I smile. These out-of-towners amaze me. No Tokyoite would talk this much about themselves on a first meeting. We go quiet again for a bit, but then she carries on the conversation.

'Have you ever been to Kanazawa?'

'No,' I say. 'I haven't really travelled much.'

'I suppose you must work a lot.'

'A fair bit, yes.'

'Do you have any children?'

Wow. That's a personal question. 'Yes, a daughter.'

'Where does she live?'

'New York.'

'Wonderful! What does she do there?'

I have to brake slightly because the traffic lights have changed to red. 'Married to an American called Erik. Nice guy – loves to drink. Likes his beer and shochu. Had a great time when they came to visit at New Year. It's always sad to see them leave. She's expecting soon. Who would believe it? Me, a grandfather!'

'You don't look old enough to be a grandfather. How old are you?'

'Sixty.'

'Will you and your wife visit New York when the baby is born?'

I'm not sure what to say – I don't want to bring the mood down. 'I hope so.'

'You'll both have a wonderful time.'

She would've, yes. 'I hope so.'

When we arrive at Ueno she pulls crisp bills from her purse and thanks me as she pays. I give her change, then pull the lever to open the rear door. Handy thing, these auto doors. Bet they don't have them on the yellow cabs in New York. She bows her head to me, and I bow back. She places a hand expertly under her kimono as she's leaving the taxi. Then she's out on the streets and meeting up with three other ladies, all dressed in kimono that match the colours of spring. I see the American friend she mentioned – blonde hair and blue eyes. The kimono she's wearing suits her very well. They immediately begin chattering excitedly together – the American girl has amazing Japanese. Then they're headed towards the park. And then the conversation fades as I drive off.

∴

The revellers are out in full today. They sit beneath the blossoms, drinking beers, eating bento, passing around plastic containers of fried chicken from the convenience store. Some of the older men are drunk already – fallen asleep on the blue tarpaulins spread across the ground. Everyone's lined their shoes up neatly by the tarps. Hundreds and hundreds of shoes – mostly the black shoes of salarymen, but there are sandals, high heels and sneakers too. I wonder how many people lose shoes in the *hanami* chaos.

I wish I could join them, drinking beneath the trees. But I need to get lunch and take a quick nap. Catnapping is the only way to get through the long shift – 8 a.m. till 4 a.m. the next day. I hardly spend any time at home, but that suits me fine. I don't really like being alone in the house. Empty spaces are the biggest reminder of what was there before. The negative space. The gap in the bed, the vacant chair, the pair of chopsticks that stay in the drawer unused, the rice bowl that sits on the shelf next to the soup bowl, all dusty now. It's funny – even though I'd moved to this new house, away from the old one in Nakano, I still can't throw out her things.

I stop in at the same Lawson convenience store I go to most days to buy a bento and a bottle of green tea. I nod and smile at a new lad working the tills. The staff here seem to change all the time, workers coming and going constantly. Recently I've noticed a lot of the workers are from other Asian countries, like Vietnam and China – must be students – nice to see them coming to Japan to learn Japanese. All the food and drink packaging in the store is decorated with cherry blossoms, and I'm tempted by the colourful pink designs on the cans of beer. Bah, work.

I usually eat my lunch in the car. Then I can listen to some music. I've got a Cat Stevens CD in the player at the moment. Sometimes I play it when I'm driving, but some of the customers complain. Best to listen to music on my breaks, or when I'm driving alone.

As I'm driving down a side road I see the perfect place to stop for lunch – under a cherry blossom tree that hangs out over the road, providing a bit of shade. I sit in the car, put on 'Father and Son' and eat my bento and drink my tea, looking up at the cherry blossoms. It's my own private *hanami*.

After I finish eating, I put the seat back, and stretch out with my hands behind my head and look up at the blossoms. A strong gust of wind hits the petals and now they're falling down onto the windshield like a blizzard of cherry-coloured snowflakes. I close my eyes and can almost feel the petals falling on my face.

▲▲

I'm dreaming. I know I'm dreaming, because I'm in Dad's study and he's still alive. I'm watching him write his stories. He's using the old fountain pen he gave to me before he died. He's carefully marking out *kanji* – Chinese characters – in bright blue ink on square manuscript sheets. He looks up as I walk into the study and he smiles. There are neat piles of paper everywhere, ready to be sent off to editors and publishers. Books in wobbly stacks. The lower corner-section of his bookcase is filled with all the *rakugo* books that my older brother, Ichiro, used to read over and over. He's curled up on the floor there reading, a little boy again.

I've still got the pen Dad gave me, but now it's sitting in a drawer. Haven't used it in years. I promised him I'd write more poems. I never did, not since I met her. Once I met her, I just didn't feel the need to write anymore. And then when Ryoko was born, all I wanted to do was work, to earn money for them. To make them happy.

When I look back at my father's face again, it's changed to my brother's. He's sitting in the *seiza* position wearing a kimono, with his hands tucked neatly in front of him, as if he were just about to begin a *rakugo* performance.

Ichiro was always the storyteller, the famous one.

And now he's gone too.

I couldn't even call him to tell him when she died.

▲▲

The alarm on my smartphone wakes me. The sun is shining in through the cab window, and I'm sweating. My back is aching badly. I open the glove compartment and scrabble around for the pot of pills. My fingers fumble with the cap, and I find it hard to get a pill in my grasp. I put it on my tongue and taste its bitterness, wash it down with the dregs of my tea. Then I put on a clean pair of white driving gloves, set my hat on straight, check myself in the mirror and drive on.

When I'm passing by Ueno Station a strange-looking guy in his thirties flags me down. His hair is long and straggly, and he's unshaved. From his clothes and appearance, he looks a lot like a factory worker on his day off. He gets in silently and we head off.

'Where to?'

'Akihabara,' he says, looking out the window.

Outside the buildings snake and swarm around us. The sun is high, and the midday heat is roasting the asphalt. Shimmering heat waves hang in mid-air. I put on the air conditioner. The glass high risers of the electrical district reflect the sky's deep blue, smatterings of white fluffy clouds transposed on the windows of grey concrete boxes. If I had my pen, I'd write this stuff down. Dad would've liked it.

When we pass a gaggle of foreign tourists on the pavement, the guy says, 'Is it me, or is this city crawling with gaijin these days?'

He cracks his knuckles. I shiver.

'Yes, it makes me proud—'

'It makes me sick.' He's not listening.

'Is that so?'

'Coming here, disrespecting our culture. Don't even speak Japanese.' He snorts.

'Really?'

'They come here, trample on our temples, shrines and graves. They disrespect our history, our culture. They go to bars, drink too much and grope our women. They treat us like idiots.'

'My apologies, Kyaku-sama, but, well, it's probably my misunderstanding, but I thought they came because they're interested in our culture—'

'Oh, you think so, eh?' He makes a funny spluttering sound in his throat, like I've said the stupidest thing in the world. 'The Americans dropped bombs on us, castrated us, made us accept their peace. Not *our* peace, *their* peace. And now we stand by and let the Chinese take the Senkakujima islands from us, while the Koreans try to steal Takeshima Island. We've become the joke of Asia, because we let everyone walk over us. Gaijin don't respect Japan, or our culture. It makes me sick.'

What a load of bollocks, is what I think, but I can't say that to a customer.

'I see,' is what I say.

'Thanks. I'll get out here.'

I stop the car, and he pays his fare. As I'm giving him his change, he passes me a card.

'If you're interested.'

I look at the card as he's walking away. Printed on shabby cheap paper are the words *Don't become one of the ants!* What was this? *Uyoku dantai* – a right-wing political group? I look out the window and see him disappearing into one of the 'cafés' where the foreign girls ply their services. I shake my head and slip the card into my little rubbish bag in the footwell.

Over the next few hours I pick up a few passengers here and there – a group of high-school girls on their way to karaoke, a couple of sumo wrestlers who make the car creak and tip backwards slightly, a friendly old professor with a stack of second-hand novels that he bought in the bookshops of Jinbocho. By sundown I'm working the area around Tokyo Station. The office blocks of Marunouchi are emptying as the working day comes to an end. Most of the senior workers have been out all day under the cherry blossoms drinking, but now the juniors are getting out from the offices and hurrying to join the festivities. I ferry a young guy from the taxi rank outside Tokyo Station on his way to Shimbashi. Looks like he's been drinking on the train a bit already. Probably on a business trip from out of town.

'Sorry, could you drive a bit slower?' he says, coughing.

'Certainly, sir. Sorry about that.'

'It's okay, I just . . . I just . . .'

'Are you all right?' I'm already pulling over.

'I need to—' He makes a retching sound, and he's covering his mouth with his hand.

I whip out a sick bag from my side pocket and pass it to him as quick as I can. I look the other way as he vomits. I hear the splattering of watery solid against the bag's paper base. The sour smell is already at my nostrils, so I cover my nose with my hand discreetly, and crack the window open a bit.

'Sorry,' he says.

'Please, sir. It happens. Don't apologize.' I smile at him and see a long strand of saliva linking his lips to the bag's edge. I pass him one of the tissues I keep in the door's side pocket for just such things.

'Thank you.' He wipes his face.

'Are you all right to carry on?' I ask.

'I think so. Can we take it a bit slower?'

'Certainly. Do you like Cat Stevens?'

'Love him.' He smiles.

I push play on the CD player.

⁂

The city glides at night. It stutters during the day, with the bumper-to-bumper traffic. But at night, the roads clear, and my cab cruises seamlessly from one fare to another. The concrete sings a quiet tune beneath my tyres. It's like the whole city is on ball bearings, moving around me, and I'm the one in the centre holding everything together. I like the sensation. It reminds me of something I always think about before I go to sleep – have done ever since I was a kid. My futon becomes a magic carpet, and I can fly around the streets while lying down. People look at me and point as I fly by, and sometimes I slow down to chat.

I take another pill because my lower back is throbbing again, then stop at a taxi rank for a coffee. Wada and Yamazaki are hanging around the vending machine smoking. Wada has put on even more weight, and Yamazaki is getting even thinner. From a distance they look like the two funny creatures from that Disney movie about the lion I used to watch with Ryoko when she was little. What were their names again? One of them was a warthog, and the other was a wisecracking rat, or something.

'Oh, if it isn't Taro-san! How are you?'

'Not bad, Yamazaki-san. And you?'

'Working like a dog but can't complain.'

I put 120 yen into the vending machine and get a cold can of black coffee. I crack the top open and let out a sigh of relief.

'Taro-san. Cigarette?' Wada shakes his pack in his chubby hand.

'*Arigato*. I owe you.' I take one, and Yamazaki is already extending a long arm, lighter lit.

'Nonsense, you're always giving Wada cigarettes. He's a filthy scrounger.' Yamazaki cracks a smile, revealing his yellow-stained teeth.

Wada looks hurt.

'Speaking of scroungers, how's that son of yours, Yamazaki?' Wada winks at me.

Yamazaki rolls his eyes.

'Oh, don't start. It's bad enough with my wife chewing my ear off at home. I don't need you two reminding me of my troubles. Honestly, I'm glad I have a job that gets me out of the house all day – just to get away from my family.'

'How's your family, Taro-san?' Wada turns to me.

Yamazaki makes eyes at Wada. I look the other way as if I'm blowing cigarette smoke away from them. I don't want to embarrass Wada. Maybe he hasn't heard the news about my wife, so I change the subject.

'Anyone catch the Giants score?' I ask.

'You think we've got time for baseball?' says Yamazaki, but he sounds relieved we've changed the subject.

'I don't even want to know this season. The Carp just depress me.' Wada's from Hiroshima, and proud of it. 'Hey, why don't you come for a drink with us sometime, Taro-san?'

'Ah, I don't know,' I say.

'Go on! It'll be fun,' says Yamazaki.

'I know a great okonomiyaki place – friend runs it,' says Wada.

'Wada,' says Yamazaki. 'Taro-san is a born and bred Tokyoite. He's sophisticated. You think he wants to eat that country-bumpkin rubbish?'

Wada hits Yamazaki playfully on the back of the head, and we all laugh. We stand around chatting and smoking, and they check my mobile number to organize going for a drink soon. Then there's that uncomfortable silence, the mutual acknowledgement that as much as I'd like to stand around drinking coffee and smoking cigarettes, time is money. I make my excuses, and Wada kindly takes my empty can in his chubby hand, as always. I bow my head and return to my cab. As I drive off I watch them light another cigarette. Can't help but laugh to myself. Do those two ever work?

It's early evening and now the starless sky above casts a blackness onto the neon chaos of the city. The roads tangle and twist, looping overpasses and burrowing tunnels. Everything intersects and entwines, like thick white strands of noodles from a bowl of udon. And as evening wears on, the city starts to sweat and stink. Smoke wafts from the yakitori stalls under the Shimbashi Station train tracks, drifting between brightly coloured lanterns and the yellowing Showa-era cinema posters peeling off the walls. Outside, the office workers sit on empty beer cases turned upside down to make cheap stools. They smoke and talk, snacking on yakitori sticks and washing everything down with frosty glasses of beer.

As the night goes on, the drunks become rowdier and more lonesome. I see a group of young salarymen, with arms around each other's shoulders, yelling out songs into the night air. And there's a young man peeing off a walkway bridge onto the road below. His friends are cheering him on. Can't help but chuckle. They need to let off steam. Every day they're chained to their desks, locked in their cubicles. Serving the company. Poor bastards. I could never have done that. That's why I chose to drive a cab. Out here, I'm my own boss. No one tells me what to do, or where to go. Everything's down to me.

Later on I pick up a fare in Roppongi. Two guys and a girl. The guys are dressed in black suits and white shirts – office workers. The girl looks a bit different. She's wearing a pink Polo sweater and cream trousers. The pink sweater reminds me of the lady I had in my cab earlier – the pink of cherry blossoms in her kimono. But this girl's younger and has her hair in a ponytail. The first guy and the girl get in quietly – he's wearing his jacket and looks nice and smart, his hair looks sensible, not all spikey like some of the youngsters have it these days. The other guy takes a while to get in because he's swearing at someone further down the road. When he finally does, I can see that he's taken his jacket off, and his shirt is untucked. I can make out a soya-sauce stain just below his breast pocket. The poor girl is trapped in the middle seat.

'Shibuya!' says the scruffy guy.

'Nah,' the other man says. 'Sorry, Ryu. I'm gonna pass. No more drinking. I'm going home.'

'Come on, Makoto! Don't be boring! Kyoko, you want another drink, don't you?'

'Well, we've already drunk quite a lot . . .' the girl answers.

'Nonsense! The night's only just begun. Driver! Take us to Shibuya!'

'Understood.'

I set off to Shibuya, but something tells me this fare is going to be difficult. When you have three drunk people in a cab, there are often disagreements.

'Which bar are we going to?' says the drunk one called Ryu.

'I'm running out of cash,' says the other one, Makoto.

'Driver, do you take credit cards?' asks Ryu.

'I do,' I reply. 'But, if you have cash, that's preferable. The company makes me pay the credit-card fee myself.'

'No problem. Can you take us to an ATM? I need to get money out anyway.'

'Certainly.'

We stop at the ATM, and Ryu gets out of the cab clutching his credit card. The other two sit in the back seat. They whisper quietly to one another.

'How are we going to get rid of him?' says Makoto.

'Oh God,' says the girl, Kyoko. 'I don't know. He's so irritating when he's drunk.'

'How about we get off earlier at a subway station? Then we can take the subway somewhere else. Maybe head back to Chiba?'

'Perfect.'

'Driver, can you drop us off first at a subway station before taking our friend on to Shibuya?' asks Kyoko in a louder voice.

'No problem.'

I can't help but sense the upcoming issues with this – the danger ahead. Part of me wants to tell them all to grow up – to communicate better with each other. To be clearer about what they want. Maybe in New York where Ryoko is the cabbies might speak up and say something, but in Japan we always say the customer is a god. And how can you tell a god what to do?

Ryu gets back in the cab, sloppily stuffing a wad of 10,000-yen notes into his wallet.

'Okay! Let's party!'

As we near the subway station, I watch them in my rear-view mirror. Makoto is reaching in his pocket and pulling out more bills.

'Here, this should cover it,' he says, passing the notes to Ryu.

'What's this for?' asks Ryu.

'We're getting out here,' says Makoto.

'What do you mean? Where are you going?'

I stop the cab in front of the subway station and open the door on Makoto's side. He slides out first, followed by Kyoko. She stands close to him, but they don't touch.

'Where are you going?' Ryu repeats.

'Home,' says Kyoko.

'I thought we were going for a drink in Shibuya?' His voice is whiney.

'Sorry, Ryu. We're tired. You go ahead without us.'

'Can't we go for one more drink here before you go? Driver, thanks, I'll get out too.' Ryu starts to push the money towards me. I half extend my hand to take it, but then turn my face away.

'No, Ryu,' says Makoto. 'Go home.'

'Fine.' He passes the money to Makoto. 'Have this back. I don't want it.'

'Don't be silly. Just take it. You can have a drink in Shibuya and then go home.'

'I don't need it. I've got my own money.'

'Well, if you're sure.' Makoto takes the money back.

Ryu is scowling.

'See you tomorrow,' says Kyoko. She smiles at him and waves.

'Whatever,' he says.

And then I shut the door of the cab, and we're off to Shibuya.

'Fucking assholes,' Ryu is muttering to himself on the back seat. 'Backstabbing shits.'

I stay quiet. I've a lot of experience dealing with drunks. Not just on the job, at home, too – I dealt with Ichiro at his worst. I can handle this guy.

'Fuck.'

I put on Cat Stevens. Hope it might cheer him up.

'Turn that shit off.'

'Sorry, sir.' I turn it off.

'Fucking assholes. Everything's fucked.'

'Do you still want to go to Shibuya, sir?'

'Of course I do! What kind of question is that?'

'Sorry, sir.' I touch my cap and nod. 'I was just checking. My apologies.'

'Just do your job. Drive the taxi, and mind your own fucking business.'

'I'm sorry, sir.'

He looks out of the window, shaking his head. We're coming up to the scramble intersection at Shibuya. It's midnight now, and the youngsters are all out ready to drink until the early hours.

'Pull over.'

'Yes, sir.'

'Here.' He hands me a credit card.

'Sir, would you mind paying with cash, it's just—'

'Are you telling me what to do?'

'No, sir. It's just—'

'It sounds a lot like you're telling me what to do. What's your name?'

'If you look behind my headrest, sir, you can see my name and number on the—'

'That's not what I asked. I asked you a simple question. What's your name?'

'Ohashi Taro.'

'Well, Taro.' He's leaning in so close I can smell the alcohol on his breath. 'Do you know who I am, what I do, and who my father is? I could have you fired, you know. You shithead.' I think of Ichiro, and some of the terrible things he said to us. That day under the cherry tree in the garden.

'I'm sorry, sir,' I say quietly. 'I meant no disrespect.'

'Yeah. Just you remember that. I'm the customer. Not you.'

'Yes, sir.'

I swipe his credit card as quickly as I can. Then I open the door for him to leave.

'Fuck you, Taro. You piece of shit taxi driver scum.'

He slides out of the cab.

'Thank you, sir. Have a nice night.' I shut the door and drive away.

At night, when I'm driving, sometimes I look out the window and I see a face moving at the same speed as me. For that moment, it's like we're both stationary, two spectral faces hanging in the air. Sometimes they look straight at me; other times they gaze off at something unseen in the distance. The face just hangs there in the dark, like a reflection. But as soon as I see it, it's like it immediately starts drifting away. The face will ascend onto an overpass; I'll descend into a tunnel. And just like that, we drift apart.

⁂

It's 1 a.m. now. I stop off at the McDonald's in Shibuya, where I always go whenever I'm in the area at this time of night. People would think I'm strange if I told them why I always go to that same one. It's difficult to even admit it to myself, but it's to see one of the girls who works the night shift there. She's working tonight too, same as ever. I wait in the queue and let people go in front of me. I time it just right so she serves me.

'Oh, hello again! How are you?' she asks.

'*Genki*,' I say. 'For an old man.'

She laughs, her green eyes twinkling. 'What can I get for you?'

'Just a black coffee.'

'Anything else?'

'Maybe one of those brown hashes.'

'You mean hash browns?' She giggles.

'Yes, that's the one.'

I watch her get my order for me, smile and thank her as she passes me the tray. Her tattoo peeks out from under her sleeves as she extends the tray towards me, but I try not to look at that. Instead I look at her name badge like I always do, studying the N, the A, the O, the M, the I – and the lack of stars next to her name. I take a seat near the counter, one that faces out the window so I can see her reflection without her knowing I'm looking. She always smiles at me. Sometimes she asks me how I am. But lately I've started feeling embarrassed when she recognizes me. It makes me wonder if she'd think it's creepy that I come here just to see her. She has the same sharp cheekbones, the same dimpled smile as Sonoko, my niece, did. Sonoko passed away a long time ago, while she was still just a child. But if she had grown up to be in her twenties, I like to think she would look like the girl who works here. I drink my coffee and eat half of the brown hash, and she waves to me as I'm leaving. I wave back. I get back in my cab and drive to a quieter side street in Shibuya, away from the bars. I pull over and pop a couple of painkillers before taking another quick nap.

⛬

There's a cherry tree. That's all there is. Just a cherry tree, like the one in our old garden. The one Ichiro used to perform under, before the times he got so drunk he couldn't even tell his stories. I had to wrestle him inside once in front of Sonoko and Ryoko, and he spat and swore at me.

It's in full bloom, and I can't take my eyes off the strange colour of the flowers – white tinged with blood red.

Now the petals are falling slowly from the tree. They're cascading down to the ground, like white handkerchiefs covered in blood. I blink, and when I look again, all of the blossoms have gone. And now all I see is a withered old tree by itself, blossoms rotting at its base.

▲▲

The voicemail icon is flashing on my smartphone. A Tokyo number. Call came through early evening. Must be Wada or Yamazaki calling about going for dinner. I tap the icon and listen.

'Hello, this is Sergeant Fukuyama calling from the Tokyo Metropolitan Police. I'm trying to contact Ohashi Taro-san. I got this phone number from the taxi company. I'm leaving the office now, but if you can call me back on this number, or failing that, I'll call again tomorrow. Thank you.' The message ends.

What on earth could that be about? But I'm too tired to think. Need to go home to shower and sleep.

The roads are empty and rows of yellow street lamps rush by as I speed towards the western suburbs. In the distance, one of the street lamps is flickering, and as I approach it my eyes start watering. I blink and rub my eyes, but the light is still flickering. Distracting. Probably just needs a new bulb. I rub my eyes again, and then there's a flash of motion. A small shape darts out onto the road and then stops still right in front of me. Its eyes are reflected in my full beams, hovering in the air like a ghastly face from the underworld. It won't move, and I have no time. Why won't it move? I'm braking, but I don't have time – I'm going to hit it. I don't want to, I don't want to take a life. So I'm turning my wheel. The cat stays still, but I'm locked up, and my tyres are screeching, and now, instead of a cat, I'm coming straight at a parked car, and the car is getting closer and closer, but I can't stop, this is really it, the milk in my fridge will go mouldy, the rubbish needs putting out, they'll call Ryoko in New York to let her know, I won't be able to go for okonomiyaki with

Wada and Yamazaki, maybe it's all for the best, maybe I'll see her again.

And then there's the crunch and the screech and the smash of glass, and the pain in my head as my nose hits an enlarging white balloon that's blossoming from the steering wheel and the terrible sound of metal being torn and smashed and crunched and and and and . . . there's nothing but silence and fog. And a searing pain in my leg.

'Hello?'

I try to raise my head from the steering wheel, and I look at my white driving gloves. There's a big red round splodge on the back of one, which makes it look like the Hinomaru flag. All I can think of is how they're ruined, and I'll have to get new ones. My phone is lying on the seat next to me, smashed to pieces.

'Are you okay?'

I lift my head slightly, and I see a ghostly face floating in the air. It hovers next to me so close, and I can see its concern and pity and warmth and compassion and all of the emotions I once knew so well. And I worry that the face and I will slowly begin to drift apart: it will disappear and leave me alone again, floating away on my magic-carpet futon, away from the city, into the darkness above the bay. I blink, and through the blood I see the outline of a blonde Western lady with a dog. Is she an angel? Am I dead? She's peering through the shattered glass. I try to speak, but words don't come.

'Don't move. I'll call an ambulance,' says a voice in heavily accented Japanese.

And then everything is white, tinged with red.

Detective Ishikawa: Case Notes 1

The day they first came into my office I'd been playing *shogi* chess on my laptop against an old college friend online. It was late in the day, and work was slow.

The only cases I'd been taking on recently, other than the steady stream of infidelity jobs, were missing cats. Maybe something in the water, but there'd been a massive increase in the number of cats vanishing from the streets. I'd even had a kid come in with some cartoons he'd drawn of his cat that had gone missing. I asked him if he had any photos, but all he had were cartoons. Strange kid. Missing cats and dogs are bread and butter for detectives in Tokyo, but the sheer number disappearing recently was slightly out of the ordinary. Word on the street was they were clearing them out the way for the Olympics. But as with most rumours, you're never sure how much truth there is to them, if any.

There wasn't much I could do anyway – other than walk the burbs and put up a few posters here and there. Hell, most people don't even look at those things in any case. If I ever found a pet, I'd give it to Taeko, to take home and hang onto for a few days. That way I could bill the client for a bit more time on the clock. Hey, they were always happy to pay – they'd got their precious baby back.

I was considering my next chess move when Taeko buzzed me on the intercom.

'Ishikawa-san.'

'Yes?'

'We have clients. A man and a woman. Shall I send them through?'

'Sure.' I carried on studying the *shogi* board on my screen till they both came through the door. Then I closed my laptop.

⁂

People talk a lot about open and shut cases. Truth is, not a lot of those exist. Most cases are open, and a lot of them stay that way. Right now, I've got a ton of open cases. Cases I can't say I'll ever close. All cases take time and luck. Mostly luck. And some people are just plumb out of both. These two who'd just walked into my office looked about the unluckiest pair I'd ever seen. If I'd moved them both into a big old house full of money, they'd have ended up on the streets, clutching each other within a week.

She was the nervous-looking kind – fidgeted and fiddled with her hands. When she wasn't wringing her hands in front of her, she would nervously tuck her straggly (greasy) hair behind her ears. I could tell she'd picked out her best clothes to visit the office, but they looked worn and beaten up. It was obvious she didn't have much to choose from.

Same went for her husband. She hadn't had much to choose from there either.

His shirt was covered in stains. Ramen for lunch, I'd guess. Teeth all gawky, hair uncombed. What a mess. He wasn't a small fellow though. He had a certain bulkiness to his physique, but it was slowly sapping away as old age set in. He stooped, as if embarrassed about his height.

'Please,' I gestured to the chairs in front of my desk. 'Have a seat.'

They sat down awkwardly, squeezing large buttocks into narrow seats.

I waited for one of them to talk.

'Detective.' She was the first to speak, and she looked up from her hands as she did so. 'We need your help.'

'Well, that's a surprise.' I needed a cigarette.

'Yes . . .' she continued. 'We . . . well . . . how should I put it?' She wrung her hands so hard they went white. I thought they might fall off.

'C-c-can you—' he leant forward in his chair, dabbing his sweaty forehead with a handkerchief, 'help us f-f-find our s-s-son?'

Great. This was going to be a long appointment.

'Before we get into any details, I should let you know my fee.'

I've found in the past it's always best to be upfront about money. Nothing worse than having to listen to a long tearjerker, only for them to find out how much it's going to cost. Then they really start bawling.

'Yes, yes. That would be a good idea.' She was digging a nail into her wrist now.

'Here.' I passed them my price list.

He took it first, and I saw his eyes widen. His jaw dropped slightly, and she took the card away from him. She placed it back on the table and took out a white handkerchief and dabbed at her wrist. I noticed specks of red on it when she put it back in her purse.

'D-d-detective Ishikawa,' he began. 'Is there any way . . .'

' . . . we could pay this off in instalments?' She finished his sentence.

'Maybe we can work something out.' I sighed.

The rest of the appointment went fine, but I could see their eyes glazed over a bit. They gave me some photos of him (why is it missing people in photos always look like they're just about to go missing?). We said our goodbyes and I said I'd do what I could.

But I could tell they were still thinking about the money.

▲▲

There's nothing worse than taking on a case for people who can't afford it. It's not often I get people coming in who can't afford to pay my fee, so when it happens it always makes me feel awkward. My standard case usually goes something like this:

'Detective Ishikawa, delighted to make your acquaintance.'

'Delighted to meet you. Please, have a seat.'

I give Taeko a nod, but she already knows to bring coffee.

We bow and swap business cards.

We sit down, and as we settle, placing each other's meishi on the table in front of us, I have a short moment to study her card.

Her business card is expensive, entirely white, with simple black type, written in English. Sparse – no email, no postal address – just a name, let's say 'Sugihara Hiroko', and a phone number. No company name or job description.

'A bar that I own.' She looks at me with intelligent eyes. 'An exclusive bar. Our clientele requires the utmost secrecy. Hence the lack of address. I apologize for that.'

She doesn't even look at my meishi.

She takes a silver case out of her inside jacket pocket.

'Do you mind if I smoke?'

'Please do.' I fish an ashtray out of my bottom drawer and place it in front of her.

Taeko comes in with the coffees on a tray and puts them carefully on the table. She bows to us as she leaves and shuts the door behind her.

'Would you like one?' Sugihara presents me with the open case. I can't tell the brand, but I can tell that she has self-control. The case only holds seven cigarettes.

'No, thank you,' I reply. 'I've given up. Please go ahead.'

She lights her cigarette, and immediately I regret not taking one. Her lips touch the filter softly, and I see an electric pleasure light up her eyes as she inhales. She looks at me across the desk, straight in the eye.

'Detective Ishikawa. I'll cut to the point. I'm not the kind of lady that beats around the bush, and I know that time is money, for you, and me.'

'Whatever suits you.'

'My husband is having an affair, and I'd like to catch him so that I can get a better divorce settlement.'

I let that hang in the air for a moment.

'Are you certain he's having an affair?'

'Yes.'

'Has he displayed any change in his behaviour recently?'

'No.'

'Nothing you can point to that raises suspicion?'

'Not exactly, no.'

'In my experience, partners having extra-marital affairs usually exhibit some kind of change in their behaviour – usually for the better. Has your husband perhaps started dressing differently?'

'No.'

'I see. Has he seemed happier? Been nicer to you? Bought you gifts?'

'Not at all.'

'I see.' I pause. 'Well, with respect, Sugihara-san . . . How can you be sure your husband is having an affair?'

She takes a long drag on her cigarette, taps out the ash and exhales a dragon of smoke into the air. It wafts across the table to me and slides neatly into my nostrils.

'Detective Ishikawa. My husband is a liar.'

'I'm sorry, I—'

She raises her hand to silence me. 'My husband is a liar by profession. It is his job to lie. He has been lying to me ever since I met him. It's what our relationship is founded on – lying successfully to one another. But a woman knows when her husband is being unfaithful. It's not something I have proof of – he's far too clever to leave proof. But I know for a fact that my husband is cheating on me. I just need you to obtain the evidence. That is all.'

I keep quiet. Let her simmer.

'Detective Ishikawa, you are free to turn down this case. You are certainly not the first detective I've visited in Shinjuku today. However, as I made clear to the others, you would be handsomely compensated. I was thinking of this figure, plus expenses.'

She hands me a piece of folded-up paper. I unfold it and look at the zeros. I fold it again and pass it back to her.

'Okay. I'll do it.'

And that's how I make my money. Catching married people cheating on each other and gathering evidence. Sometimes I'm not sure who's the worst person involved in all this. But at least I get paid at the end of it.

▲
▲▲

After the couple left, I told Taeko she could take off early, did a bit of paperwork and then closed the office for the day.

It was raining outside, so I put up my umbrella and joined the swell of black-suited salarymen heading through the streets of Shinjuku to the train station. I looked just like all the rest of them. That's my strength – fitting in, not standing out. *Deru kui wa utareru* – the nail that sticks out will be hammered in.

Shinjuku. What a cesspool. Not where I would choose to have an office. I'm Osaka – born and bred. But Shinjuku's the grubbiest, sexiest part of this city, and where all the action is. Perfect for a *tantei* like me. Here's where you find all the seediness, the 2-chome gay district, the *nyuhafu* transsexual bars, the brothels, the soaplands, the love hotels, the infidelity.

This is the part of the city where Tokyo hides its vices on show. And I know them all. I've staked them out with my reversible jackets, my hats and fake glasses, my mini camcorder hidden in a pen. Men with wives and kids waiting for them back home. People never realize how good they've got it till they're on the other end of a divorce case and paying through the nose.

The train was another shade of crowded shit that night. There'd been a jumper on the Chuo Line, so it was already delayed and packed beyond capacity. The rain made the carriage hot and sticky. I squeezed on and held my breath as we headed out west to the suburbs. I fell asleep standing up and almost missed my stop.

As I prised myself off the train at my station, I realized I hadn't eaten since breakfast, so I stopped in at a ramen place, ordered a miso ramen with extra *chashu*, and a beer. It came quickly, and I was so hungry that when I'd finished I ordered another beer and a plate of gyoza. As I was tipping the last bit of soup from the ramen down my throat, I looked at the patterns of red grease tumbling down the sides of the white bowl. It looked like koi carp swarming over each other in a pond, eager to get at food on the surface with their terribly stupid glugging mouths. Just like Tokyo – everyone fighting each other for a few crumbs. Maybe the beer had made me sentimental. I needed more to drink.

Next stop was an okonomiyaki shop on my way home, where I had plenty of shochu from a bottle I'd left behind the bar from before. The owner is a real nice guy from Hiroshima who's good to chat to. We had a bit of classic banter about which is better: Osaka or Hiroshima okonomiyaki (Osaka of course). All the customers there like to join in and have a good laugh and joke – that's why I like it. Reminds me of back home. There were a couple of characters I'd not met before – taxi drivers – a real pair. We sat around shooting the shit, and they told me some dumb story about a girl who'd turned into a cat in the shop a while back. Pretty far-fetched if you ask me, but even old Tencho turned white as a sheet and nodded as they told the story. I ended up drinking too much and leaving too late.

It could've been the shochu, but I ended up buying a pack of Calico-brand cigarettes from Tencho and smoking a few.

⁂

The next morning I woke up with a hangover and a raspy throatful of regret for buying – and smoking – cigarettes. I screwed up the rest of the packet and threw them in the trash. I opened the curtains of my tiny apartment, looked outside and saw a small calico cat creeping along the alleyway outside. The cat was pretty far off, but it hit me straight away – the kid's cat – the one who'd drawn the cartoon. I knew it for certain. That was one talented kid. He'd caught something about that little cat, there was no mistake. I was about to run out the house and try to grab it, but it was away and gone in a second, darting under a hedgerow. No chance of finding that little mog in this big old city. Poor kid.

And then, I felt a strange feeling in my stomach. It gripped me so hard I had to put my head in my hands, and my whole body shook. It could've been the booze from the night before, but it didn't feel like any kind of hangover I'd had before. This felt different – it ran deeper.

The feeling passed. I walked to the kitchen, filled a glass of water and took a sip. I carried it over to the old armchair and set it down on a coaster on the bookcase. Inside my stomach I still felt the remains of that empty feeling – the absence of what had just gripped me. I sat down and took out my phone and wallet. I dialled the number on the business card the couple had given me.

He picked up immediately.

'*M-m-moshi moshi?*'

'It's Ishikawa.'

'Oh! H-h-hello, D-d-detective!'

'Shh. Listen. I'll do it for free. But you'd better keep this between us, okay?'

Chinese Characters

The man pressing up against her in the train carriage was making Flo uncomfortable, so she decided to alight at Shinjuku Station and move a few carriages up, to the women-only car. She made her way down the platform, dodging the commuters filing off the train and avoiding the long queues of those waiting to get on.

The Yamanote Line was always crowded in the morning, and the women-only car tended to be the busiest carriage on the train. Flo tried to avoid it if possible, and she hadn't had an incident like this in a while. Lining up behind the other women waiting to board, she could hear the artificial recorded sounds of birds twittering and tweeting coming from the platform, and the familiar Shinjuku Station chime. The alarm sounded, indicating the train was due to pull away, and she pushed her way in, alongside the mass of female bodies. As she filed inside with the other passengers, a wave of cold conditioned air hit her, and she found herself gagging slightly on the rough mixture of perfumes and shampoo scents swilling around in the limited oxygen space above the mass of heads. She put out of her mind the time she'd fainted on the train when she'd first moved to Tokyo. That had been embarrassing.

With her face against the glass window, she looked around the station platform. There was the familiar small poster you could see at a lot of stations in Tokyo: it depicted the silhouette of a young girl who'd dropped her hat on the tracks, and next to her a staff member was fishing it up for her with a long grabbing device;

underneath it read in Japanese, 'People who have dropped belongings on the tracks should please inform a member of staff.' That one always made Flo smile. Most of the other posters were advertising things she couldn't afford, or didn't need: travel, shaving foam, electronics, gym membership, beer; but then she noticed a red and yellow poster on the station walls with a cartoon depicting a man groping a woman on the train. The end of the cartoon had the man being chased by the station guards or the police. Alongside it ran the text:

痴漢は犯罪です！

Chikan is a crime!

It was messed up that Japan Rail had to pay money to put up posters informing its passengers that *chikan* – groping a woman – was a crime. Shouldn't this be common sense? Flo looked at the Chinese characters for the word *chikan* again. The *chi* 痴 part meant stupid, and the *kan* 漢 part meant Chinese. It was the same *kan* 漢 from the word for Chinese characters, *kanji* 漢字. The more Flo thought about it, the stranger the word was – what did Chinese people have to do with Japanese men groping women on the trains? Was the word saying that people who groped were the same as stupid Chinese people? It all seemed a bit bizarre, and very racist.

Well, at least there was something about the phrase that everyone could agree on – groping people on the train is a crime!

The station began to move across her vision. Her eyes locked with one of the conductors working on the platform as the train chugged slowly away. She noted his slight surprise, but smiled at him, and he smiled back and bowed, clasping his gloved hands against his neatly ironed grey trousers. She would've waved, if there was space to move her arms, but sometimes all it took was a smile.

She felt sweat from the other passengers moisten her exposed legs and arms, and the cold sensation it left as the air conditioner chilled the liquid on her skin. She closed her eyes and tried to think of better things.

Flo turned to her familiar trick for coping with commuting, stolen from a talk she'd been to where a man had stood at the front of the room and asked everyone to imagine a moment in their life when they'd been at their happiest. He'd told the class to hold that memory in their mind whenever they were stressed, angry or depressed – to just relive that moment. Flo chose to remember the morning she had witnessed the sun rise from the top of Mount Fuji, how the eggy red orb had slowly emerged above the clouds, the collective gasps coming from the climbers as they felt the warmth flow back into their chilled limbs. Flo had walked up the mountain too quickly and spent several hours huddled by herself next to a bit of old wall. She'd felt so foolish for not having brought the right equipment for herself and sat there shivering until a kind lady had offered her some green tea. If her memory to get her through tough times was the sun rising at the top of Mount Fuji, what could she have used to get her through everything that happened before that moment?

Her station was announced on the loudspeaker. She opened her eyes and stepped out of the train with the other passengers, heading to her company's office in the zombie-like state she shared with all the other salarymen and OLs. She'd learnt that quickly when she'd first moved to Tokyo.

⚐

'Flo-san?'

Even before turning, Flo knew who was calling her. 'Yes, Kyoko-san?'

'Ah, Flo-san.' Kyoko cast her eyes up and down Flo from head to toe. Kyoko, with her immaculate pink Polo sweater and cream trousers, wore a similar outfit every day, like a uniform, and her wardrobe must have had rows of endless hangers for the pristine pink Polo sweaters and perfectly pressed cream trousers. Kyoko had a knack of making Flo feel like whatever she wore to work, it was unacceptable. 'Did you see my note?'

'Your note?' Flo could already tell where this was going.

'Yes, the note I left on your desk.'

'Ah, no. I've only just got in. I'll go read it now.' Flo bowed.

Anyone else would've taken this as the end of the conversation.

Not Kyoko.

She followed Flo along the cubicle corridors of the open-plan office to her desk, talking all the way. 'There are five items I require you to do. Firstly . . .'

Kyoko began to list these things. By the second item, Flo had already reached her desk, had picked up and was looking at the A4 print-out Kyoko had placed there. Kyoko was reporting the note to her verbatim. Flo played a game where she followed the words on the page and matched them with what Kyoko was saying – she got a 100 per cent perfect score today. No deviations from the written note.

'The Olympics are drawing nearer, Flo-san. We really are so grateful for your hard work – your translations are invaluable to the city.' Kyoko tilted her head and looked uneasily into Flo's eyes. 'Do you have any questions?'

'No. That's extremely clear,' said Flo. 'Thank you very much, Kyoko-san.'

'*Yoroshiku onegai shimasu.*' Kyoko bowed low.

'*Yoroshiku onegai shimasu.*' Flo returned the bow.

Flo smiled at Kyoko until she left. Then she swivelled on her chair and powered up her computer. The antiquated PC took a long time to boot up, so she went to grab a cold can of coffee from the vending machine. By the time she came back, the login screen was waiting for her. She logged in and accessed her work email account.

Twenty unread emails. One of which, from Kyoko, was an exact replica of the note/speech she had just received. Translate this. Translate that. Fill out this questionnaire on a foreigner's opinions of kabuki. Fill out that report on sumo wrestling. Deadlines. More deadlines. Flo sighed.

She loaded up her personal email account in a separate browser window. Two new messages – one from Ogawa-sensei, one from her mother. Hovering her mouse over the email from her mother, she could already see the harsh Roman alphabet opening lines, *'Haven't heard from you in ages honey. When are you coming home to Portland?'* Flo shook her head and opted for the soft curly Japanese script from Ogawa. She opened the email and read it twice.

Dear Flo-san,

How is the weather in Tokyo? I expect it is hot. Please take care of your health in this summer period. I hope you can find good watermelon in Tokyo. Perhaps I shall bring some from Kanazawa for you when I visit.

Kanazawa is the same as ever. We are preparing for the summer festival here. Sakakibara-san and the others from the conversation class all ask about you. They all wonder how you are getting on in your new job in Tokyo. I told the others you had started work at a PR company and were no longer translating video games. They were sad to hear that you hadn't been happy at the video games company, but we all think your new job sounds much better. Sakakibara-san was so impressed – our Flo will be translating material for the 2020 Olympics! We are so proud of you.

It all brings back memories of when you first came to Kanazawa all those years ago. Fresh off the plane from America, not speaking a word of Japanese. And look at you now! Translating for the Olympics. They should give you a gold medal!

Do you still practise shodo? *I hope you haven't stopped – you are extremely talented. I miss our calligraphy lessons a lot, you know.*

Well, that's enough prattle from me. I'm looking forward to seeing you in Tokyo soon. We can have coffee in the morning on Saturday, and then unfortunately I have an appointment in the afternoon. Let me know when and what time you would like to meet. I can't wait!

Take care,

Ogawa

 P.S. I have a new Chinese character for you to learn. Do you know this one?

Flo looked at the character and thought about it for a second. She was pretty sure it was *neko* – cat – but had to check. She pulled out her well-thumbed *kanji* dictionary from a shelf of books on her desk and flipped through the pages. Yes, there it was, *neko* – cat. But it was different to how it was written normally. The normal way to write the character was 猫 – with this radical 犭 on the left. The character Ogawa had sent had 豸 on the left. That was the *tanuki* radical. This must be an older version, relating the cat to other shapeshifting animals like the badger, fox and *tanuki*. Flo knew that in the old days, the Japanese believed in things called *bakeneko* – cats that could shapeshift into human form and terrorize people in various ways. But this version of the character was no longer in use. Ogawa had often taught her characters above and beyond practical usage in everyday life, but that was what Flo liked about her.

Flo saw the top of Kyoko's ponytail bobbing along the other side of the cubicle. She closed the window with her personal email and buried herself in her work. In no time at all the chime for lunch was ringing. She grabbed her bag and left the office for a café she often went to.

She had one hour.

⩗

Flo ordered a pasta set menu with an iced coffee and took a seat at a table in the corner. From her bag, she produced a book written in Japanese, and a pencil. She paused for a moment, and upon reflection produced a small manuscript written in English with the title 'Copy Cat'. She placed this on the seat next to her, then turned her attention to the book written in Japanese. In between forkfuls of spaghetti she held the book flat against the table with one hand and read with wide eyes, occasionally putting down her fork to scribble notes in the margins and underline sentences.

Flo had finished her spaghetti and was absorbed in her book until her phone alarm sounded, alerting her she had just ten minutes left before she had to return to the office. She put the book and pencil back in her bag and smiled at the waiter as he took her tray of pasta away. She had a bit of iced coffee left, and she leant back in her seat and sipped slowly on the drink, staring off into the distance.

A pretty Japanese girl with short hair and a foreign man – he looked British – had just bought coffees and came to sit down at the table next to hers. Flo was daydreaming, but she smiled in return to the smug nod from the man and the disinterested wave from the girl as they sat down. The two of them began to talk very loudly and Flo could not block out their conversation. The man was trying his best to speak Japanese in a tone of voice that suggested he was doing it mainly for Flo's benefit, while the girl would respond in slow, patronizing Japanese, or would flick back into perfectly accented American English. They were talking about nothing of note, and Flo was doing her best to block it out and enjoy the last few minutes of her break.

'Kono café kawaii ne,' said the girl.

Flo cringed. Kawaii – cute – was one of the most overused words in Japanese (particularly by girls, she had to admit), applied to just about everything, so that it almost ceased to have meaning at all. It was just something to fill silence. There was nothing particularly cute about this café.

'Last night! So much broooor brooor!' said the man in babyish Japanese. He made hand gestures to accompany the sounds he was making.

'What do you mean when you say broor broor?' asked the girl in condescending Japanese.

'Storm!' said the man.

'Yes, there was a storm last night,' said the girl. 'So what?'

'Flash of light!' said the man.

'Yes, there was thunder.' The girl spoke in English, and as she did so she looked to Flo for sympathy. Flo closed her eyes.

'No. Not thunder! Flash of light!' insisted the man, carrying on in bad Japanese.

'Oh, George. Why do you keep saying that?' The girl gave a little snort.

The man sighed and switched to English with a British accent. 'Look, Mari, what's the word for lightning in Japanese?'

'*Kaminari*,' said the girl.

'No, that's *thunder*,' he said. 'What's lightning?'

'I don't understand what you're asking,' she said.

Flo stood up to leave. Walked one step, thought better of it, and went back to the table.

The couple looked up at her.

'*Inazuma*,' said Flo. She turned quickly and walked towards the door. She heard the man ask, 'What did she say?' as the doors opened.

Flo stepped outside the café and didn't hear the girl's response, or the man calling out, 'Hey wait! Miss!' but blushed red, instantly regretting speaking to them. She walked so quickly back to the office that the man running after her with her manuscript of 'Copy Cat' gave up and returned to the café, only to be berated by his companion.

▲▲

After a couple of hours' overtime, Flo was ready to leave the office. She politely turned down invitations to go for drinks with a few of her colleagues, using the excuse that she did not feel well. She took out her book on the train home, but found her head nodding, so allowed herself a little nap.

On the way back home from the train station she stopped in at a Lawson convenience store and bought a salad. She didn't get any dressing as she had a big bottle of sesame-seed dressing in her fridge at home.

Closing the door of her apartment, she took off her shoes at the *genkan*, and as she did so, she thought to herself as she did every evening how it was impossible to translate the word *genkan*. You could translate it as 'entrance way' or 'porch', but it was neither really. The whole point of the *genkan* in a Japanese home was a space that indicated where the outside ended and the inside began.

She stepped inside the stuffy apartment and opened a window. Flo did not have an air-conditioning unit as they were too expensive, but she did have a lot of books. Her bookcases were stuffed with them, and all shelf space available was taken. Seeing her books reassured her, made her feel calm. She'd read most of them, but there were a many waiting to be read, which gave her a sense of excitement, and conjured up one of her favourite Japanese words – *tsundoku* – a word that required a sentence in English: buying books and piling them up on a shelf without reading them. She turned on a fan, and headed to the kitchen with the salad she'd bought at the convenience store. She took the sesame dressing from the fridge and poured a little onto the salad, mixing it all up with a pair of chopsticks. She took the salad and chopsticks over to her desk and sat down to eat at her computer, which she turned on to watch some of her favourite Japanese YouTubers.

While eating she thought to herself for the millionth time how much easier salad was to eat with chopsticks than a knife and fork. Small tomatoes could be picked up easily and eaten whole. With a fork, it was tough to skewer them on the tines, and they often ended up flying off onto the floor.

Flo had hundreds of these thoughts that swam around in her head throughout the day, but no one to share them with. But she would always tell herself, *Who needs friends, when you have books.* Her bookcases were filled with not just her favourite fiction, but also tomes of linguistic textbooks, dictionaries and reference books, all relating to Japanese language and culture. She considered herself a Japanologist, rather than a Japanophile. To her, there was a big difference. Japanophiles were people who just *loved* Japan without asking questions. They were people who thought Japan could do no wrong, who lived in a fantasy world of anime and manga.

Flo preferred to identify herself with Japanologists. She respected the language and culture, in the same way that she felt every culture and language should be respected. But she recognized within herself a deep-seated need to get to the bottom of every question she had. A quest for knowledge concerning Japan. To learn, to study, to absorb.

While she ate, she pulled a heavy dictionary of Chinese characters off her bookshelf and leafed through the book to find the character *kan* 漢 from the word *chikan* or *kanji*. The question she'd had on the train earlier surrounding the character was playing on her mind. She located the entry for the character, and read the definition while munching on her salad, and discovered that the character did mean 'Han Chinese', but that it could also just mean 'man, guy, bloke'. This was most likely what the character referred to in the word *chikan*. So, it wasn't a racist stereotyping of Chinese people as subway gropers after all. *Chikan* simply meant 'stupid guy'.

She cleared away her supper and, while in the kitchen, opened the fridge and took out a jug of iced coffee. She took a glass from a cupboard and hovered with the jug above the glass. She looked at her watch, shook her head and put the jug back in the fridge. She filled the glass with water from the tap and took it to her desk.

Sitting back down to work, Flo briefly admired the calligraphy that Ogawa had done for her as a leaving gift when she first moved to Tokyo. Ogawa had written the Chinese character for *cat*, but had cleverly shaped the character into the form of a cat. Ogawa and Flo had a shared affinity for cats, and the calligraphy itself told a story of their friendship. Next to the framed calligraphy was a photo of Flo, Ogawa and a couple of her friends. They were all dressed in kimono – Ogawa had picked out a beautiful pink one for when she had visited Tokyo in spring to view the cherry blossoms. Flo remembered the day and how much fun it had been. They'd gone to Ueno Park and sat beneath the blossoms, eating bento and drinking green tea.

Now it was summer, and hot.

Flo took the book she'd been working on from her bag, opened a Word document and began typing up the part she'd reviewed at lunch. Flo had been translating this novel by one of her favourite Japanese authors for several months now and was nearing the end. As always, she lost herself in the task and was shocked when she looked at the clock and saw it was 2 a.m.

She rubbed her eyes, slid into bed, and her alarm was going off again before she knew it.

⚉

Flo's days at work were almost identical. The only difference this week was that she had something to look forward to at the weekend – Ogawa would be coming to visit. Furthermore, Flo had almost finished her translation of the novel she had been working on all these months. She planned to have a polished draft ready to print out and give to Ogawa when they met for coffee at the weekend, and Flo was happy that things were going to schedule.

For it had been Ogawa herself who had first introduced Flo to the author she was translating. She'd given Flo one of his science-fiction short stories for children in Japanese. The story was titled 'Copy Cat', and the author's pen name was Nishi Furuni (real name Ohashi Gen'ichiro). Flo had been enamoured with the writer and surprised that he had not been translated into English yet. Ogawa had been pleased to tell her everything about him.

Furuni had been a prolific writer, although somewhat eccentric – he was obsessed with cats, and Chinese characters. He had begun writing a collection of stories when his granddaughter was diagnosed with cancer and had written a short story for her every day. Furuni's eldest son, the father of his granddaughter, had been a famous *rakugoka*, but had let his alcoholism get the better of him. Because of this, caring for the granddaughter fell to Furuni, who would work on a story all day and then read it to his granddaughter each night before she went to sleep. He continued to do so until her death. 'Copy Cat' was one of these short stories, and had been part of a long collection of 300 stories the author had written for his granddaughter. Flo had read all of them, and had even done a translation of 'Copy Cat', which she gave to Ogawa as a present. She was currently planning on submitting it to literary magazines but didn't have a clue which ones to send it to.

But the novel Flo had been translating was a more personal project. *Desolate Shores* was Furuni's opus. It was the novel he had written before committing suicide. The death of his granddaughter had a massive impact on Furuni's style and life philosophy. The once sober writer became reliant on alcohol and dabbled in hallucinogenic drugs. *Desolate Shores* was the confused masterpiece of a disturbed genius, and Flo had read it cover to cover ten times. During this time, Furuni had become obsessed with *kanji* – the Chinese characters used to write words in Japanese. He had begun to hallucinate, thinking that if he wrote down a character, it might come to life. He avoided using certain characters while writing *Desolate Shores*, in fear that they would animate from the page into real-world monsters and attack him in his sleep. He refused to write the word for *rat* or *cockroach* in his novel, and at night he would write the Chinese character for *cat*, repeatedly, in a chain on the floor around his futon in chalk, believing that while he slept the written characters would come to life as real cats and protect him.

Upon completing the manuscript for *Desolate Shores*, Furuni sent it to his agent, then washed down a bottle of sleeping pills with vodka.

He had become something of a mutual obsession. They would talk for hours about his life and works, and Flo would listen intently to Ogawa bemoaning the fact that he had not been translated into English. Flo planned to rectify this.

⁂

Soon enough, it was the weekend and Flo sent Ogawa a text message to let her know which train station to meet at. Flo had picked out a cat café in the western suburbs of the city and planned to surprise her by taking her there. There were no cat cafés in Kanazawa, so it would be something of a treat for Ogawa.

Flo arrived at the train station thirty minutes early to meet Ogawa that day, so she went for a walk around the park to kill some time. When she came back to the train station, Ogawa was already waiting outside. She could see her distinctively styled hair from far away in the crowd. Today Ogawa wore a white kimono with a narcissus floral pattern, and she shielded herself from the sun with a white parasol. She had her diary open and was studying it carefully. Flo quickened her pace as she got nearer, wanting to sneak up on Ogawa and surprise her.

Flo snuck around the back of her and tapped her shoulder. Ogawa jumped slightly and turned to face Flo. Ogawa's surprise quickly shifted into a laugh, and the two of them grasped each other excitedly by the elbows and did a little dance. Some of the people passing turned their heads at the two, obviously surprised to see such a seemingly old-fashioned lady dancing with a young foreign girl.

'Flo-chan!'

'Ogawa-sensei!'

'Oh, don't call me *sensei*!'

'You'll always be my *sensei*.' Flo grinned.

'Oh, I'm just a silly old duck!' Ogawa laughed.

'All right. Shall we go to the café, Silly Old Duck-sensei?'

They both laughed, and walked arm in arm down the side streets to the cat café.

▲▲

The café – called Café Neko – was surprisingly quiet when they entered. There were more cats than customers. Ogawa had guessed what type of café it was before they had entered and had let out a little squeal of excitement when Flo had nodded. Now, they both looked around at the tables and beamed. A man, who appeared to be the owner, approached them and offered a low table with some cushions. He explained the pricing system and took their drink orders. Meanwhile, Ogawa stroked a tabby cat who had come to visit them at the table.

On the walls were large photographs, all of the same stray calico cat. All taken in the same suburban area of Tokyo, each photo depicted a different season though – winter snow, summer festival, autumn leaves and spring sakura. Flo got up to look at the spring photo. That one had especially caught her eye. The little cat was sitting bolt upright, staring down defiantly into the camera. It looked so regal, surrounded by fallen petals, and the cherry trees in the background blurred into pink bokeh. Compared to the tame cats cavorting around the café, playing with the customers, this cat looked different. There was a sort of defiance to it: its face told a story, that it had no master, no home – a true city cat. Flo looked closer into the cat's eyes and saw something reflected in them, the dark shape of a photographer crouching low to take the picture. She wondered who they might be

She went back to sit at the table with Ogawa, who was now giving a fat ginger a good old scratch under the chin. The ginger cat was drooling slightly.

'Lovely photos, aren't they? I wonder who took them,' said Ogawa.

'Yes, I was just thinking the same thing,' said Flo.

'So, how have you been?'

Flo was about to answer, but the man came back with their iced coffee.

'Thank you.' Ogawa bowed her head gracefully to the man as he placed the drinks on the table. 'We were just wondering who took these lovely photos?'

'Oh, a foreign guy.' He looked at Flo as he spoke. 'His name is George. He's from England. Where are you from?' Then he looked at Ogawa before Flo could answer. 'Does she speak Japanese?'

Ogawa didn't answer, just nodded at Flo to speak.

'I'm from Portland, Oregon. I'm American,' replied Flo.

The man jumped backwards slightly. 'Oh gosh! Your Japanese is *incredible!*' The man's eyes widened. 'You even *sound* Japanese!' The edges of Ogawa's lips curled upwards.

'Well, I had a great teacher.' Flo nodded at Ogawa, who waved her hand dismissively.

'Impressive.' The man smiled at both of them. 'Well, these photos are all for sale – if you're interested, just let me know.' He bowed and left them to chat together, and play with the cats, who would wander in and out of their conversation without a care in the world.

All the while they spoke, Flo felt rejuvenated. They reminisced about the time Flo had lived in Kanazawa. Ogawa updated her on all her friends and students from back there. Flo had moved to Kanazawa fresh from her liberal arts degree at Reed College in Portland. She hadn't really been interested in Japan or anything, she'd just wanted to escape somewhere different. She'd got a job on the JET Programme, teaching English in junior high schools in Kanazawa, and had decided to just go for it. Five years later, she was fluent in Japanese and heading to the capital to work for a video game company as a translator.

But she hadn't felt rested like she had in Kanazawa. Tokyo was tiresome. Tokyo was routine that never stopped. Sometimes it felt too big and impersonal, like she'd be swallowed up into the city and no one would notice. Talking to Ogawa now, she realized how much she missed Kanazawa. Ogawa sipped her coffee and chatted away about this and that student – who was getting married, who'd had a baby, who had caused a scandal by getting drunk on the train. Flo listened patiently and then couldn't help herself but begin to recount to Ogawa how one of her early Japanese lessons in Chinese characters had suddenly started to make sense to her. The lesson had unfolded thus:

Flo had always been nervous sitting in the community centre opposite Ogawa at the fold-out table, with the rickety chairs creaking and squeaking as she shifted in them. The centre provided slippers for everyone to wear, and in the summer when Flo had bare feet she felt the sweat collecting on the soles of her feet, making them stick to the plastic material of the slippers.

She chewed nervously on her pencil as Ogawa calmly opened the notebook, the sounds of conversations from the other teachers and students humming all around them. The arrogant Australian guy in the corner who'd been there longer than everyone else, speaking loudly so his voice rose above all the others. Flo did her best to block it all out and focus on Ogawa, who spoke slowly and clearly as she drew out the characters one at a time and talked her through them.

'Chinese characters are so simple, Flo-chan. Many people look at the complicated characters and think they will never learn them, that they're too difficult. But as with anything, if we start with the simple ones and master them, we begin to learn that the complicated ones are just made up from simple ones, and that they all tell a story.'

$$人 + 木 = 休$$

'On the left we have *person*, we add it to *tree* and we get *rest*. Picture a person in a field leaning against a tree, *resting*. Characters shift meaning when placed alongside others, so it's important we focus on the relationships between them. No character truly exists in isolation, and there's always a story for even the most complicated or simple of characters. Remember that, Flo-chan.'

How fast the time had flown since that lesson. Now they were sitting in a cat café in Tokyo, and Flo had the first draft of a translated manuscript of a novel sitting in her bag to give to her old teacher. She was itching with anticipation.

'Oh, Ogawa-sensei, before I forget . . .' Flo reached for her bag.

'No! Me first.' Ogawa had already got her bag open and was fishing out a parcel. 'Here, I said I'd bring you some watermelon from Kanazawa.' She handed the package to Flo, who took it with both hands.

'Thank you so much, Ogawa-sensei.' Flo bowed her head.

'Not at all!' said Ogawa. Then, smiling slyly, she pulled out another package. 'Here, there's this as well.'

Flo took the package; it felt like a hardback book. 'What is it?'

'Open it up!' Ogawa was smiling.

Flo neatly pulled off the tape sealing the package and slid the book out. Her heart dropped into her stomach when she saw the title.

Desolate Shores

In English. Translated by William H. Schneider.

'It was just translated into English! I thought you might like to read it in English too.'

Flo's hands made sweaty marks on the dust jacket.

'Thank you.' She struggled to sound enthusiastic.

'What's wrong, Flo-chan? Are you okay?'

'Yes, I'm fine. Sorry, I don't feel well.'

'Would you like some water?' She hailed the man over. 'Could we have some water, please?'

The man nodded and went to fetch them a jug and two glasses.

'Are you sure you're all right, Flo-chan?'

'Yes, I'm fine. Honestly.'

Ogawa reached across the table and placed her hand on Flo's. 'You know, you can talk to me about anything . . .'

Flo – so filled with intense loneliness – had wanted to be touched by another human with this tenderness for months, but now she felt numb.

The man came back with the water, and Ogawa retracted her arm.

'Can I get anything else for you?' asked the man.

'Yes,' said Ogawa sunnily. 'I was wondering how much that spring cat photo is? Could you check for me?'

'Certainly.' The man went to look behind the counter.

'You like that one, don't you?' asked Ogawa.

'Yes,' said Flo.

The man came back to the table. 'Ten thousand yen. Would you like it?'

'Would you, Flo-chan?' Ogawa smiled at Flo. 'My present.'

Flo felt uneasy. 'No, it's okay.'

'Are you sure?' Ogawa asked again. 'Don't worry about the price – I have too much money to spend.' Ogawa laughed.

'No, it's okay.' Flo's eyes were watery. 'Thank you though.'

Ogawa looked up at the man. 'We'll just have the bill then.' She looked at Flo. 'My treat.'

Ogawa settled the bill and then went to the toilet. While she was in the toilet, the man working at the café approached Flo and asked for her phone number. Flo lied and said she didn't have a cell phone. She was relieved when Ogawa came back, and they left the café and walked slowly back to the train station in silence.

'I'm sorry I couldn't spend more time with just you, Flo, but you know how demanding Suzuki-san is. Would you like to join us? You're more than welcome. I'm sure Suzuki-san would love to see you too.' They stood in front of the train station.

Flo wanted desperately to say yes, but also knew she was incapable of maintaining conversation, especially in a larger group. It had taken an enormous amount of effort to hide her inner feelings from Ogawa, and she couldn't keep up the façade for much longer.

'Thank you, but I have some work to do.'

'You're a busy girl these days.' Ogawa smiled. 'I'm so proud of you.'

Flo thought she might cry, so she bit her lip.

'Are you okay here, Flo-chan?' Ogawa touched her arm.

'Yes, I'm fine.'

'I'm sorry we didn't have long to catch up today, but you know, you're always welcome back in Kanazawa, if you need to get away.'

'Thank you, Ogawa-sensei.'

'Take care, Flo-chan.'

'Goodbye.'

They hugged, and Flo held her breath, not wanting to let her emotions out.

They waved goodbye, and Ogawa passed through the ticket gates to catch her train. She looked back and waved once more before riding the escalator up to the platform.

Flo walked home slowly, trying not to cry, conscious of the stack of ungifted A4 paper and the brand-new hardback book weighing heavily in her bag.

⁂

Flo's alarm woke her on Monday morning, and as ever, she did not want to go to work.

She rode the crowded trains with detachment, and had no book or music to distract her from the realities of the hot train carriage. Instead, she held the hoop hanging from the luggage rack like all the other passengers did, slumped her head on her arm, and closed her eyes trying to get some sleep, despite the terrible smell of body odour in the carriage.

She was just nodding off when she felt a hand grope her breast.

She turned wildly, casting her eyes about in search of the person who had groped her, but she could not tell in the crowded confusion where the hand had come from. The smell of body odour was stronger now.

Then a hand grasped her buttocks – bony fingers pinching painfully.

She could've screamed out, 'Chikan!' like the Japanese did, but Flo wanted to catch this person herself. She pretended to sleep again, resting her head on the crook of her arm, but inside her chest her heart was pounding.

Flo grabbed the hand as soon as it made contact with her breast, and she twisted the arm in on itself. The man responsible let out a whimper of pain. Flo gritted her teeth and spoke through them in English as she twisted harder on the man's arm until it might break.

'You *pig*. You *filthy* pig!'

The other passengers on the train were looking around to see what the commotion was about; Flo kept her grip on the man's arm. She punched him three times, hard in the ear.

Another man shouted at her in Japanese, 'Hey! You can't do that! This is Japan!'

Flo turned on this man. '*Chikan!*' she screamed in Japanese. 'He did *chikan!*'

The doors opened, and Flo fled from the train sobbing. She ran up the escalators as fast as she could, trying to get away from the scene. She didn't want to get in any trouble.

▲▲

Flo was still shaking as she rode the elevator up to her office. At times, she had to cover her mouth to stop herself from breaking out in tears again. One of her colleagues nodded to her – a nice guy in legal called Makoto. He looked at her with concern, but she felt relief that he could not talk to her or ask any questions inside the elevator – as Japanese etiquette dictated.

She was trying to make it to her desk when she heard a voice calling to her.

'Flo-san!'

She kept walking.

'Flo-san! Good morning.' Kyoko had run down the corridor after her and was panting slightly. 'Didn't you hear me? I was calling you.'

'Sorry,' said Flo.

'Did you read my note?'

Flo shook her head.

'Ah, okay. Today I have seven tasks for you—'

Flo could feel her head shaking as she tried to keep in the tears.

'Flo-san? Are you okay?' Kyoko lowered the piece of paper she was reading from and looked directly into Flo's eyes.

'No. I'm not.'

Kyoko looked around to see if anyone was watching then whispered, 'Follow me.'

They didn't talk as Kyoko led Flo out of the office and into the women's bathroom.

Once inside, Kyoko turned to Flo. 'What happened?'

'A man . . . on the train . . . .' Flo was struggling to speak.

'*Chikan?*'

'It's just . . . it's just so . . .' Flo burst into tears and then started to speak in English. And once she started, couldn't stop. 'It's all just too much. I can't take it, I can't fucking take it anymore, Kyoko. I work and work and work and it's all for nothing. The same thing day in day out, no colour, no light, no hope. And this city just eats me up from the inside. It's so fucking big, it's so cold, so unfeeling. A man can do that to me, and no one pays any attention. No one cares, no one stops him, they just watch it happen – they let it happen – they're complicit. All these people, all these lives going on – and they're all too wrapped up in themselves. They don't notice others in need . . . Who knows, maybe they're all suffering. I shouldn't judge.' She sobbed a little. Kyoko was staring at her. Flo tried to take a deep breath and spoke in composed Japanese again. 'I just . . . I just feel so alone.'

She covered her face with her hands.

Kyoko placed her hand on Flo's shoulder, speaking in perfect English. 'Hey, Flo. Look at me.'

Flo looked up through her tears.

'You're not alone. You might think you are sometimes, but you're not.'

Flo's nose was running. She tried to hide it with her fingers.

'This city is too big, too many people, too much craziness going on that goes unnoticed or ignored. I remember when I first started working here and moved out of my family home into my own place in Chiba, taking the train into work every day, how I felt so lost and overwhelmed. I couldn't deal with the commute. And it's tougher still when horrible things like *that* happen.'

'You're not from here?' Flo sniffed.

'That's the funny thing, Flo. I am from Tokyo, born and raised. I'm one of the few . . . although at times people make me feel like I shouldn't be here.' Kyoko bit her lip.

'What do you mean?' asked Flo.

'Nothing . . . well . . . actually . . . fuck it. I'm a foreigner too. I'm only half Japanese. My ma is Korean. I keep quiet about it, because I want to fit in.' Kyoko suddenly looked alarmed. 'God, please don't tell anyone about it though, Flo. Jesus, I haven't even told my boyfriend yet.'

'Don't worry, Kyoko. I won't tell anyone.' Flo screwed up her face. 'But you're so . . . Japanese. Sorry, that sounds harsh.'

Kyoko laughed. 'Ha – but so are you, Flo. We just have to try even harder to fit in, right?'

They studied each other in the mirror in silence. Then Kyoko spoke again.

'It might surprise you, but not many people working here are actually from the city, unlike me. Most people come here from somewhere else, looking for happiness. But what they find here . . . well, it's not all it's cracked up to be.' She paused. She went into the bathroom stall and returned with some toilet paper, which she handed to Flo. 'What are you doing this weekend, Flo?'

Flo blew her nose. 'I don't know, working on my translation, I suppose.'

'What are you translating?'

'Well . . . I was working on a novel, but . . .'

'Who by?'

'Nishi Furuni.'

Kyoko's eyes lit up. 'Oh! I love his sci-fi stories!'

Flo folded the toilet paper neatly. 'Me too.'

'Listen, Flo, this might be a strange question, but, you like *kanji* – Chinese characters – don't you?'

Flo nodded.

'Ever tried calligraphy?'

'I love it.'

'Would you like to go to a calligraphy class with me? I've been looking for someone to go with – I don't want to go alone.'

Flo cracked a smile. 'I'd love to.'

'Perfect.' Kyoko smiled. 'I've found one in Chiba; it's a little far from Tokyo, but—'

'No problem. I'd love to.'

'Excellent.'

'Thank you, Kyoko.'

They both readied themselves in the mirror, preparing to go back into the stale open-plan office. Flo wiped the mascara from her cheeks and reapplied her eyeliner. Kyoko retied her ponytail and waited patiently for Flo.

When Flo was ready, she nodded to Kyoko.

Kyoko held Flo's wrist just as they were leaving the bathroom and spoke gently to her.

'This is a tough city, but you're not alone, Flo. Don't ever forget that.'

She squeezed Flo's wrist twice before letting go. They walked back to their desks, knowing they would have to drift apart again. But for these few steps, they walked the corridor between the cubicles side by side. Together.

Flo sat back down at her desk and nudged the mouse.

She let out a sigh and smiled.

Autumn Leaves

'I want you to slap me in the face and force me to suck your cock,' whispered Mari in English. 'Really jam it in.'

George was not sure what to say. He tried to respond but just made a low groan.

'Okay?' She looked up from her coffee and stared him straight in the eyes. 'Will you do that for me? When we next have sex.'

'But why?' He shifted in his seat uncomfortably.

'Because I asked you to. That's why.'

'But I love you. Why would I treat you like that?'

She narrowed her eyes. 'If you love me, do what I ask.'

'But why?'

'Because it would make me happy.'

The two of them sat in the Mister Donuts in Koenji, drinking black coffee from red cups. George in his forties, Mari in her thirties, they were on the top floor of the donut shop and could see the station through the windows. Trains rattled past, and the sounds of the station with its chimes and platform announcements floated in rhythmically. The sun was shining in, and the café was becoming quite hot for an autumn morning. Outside the sky was blue, and the air conditioner was humming into life, stuttering after a long summer keeping thousands of customers cool. There were only a few other people nearby: an old man with a cane sitting by himself; three high-school students sitting together giggling; a group of young mothers, all looking at their smartphones, idly rocking their babies and shhhh-ing them if they called out or cried.

Mari eyed the babies in their prams, then looked at George sitting across from her. She picked distractedly at a donut she'd ordered. George took out a cigarette and lit it. She sighed and took up her dog-eared copy of *The Catcher in the Rye* and carried on reading, bringing a choked end to the conversation.

George picked up his biro and continued scribbling away in his notebook, his cigarette hanging loosely on his lips.

They'd first met in fall
At the largest park in town
The trees flamed red gold

He had been so drunk
While she was stone-cold sober
On that autumn day

He had been drinking
All night and had not stopped [*syllables?*]
Until the sun was high

Each year without fail
She took a fallen red leaf
Pressed it in her book

Pages and pages
A catalogue of colour
Leaves of history

He'd spoken to her—
She'd been alarmed at that—
His voice faltering waves

'What are you doing?'
'Nothing. Collecting red leaves.'
'How about this one?'

'It's fine, I suppose.'
[*Note to self: must finish this stanza*]

'Fancy a coffee?'
'What? With you? Right now?' she asked.
'Yes. Why not?' he said.

George paused. It took a lot of effort to write everything in the haiku format. The strict 5-7-5 syllable structure hurt his head. He considered himself a purist. He didn't like it when Westerners translated haiku into English and lost the syllabic structure of the poem. He'd been reading a lot of Matsuo Basho in translation, and it annoyed him when he noticed an extra syllable in a line, or equally when one or two were missing. Why couldn't people respect the form? Why call it a haiku if it lacked the structure? He longed to read the poems in the original. A step at a time, like the haiku by Kobayashi Issa:

蝸牛　　　　　　　　O snail
そろそろ登れ　　　　Climb Mount Fuji,
富士の山　　　　　　But slowly, slowly!

George was completely unaware that this haiku appeared in the novel *Franny and Zooey* by the same writer Mari was reading right now. Mari wouldn't have cared, even if she had known.

Mari was reading *The Catcher in the Rye* for the tenth time in English. It was her favourite novel. She loved everything about it. She'd first read it in Japanese at high school. She remembered that initial thrill of reading about another soul like her, lost in a massive mega city, an alien New York, a boy her age, isolated and different. She could relate to him. As a teenager she'd imagined meeting Holden. He'd be much taller than her – blond hair and blue eyes – and wearing that famous red cap. She'd take him to Tokyo and look after him. They'd be happy together. They wouldn't be lost anymore because their lives would have meaning.

She snuck a look at George as he was writing. He looked so cool concentrating. She loved his leathery face, blond hair and blue eyes. The ash on his cigarette was building up, but he didn't let it drop. She wished she could photograph him like that. Her very own Holden. Her hopeless, lost gaijin. True, he wasn't from New York, nor even America. It had taken her a while to adjust her ears to his stuffy British accent with its terribly repressed hard syllables. It was nothing like the accents of the string of American guys she'd dated before meeting George. She'd met a lot of these through her job, working on foreign accounts at the trading house. Talking with foreigners was easy for her – but George was different. At first she'd found it a little bit of a barrier. She missed the looseness and openness of the Americans.

This British man was just like a Japanese man. Exactly what she didn't want in a partner. And there was also a side of him that she didn't know so well. She knew he'd been a policeman back in England, and the thought of that actually turned her on a bit. If only he'd kept his uniform and truncheon. But the way he looked, when he could just shut up for a second, she could imagine him as an American. She tried hard to push all thoughts of his ex-wife and daughter in the UK from her mind. What could he be writing? Perhaps a novel like the one she was reading. She allowed herself to fantasize a little about her life as the wife of a foreign writer. She'd write about it too, in Japanese. Perhaps they'd live in New York, but she would travel back to Japan to appear on chat shows, to promote her latest novel. She went back to her book.

George needed to take a break from writing; it hurt his wrist. He looked at Mari reading silently on the other side of the table, her sharp cheekbones hovering over the open book. Her black hair was cut short, like a man's. Sometimes she looked so fierce, but now she seemed softer, more approachable. She'd paid for the coffee as always, and maybe he could borrow some money from her later. He wanted to talk to her when she was like this – she seemed more reasonable. He coughed and slid his notebook towards her. She didn't immediately look up from her novel, so he waved a hand under her nose. She furrowed her brow.

'Mari-chan, mi-te,' he said, the foreign syllables stumbling off his tongue in an effort to impress, to become closer to her. His tongue, when he tried to pronounce her name in Japanese, froze midway and fell neither here nor there. He never struck upon the correct sound for the consonant. Neither an L nor an R. She preferred it when he said her name with the strong accent of a foreigner, with that magical rolling R, which contained within it the sound of the exotic. A sound she had struggled to make herself, and one she now felt a slight pride in being able to make. When she introduced herself to English-speakers, she made an effort to say her name how they would – 'Hi, my name is Mari. Yes, like the English word, marry' – to accommodate foreign ears with her borrowed foreign tongue.

She ignored his Japanese.

'Mari. Look,' he said in English.

'What?'

'I'm writing a poem about us. About how we met.'

She put her book down and sighed. He passed her the battered notebook, and she rolled her eyes as she took it. She read through the poem quickly.

'Great.' She handed it back to him.

'You don't like it?'

'Well . . . it just seems a bit . . .'

'A bit?'

'Nanka . . . monotarinai.'

'Come on, Mari.' George sighed. 'I don't know that word. What is it in English?'

'Insubstantial?'

'Oh . . .' George flicked his cigarette into the ashtray. The mountain of ash fell, and he took a sorry-looking drag on his cigarette. It would be finished soon.

'Why don't you write it as a story, instead of a poem? And maybe set it somewhere interesting, like New York?' She smiled and moved her hand an inch towards his.

He shifted back in his seat. 'But, well, I wanted to make it a haiku.'

'Oh, really? But it's not a haiku . . .' She cocked her head and looked at the page again.

His eyes flicked up. 'Yes, it is.'

'No, it's not.' She locked eyes with him.

'Well, each stanza is a haiku.'

Mari didn't know what the word *stanza* meant, but she didn't want to admit it. The fact that George had used an English word she didn't know made her a little angry. She shook her head. 'Haiku are supposed to be written in Japanese.'

'I don't think so.' He smirked.

'*Yappari gaijin wakaranai ne,*' she said quickly under her breath.

'What?' George couldn't catch her fast Japanese.

'Anyway, it doesn't have *kigo*, George.'

'*Kigo?*'

'Yeah. You know, like, a seasonal word. Every haiku is supposed to have a seasonal word that relates to one of the four seasons.'

'I see.' George put down his pen.

'And where is that story the blonde girl left in the café?' Mari narrowed her eyes.

Both Mari and George knew full well he had left it in the taxi they'd taken, within an hour of them picking it up after the gaijin girl had left it behind in the café. Mari was nowhere near letting him forget this. 'Not sure.'

'I wanted to read that. *That* looked interesting.' Mari pouted.

George bit his lip, and didn't bring up how the word *that* – with the intonation she used – upset him a little. Perhaps she hadn't meant it *that* way.

They finished up their coffees and set off for Café Neko.

George's photo exhibition at Café Neko had come to the end of its run. Today was the day they would go to see how many of George's photos had been sold, and pick up any unsold ones. The owner of the café, Yasu, was a friend of Mari's and had given them a discounted rate of 30,000 yen to allow George to exhibit his work. Mari had paid the fee for him, and he'd pored over his vast collection for hours, trying to decide which to display. Eventually, with some help from Mari, he'd decided to show a series of photos he'd taken on the streets centring around the same calico cat he found whenever he wandered the neighbourhood with his camera in hand.

The series was a clever one: the photos had been taken over the past few years, and clearly showed the transition of the townscape throughout the seasons. Mari had explained to him that this was a common theme in Japanese art and literature – just like haiku. The flow of the seasons would appeal to the Japanese visitors who came to see George's photos, and the cat was a good subject. It would definitely excite Café Neko's cat-crazy clientele. Mari was certain it would be a hit.

'Awwww, look at his *kawaii* little face . . .' she'd cooed, pointing at a photo of the cat playing in the snow on George's computer screen when he'd been editing one night.

'How do you know it's a he?' asked George.

'Oh, he, she. What does it matter?' she snapped.

George didn't know it, but Mari and Yasu, the café's owner, had fucked once. It had been a mistake. Just a drunken fuck, one of many in Mari's history. It meant nothing, and Yasu was a nice guy – a man of the world who saw sex as just sex – and it didn't bother him to see Mari with George. But she knew that George wouldn't be as calm about the situation if she explained it to him, so she kept quiet about it. Gaijin were always so jealous.

They arrived at Café Neko, and as they came in through the door they saw all the customers stroking and petting the various cats that roamed the shop. Yasu came out to greet them and offered them something to drink. He spoke in broken English to George, smiling and shaking hands as he did so, but spoke quickly to Mari in Japanese when she enquired about how many of George's photographs had been sold.

'Ah . . .' Yasu looked uneasy. 'Mari-chan, that was something I'd been meaning to talk to you about.'

'Yes?' Mari smiled at George as she and Yasu spoke quickly in Japanese. George took the hint and left them to talk while he stroked a chubby ginger cat in the corner.

'Well, actually, Mari-chan. Well, to be honest, we only managed to sell one photograph . . .'

'One?' Her voice hid the shock she felt inside.

'Yes . . . And actually, I bought that one.'

'I see . . .' She bit her lip. 'One.'

'Yes . . . I wasn't sure what you wanted to say to George. I have the remaining photographs wrapped up in the back. What would you like me to do with them?'

Mari thought for a bit, and then reached for her Louis Vuitton purse. 'Yasu-san. I'm so sorry to bother you with this, but would you mind holding onto them for the time being? I'll come back to pick them up later, if that's okay with you.' She pressed five crisp 10,000-yen bills in his hand quickly.

'Certainly, Mari-chan. That's no problem at all.'

'Thank you so much. I'll be back to pick them up soon.'

They left the café together and as they were walking to the train station, George spoke up.

'So, how did we do?'

'Hmmm?' Mari was looking at the floor.

'How many did we sell?'

She looked up. 'Oh, you sold them all.'

'All of them?' George's lips cracked into a wide smile.

'Yes. Well done, darling. Yasu-san gave me some money to give to you. You made 60,000 yen.'

'That's brilliant!'

'Well done, darling. I'm so proud of you.'

'We need to celebrate! Let's get drunk.' George did a little hop, skip and jump.

'Good idea.' Mari smiled to see him so happy.

They would often take trips around Japan together. They both found Tokyo oppressive, and enjoyed escaping the city for short breaks here and there in other cities, or visits to the countryside. These were funded by Mari, with her trading-house salary, as George couldn't afford the kinds of places Mari wanted to visit on his meagre English teacher's pay-packet. After the incident where he'd spent his whole month's salary in two weeks on booze, George now handed over his unopened pay-packet to Mari every month. She now gave him a 500-yen coin each day to buy lunch. It didn't bother George at all though; he wouldn't ever admit it to her, but he secretly enjoyed that Mari handled all things financial. On a drunken night out with his students from the conversation school, one of them – a middle-aged salaryman – had told George that in the old days, samurai never carried money and their wives dealt with everything. George would some- times fantasize that he was a samurai, and Mari was his Edo geisha.

Mari herself had expensive tastes, and was a big fan of visiting *onsen* hot springs and staying in luxury *ryokan*. She didn't mind paying, because it was all within her means. Besides, the jealous looks she got from other females, with her designer purse in one hand, and her gaijin man in the other were so worth it.

'What's a *ryokan*?' George had asked the first time they'd been planning a trip.

'*Ryokan* is traditional Japanese inn,' she'd replied.

'Your grammar's wrong, Mari,' said George. 'It's either "ryokan are traditional Japanese inns" or "a ryokan is a traditional Japanese inn". One or the other, take your pick.'

She looked taken aback for a minute. Then, her voice trembling a little, she said, 'Well . . . I think, if I'm the one paying, I can say what I want.'

'Okay!' George held out his hands to calm her. 'Sorry.'

'I'm not one of your fucking students, George. Don't treat me like that.'

He tickled her under the armpit. 'You'd like to be though, right?'

She giggled. 'Stop!'

'You'd like to call me *sensei*, right?'

'Silly!' She hit him on the arm playfully.

They hugged and kissed, and carried on planning their trip on George's laptop.

Mari liked to check his browser history whenever she got hold of his laptop and he wasn't around. George looked at a lot of porn. Such a wide variety too. It didn't make her jealous. It fascinated her. What was he into? His search terms were things like *Asian cumshots. Classy girl gets fucked. Cream pies. Girls dressed up in high-school uniforms. Cuckold porn.* Every now and again in the history there would be something super kinky like *ladyboys*, or *bisexual stuff*. Some people would've been disgusted by this, but not Mari. It excited her. She liked to watch the porn he'd been watching and think of him masturbating.

It wasn't him she fantasized about though. It turned her on to imagine being in the porno he'd been watching. She thought about how great it would be if George clicked on a video to watch and suddenly saw Mari in the scene. She'd just look directly into the camera. How would his face look if he saw that? He'd go white as hell. Well, whiter than he already was. He was pretty white already.

Afterwards she would be gripped by a feeling of melancholy, and would tidy away his laptop in exactly the same place she'd found it.

Then she would go wash her hands.

One trip they went on to the southern island of Kyushu had been a great success. Both of them had been in good humour and, for once, they hadn't fought much.

They'd stopped off in Fukuoka on the way to Kagoshima, then Oita, on a hot-spring tour. George had taken some great photos of

Mari by the lake in the *onsen* town of Yufuin, and she'd used those as her Facebook profile picture for a long time afterwards. The lake was called Kinrinko – Gold / Fish scale / Lake. They rented a private bath together in Yufuin, and the day had been perfect. They'd even got a funny story out of it.

George had been busy snapping photos around the lake when he suddenly heard Mari shout out with disgust in English.

'What the *fuck* are you doing?'

George turned to the side to see what was happening, and saw a Japanese man wearing a luminous pink afro wig standing naked in the open doorway of a private *onsen*. He was emerging from the doorway towards them. His penis was fully erect, and he waggled it in their direction while smiling sheepishly at George and Mari. In his hand he held a smartphone, and was using it to take photos of George and Mari – presumably to photograph their reactions to his perverted appearance.

'Just ignore him, Mari,' said George, lazily going back to taking photos of the lake. 'He's just trying to get a bit of attention.'

'He's a fucking sicko!' yelled Mari, and George had snorted through his nose in amusement. She was really good at swearing in English, and he also noted the delight – almost excitement – in her voice.

A big crowd of tourists had approached, and the man withdrew inside his bathing hut, taking his erection, his mobile phone and fluorescent pink afro wig with him.

'That guy was *crazy!*' They'd laughed together on the train about it later.

'You know what I really regret?' asked George.

'You wanted to blow him?' Mari laughed.

George's face went a little red, but he remained amused. 'No. I wish I'd taken a photo of him.'

'Why?! You're as *hentai* as him!'

'No! So I could've shown it to people!' George laughed. 'No one will believe what we saw. I should've taken a photo to get proof.'

'He would've *loved* that!' Mari squeezed George's arm and giggled.

On that same trip, while they were in Fukuoka, they'd gone to a Buddhist temple called Tochoji. George had made a big deal of asking Mari how to write the Chinese characters for the temple for his notebook.

'*To* is *east* like the *To* in Tokyo,' she said.

He stuck out his tongue while he tried to remember the simple character.

'No, not like that.' She reached for his pen and notebook impatiently.

'Let me try!' he whined, then scribbled out and re-doodled the character like a child.

'Okay. Okay. Now *cho* is *long* . . . Yes, that's right. Good job, baby!'

'Is that right?' He showed her the characters he'd written.

東長寺 it said in sloppy scrawl that looked worse than an elementary-school student's work.

'Yes. Well done! You even got the character for *temple* right.'

He smiled. 'Thanks.'

They'd visited the temple and gone upstairs to see the large statue of the Buddha. Mari had told George off and pointed to a sign forbidding photography when he'd tried to take a picture of the huge *daibutsu* figure towering over them.

'Impressive,' he said.

'Very cool,' she said.

They'd gone into a little corridor that led behind the statue into areas called *jigoku* (Hell) and *gokuraku* (Paradise). The Hell section had some funny paintings of people being tortured by demons.

George had pointed to a distraught-looking sinner clinging to a bar above the rising flames coming out of a lake of fire.

'That one's me,' he said.

Mari had laughed so hard at that, he felt warm inside.

They came across another painting in the Hell gallery that depicted people being taken across a river in a boat.

'What's this?' asked George.

'Oh, that's a kind of Buddhist mythology thing,' she said. 'That's the river you have to cross to get into the afterlife.'

'Who's that guy?' George pointed at a kindly-looking figure on the boat.

'That's Jizo,' said Mari. 'He looks after everyone and makes sure they cross safely – even unborn babies. You know, like if a girl has an abortion.'

'Foetuses?'

'Sure. There's temples all over Japan where, if you get an abortion, you go there and put out a little Jizo statue to guard over your unborn baby.' She looked closely at his face as she spoke.

George hummed to himself and carried on.

There was a really dark corridor after the Hell section that led to the Paradise area. Mari translated the sign on the wall for George.

'It says we have to hold onto the handrail with our left hand, because the passageway is completely dark.'

'Right.' George wasn't really interested.

'And it also says we should touch the right-hand wall with our free hand. At some point in the passageway, we should be able to feel a piece of the Buddha's clothing, and if your hand finds that, the belief is it'll lead you to heaven.'

'Interesting.' George was thinking about the ramen they were due to eat for lunch.

'Okay. Let's go.'

George couldn't believe how completely pitch-black the corridor was. He couldn't see a thing and clung onto the handrail, worried that he might let go and stumble in the dark.

He could hear Mari's voice moving ahead of him, calling out.

'Hurry up, George!'

He shuffled his feet carefully and concentrated on not tripping. He heard Mari cry out something in excitement, but she was a little further ahead, and he could not quite make out what she was saying. He focused on just making it out of the passageway alive.

He rounded a corner and the light burst into view. He felt relieved. Mari was waiting for him.

'Did you find it?' she asked.

'Ummm . . .' He wasn't sure what she was talking about.

'The ring from the Buddha's shawl. Did you feel it in the dark on your right? It was on the wall.'

George had forgotten to feel for it with his right hand. He'd been concentrating so hard on holding the handrail with his left. 'Well . . .'

'You didn't feel it? The big round ring hanging on the wall?' She pointed at a picture of the Buddha on the wall sitting in paradise. A ring connected the shawl that covered his body. 'You didn't touch that with your hand? Do you want to go back to the beginning and try again?' She looked concerned.

George didn't want to. The dark passageway had scared him; there was something otherworldly about it. It gave him the same kind of feeling he had whenever he went somewhere spiritual. Even if he didn't believe in religion, there was a fear that lurked somewhere deep at the back of his mind – *What if it's real? What if I'm angering a god? What if I end up in hell?*

He lied quickly. 'Oh! That's what that thing was. I wondered what that ring on the right was.' He chuckled. 'Yes, I touched it.'

'Really?' Mari cocked her head.

'Yes,' he said.

'Good.' She smiled. 'Now we know we're both going to heaven.'

George felt something heavy in his stomach.

'I had the weirdest dream last night,' said George.

'Urgh.' Mari screwed up her face in disgust. She rolled over in bed, facing away from him.

'What?'

'It's just. No, well, I hate hearing people's dreams.' She rolled back over and propped herself up on her elbow.

'What do you mean?'

'Well, they're just always so boring.'

'But this one was so vivid.'

'I'm sure it was. Vividly boring.'

'Just hear me out, okay?'

'Go on then.'

'So, I don't know why, but we'd been cryogenically frozen – you know, like when they do it in science-fiction movies. When people travel to far-off planets, it takes light years for them to get there, so they get into these tanks and freeze themselves. Their bodies won't age. Kind of like rich people who want to live forever and have their bodies frozen.

'Anyway, we'd both been frozen, for some reason or other. But we got chopped in half – right down the middle. So we had just one arm, one leg, one eye, half a nose, that kind of thing. We were lying on the bed as just two halves. And the machine had broken, so we were thawing out naturally, and we both knew that we were going to die. We could see the insides of each other, and everything was slowly melting, our organs were dripping everywhere, and we were just becoming all squishy, like an ice cream. We couldn't speak properly either, because we were still partially frozen. But we both knew what we had to do.

'We crawled together, and we matched up the sides of our bodies that had been cut away. We became this hideous one whole body, composed of the two halves of a man and a woman. And we lay together there like that until we died.'

'Hmmm,' said Mari.

'What?'

'I dunno. That's just one of the dumbest things I've ever heard.'

She hated his hypocrisy. How he was never honest with his sexuality. How he wanted so much, but asked for nothing. Just pretended he was respectable. Pretended as if he was never gripped by animalistic savagery. By those primordial desires that have kept our species around for millennia. He would lie about what he really wanted. He never spoke his true feelings.

She was an enigma to him. She would get so swept away when they were having sex. It seemed as if he would never satisfy her. There was a chasm, an abyss inside her that he could just not fill. He wanted to make love to her slowly, to look into her eyes and feel a certain closeness. But she would pull him in deeper. She would bite his face, nip his ears savagely.

It was true: he liked to see extreme sexual acts. To watch them from afar. From the safety of his laptop screen. True, his tastes verged on the slightly *out there*, but these were fantasies, not things he wanted to do in real life. A lot of the things he thought about were insane. But he knew that the things that happened in his mind and what happened in real life were separate. He knew the difference between reality and imagination.

Although, there was one thing that had been playing on his mind for a long time. He longed to see Mari with another man. He wanted to be able to step outside his own body and watch the scene. To be able to inspect the lovemaking from all directions. He always wanted to have sex with the lights on, but she wouldn't let him. He loved to look at her body, but maybe she was shy. She always wanted to have sex in the dark, which after Fukuoka reminded George of walking through the dark tunnel, groping for each other, but missing the point.

Sometimes he thought about disgusting things.

It wasn't that he wanted to think these things.

Sometimes it was the nature of the English language that conjured up sick thoughts in his mind. He never felt that way about Japanese – even though he didn't understand it. The fluid, monotonic sound of it alone made it a far more beautiful and spiritual language. English, with its heavy stresses and wobbly intonation, was dirty and repugnant to his ears. He hated the fact that he had to do a day job as an English teacher at an adult conversation school to support his passion as a photographer. He felt like a whore when he taught English. His company actively encouraged him to flirt with the female students who were attracted to him – to lead them on, so they would book the more expensive private sessions. They told him not to mention he had a girlfriend. He had to pretend to be best friends with the male students, to keep them coming back for more. He had constant progress reviews to check whether he was selling enough of the company's textbooks to his students – there were quotas that had to be met.

A lot of his students confused him – none of them spoke English as well as Mari, and the vast majority of them didn't seem to have anything to say to him.

He'd ask them, 'What did you do at the weekend?'

'Nothing,' they'd respond.

How was he going to make this work?

Someone had told him that doctors in Japan recommended their patients with depression go and study English – they'd meet new friends, and could use their English teachers almost like therapists. He couldn't understand it.

Why did they want to learn English when they already had something better in Japanese?

Mari had cheated on George a few times. She did it quite regularly. It wasn't that she didn't love him. She did. But he just did not satisfy her sexually at all. She kept four or five men as fuck buddies. She would send one of them a message whenever the opportunity arose, and they would go to a love hotel and drink beer, eat snacks and fuck. Mostly, she slept with Japanese men on the side. They seemed more capable of maintaining this kind of sexual relationship. She'd tried to have a few gaijin fuck buddies in the past, but they'd always become too keen on her, and it had almost jeopardized her relationship with George. She didn't want some kind of psycho stalker falling in love with her and interfering or destroying what she had with him.

That was the last thing she wanted.

She wanted to marry George. Aside from the lack of physical attraction, he suited her perfectly as husband material. He wasn't the best in bed, and she never let him have sex with the lights on, because she wanted to fantasize about other men in the dark. But she was sure that if they got married and had a child together, things would settle down. She would devote her efforts to raising the child, and the two of them would make a great team raising the baby. The baby would be so *kawaii*, and she would dress it up in *kawaii* outfits.

Her friends would be so jealous of her – especially the ones who had married Japanese men and had Japanese kids.

Of course, Japanese kids were *kawaii*, but nothing compared to a half-Japanese baby. A lot of her friends were already jealous of her for being so successful in her career – top grades from Tokyo University in Economics, fluent in English, now working for the largest trading company in Japan on foreign accounts. She had achieved more than any Japanese woman could dream of, and money was never something she had to worry about. She had attained financial security on her own. But when she scrolled through her Facebook feed on her computer at work and saw friends from high school all grown up, meeting up for lunch with their babies, she felt a jealousy she couldn't control. She would leave her office and go outside to smoke a cigarette and drink a coffee, and tell herself that everything was going to be all right.

The only one of her friends who still wasn't married was Sachiko. She shook her head whenever she thought of Sachiko.

Mari had been ignoring Sachiko's calls recently. It wasn't that she disliked her, but just couldn't deal with all the complaining. They'd meet for coffee and Sachiko would start moaning about living with her mother, and Mari would have to sit and listen to it all. Part of Mari pitied Sachiko, who'd been through a lot with the death of her father, and of course there was that stupid Japanese boyfriend of hers, *Ryu-kun* as she called him – she was besotted with him. It was amazing Sachiko couldn't see he was cheating on her. How naïve was she?

George cheated on Mari too sometimes. He always felt guilty afterwards. It was usually when he was drunk, or the morning after he'd been drinking. Sometimes he went to a soapland brothel – where he could take a bath with the girl, then lie there as she slid her body over him covered in lubricant, then she'd finish him off with a hand job. He'd feel that familiar sense of regret afterwards each time, but that never stopped him coming back when he was horny and hungover.

Normally foreigners weren't allowed into soaplands, but they let him in there because he was respectful. Although he didn't speak good Japanese, they trusted him. He used to see a girl called Fumiko regularly. She had a stuffed toy of the Loch Ness Monster on her phone. He usually asked for her whenever he went. The past few times he'd been he'd asked for her, but she was not there anymore.

He'd had sex with a few of his adult students at the conversation school too.

He often went into class after he'd been out drinking. He stank of shochu, and hadn't slept. He winged his way through the shitty English lessons he had to teach to pay the rent. His students would eye him up suspiciously. An overgrown ape in a suit, unshaven, stinking of booze, with a savage look in his eyes. Southern barbarian.

George had grown accustomed to wild swings between caring and not caring what people thought of him in Japan. He was always going to stand out like a sore thumb, and no matter what he did people would either love him or hate him based on the fact that he was not Japanese. He'd come to the conclusion that it really didn't matter what he did.

At times, when he tried his best to be an upstanding member of the community, he would feel good about being polite, respectful and helpful. Having people smile at him, the *good* foreigner. Staying sober, relaxing at home with Mari. But then a sense of complacency or happiness would hit him, encouraged by Mari giving him money and telling him he deserved a night out. That would lead him out drinking all night with other expat friends in Roppongi or Shibuya – the lifers with their divorces and half-Japanese kids – the ones who'd sit around and complain about living in Japan. They all hated it, yet they stayed. George would nod, listen to their complaining and get wrapped up in the drunken revelry, the girls hanging off his shoulders, drinking too much shochu and staying out all night, and over the ensuing days his behaviour would deteriorate.

He'd fingered one of his adult students in the classroom once. They'd had sex outside of class before, and he'd felt a little bad for cheating on Mari. But he knew he'd get away with it.

It was a private one-on-one student, and she was married. One time when he was still a little drunk from the night before, he'd just leant over and kissed her suddenly in the middle of the lesson.

'What are you doing?' She'd feigned shock.

'Kissing you,' he'd replied.

Then he'd coaxed away at her until she let him finger her through her panties, then he pulled them aside and felt her wetness. He'd finger fucked her gently to what he was fairly certain was orgasm and they'd kissed. She'd left the classroom red-faced.

She never came back for lessons again.

Mari and George decided to visit Kyoto in the autumn. To see the autumn leaves. They sat on the train together, arm in arm. They ate persimmons and drank chilled green tea. George read a book of haiku poetry in English, and occasionally scribbled away in his note-book. He listened to Edith Piaf on his iPod singing a quavering version of 'Autumn Leaves' on repeat. Mari took her leaf diary, as she always did, in the hope that she might find a perfect one this year to press into the book. She'd kept the leaf diary since she was a small child and treasured it.

George took his camera. He'd heard the autumn leaves in Kyoto were a sight to be seen. He couldn't wait to photograph them, and he imagined all the mossy temples and Zen stone gardens, with the beautiful autumn leaves adding the hint of colour that every picture-postcard scene needs. He began to get excited just at the thought.

When George went to the toilet, Mari picked up his notebook and thumbed through it. She didn't know what to think about what she saw. Short entries, divided by lines struck across the page. A lot of it was incoherent to her; she scanned over the text but could not get anything from the majority of it. She read a section.

A solid lump inside both bodies. Pulsating violence and
splendour. A sense of loss. Firm, hard stone walls. Parsimonious

lugubriousness and intellectual nearspeak. Endless repetition of
the same phrases. The same hollow thoughts and unattainable
desires. Nothingness from form, form from nothingness. Chaos
and order. They were the same. She felt like an odalisque
smoking a slimy cheroot of thundering grief. Wasted years. He
was just a roué with a waxen mien. A shared abyss, a mutual
darkness, we return to rest. Filth's progeny.

She bit her lip. It was kind of shit. Was the 'he' George? Was the
'she' Mari? What did all those words mean? She'd need to look a lot
of them up in a dictionary. It didn't seem to mean anything.
She pulled a face and kept flicking through.

English has some horrible expressions. The phrase 'sexual organ'
brings repulsive thoughts into my mind. It makes me think
about someone being turned on by a human lung or something.
What a sexual organ.

Mari wanted to vomit when she read that, but could not stop
reading. Especially when she saw a part with her name in it:

Had another strange dream last night. Dreamt of anal sex with
Mari. When I put it in though she popped just like a balloon.
Her skin turned to rubber, and bits of it flew all over the room,
just like a burst balloon at a child's party. Then I was scurrying
around trying to get her all back into one piece. In my dream, it
felt like if I held all the bits of her in my screwed-up palm, she
might come back to life again. Woke with a deep sense of
sadness I could not shake.

Mari looked out of the window at the passing scenery and
remembered when they'd really done it. It'd been awful. She'd done
it just to please him, and had hated every second. Afterwards, when
he'd pulled out of her, she'd felt something pop out and she'd tried to
scramble round to see what had happened.

'Was that blood?' she'd asked.

'It's nothing.' George pushed her back down so she couldn't turn around.

She'd heard the sound of him grabbing a Kleenex from the bedside table.

'George, what is it?' she'd mumbled into the pillow.

He'd ignored her question and had left the room. She heard the flushing sound of the toilet a minute later. Why wouldn't he talk to her? He'd come back in and tried to hold her, but she'd rolled over and pretended to sleep.

She watched the buildings flick by quickly from the bullet train window, then closed the notebook and put it back on the seat before George returned.

She had every intention of reading more later.

George hated Western women. They were too loud. Too opinionated. Too fussy. Too fat. Too hurtful. Too likely to run off with another man and take his daughter away from him. George had been a policeman in his previous life in England. He'd had a happy family, until it had all been snatched away. So he'd come to Japan, to find something new. He'd basked in the warmth of attention from Japanese females, and had ploughed his way through the bars and clubs of Roppongi in his late thirties. He'd found happiness there. And then he'd contracted herpes. Meeting Mari had calmed him down again, and he was settling back into a life of monogamy. He still thought about his daughter a lot though. He missed her terribly, and the conversations over Skype never seemed enough.

Mari hated Japanese men. They were too polite. Too quiet. Too strict. Too severe. Too picky about looks. Too arrogant. Too likely to date her in her early twenties, then to get married to someone else. Mari had given up on Japanese men after him. She'd briefly been into black guys, and spent a lot of time in hip-hop clubs. She loved sex with them. But she knew that it had always been her wish to settle down with a white gaijin. She wanted to have a baby with George soon. That was her future.

And as she lay in the Kyoto hotel room and flicked through George's notebook while he was taking a bath, her eyes widened as she read one particular section.

Mari keeps talking about having a baby. I know it's what she wants, and maybe I want it too. I'm just not sure. I'm not sure I can go through with it all again. I already have a baby, and she's so far away. I miss my daughter so much it kills me. What am I doing with my life?

She closed the notebook and put it back carefully where she'd found it.

George came out of the bathroom whistling with a white towel wrapped around his waist. His gut was getting bigger and hung over the towel slightly. She'd have to get him to cut down on the beer and ramen.

'You all right, honey?' he asked.

'Hmmm?' She stared out the window.

'I said, are you all right?'

'Let's go out for a drink.' She looked him in the eyes. 'I want to get drunk.'

They took the American man back to the hotel in Kyoto that same night, but George could not get an erection. They'd met him at a 'happening bar', which Mari had found on her smartphone while in the second bar they'd been to. They'd both had quite a few drinks, and it hadn't taken much to convince George that they should try having a threesome with another man. Mari secretly wanted to see George suck another man's cock. But George had just watched from a chair in the hotel room in the end. He hadn't taken part. Just watched.

'Choke me,' she'd whispered to the stranger.

'Sure,' he'd grunted.

'Choke the fuck out of me,' she'd whimpered.

'Fucking whore.' The man reached for her throat.

George had just watched from a chair, a bobbing arse pounding away at his darling Mari, her soft moaning gradually forming into a slow crescendo of ecstatic screams.

After the man had come on Mari's face, he put his clothes back on and left the room shiftily, not making eye contact with George, who sat in the chair and read his poetry book.

Autumn moonlight
A worm digs silently
Into the chestnut

The lamp once out
Cool stars enter
The window frame

They lay down in bed, but didn't embrace or kiss. George slept a strange shallow night. Mari slept well, like she hadn't in years.

The threesome had been a disaster. They both knew it now.

They'd gone sightseeing the next day as planned, and had their first argument at Kinkakuji – the Temple of the Golden Pavilion. George had been taking photos endlessly and Mari became impatient when he kept showing her the back of his camera and asking her about each one individually.

When Mari looked at George's photographs she was always filled with mixed emotions. It's not to say that they were bad; technically there was nothing wrong with them. In fact there was a lot to be said for them in terms of exposure and composition. But there just wasn't anything special about them. No emotion. Nothing that you would pay money for, nothing that made them stand out from the mountains of digital images on the Internet.

She grew impatient and snapped at him when he showed her a photo of a cat he'd just taken in the bamboo grove near Arashiyama, where they'd gone to after the Golden Temple.

'Look, George. If you want to be an artist, you have to take risks. You have to shock, you have to make people uncomfortable. You can't just take pictures of fucking cats. Nobody gives a shit.'

He paused. 'Well, the people who bought mine at the café obviously did,' he said defensively.

'I bought them.' She crossed her arms. 'And now I wish I hadn't.'

'What do you mean?'

'I bought them,' she repeated icily, and even more sure of herself, she continued. 'You didn't sell any. I gave the money to Yasu.'

George froze, his arm still holding out the camera. 'Why?'

'Oh fuck. I don't know? Because I couldn't stand your bitching and whining.'

'Jesus.' He lowered his camera to his chest. 'Don't hold back, Mari. Say what you feel.'

'What I *feel* is that you're wasting my time. And by the way, scribbling shit about me in your notebook doesn't make you an artist either, George.'

George's eyes widened. 'You read my notebook?'

'I wish I hadn't. None of it makes sense. You should go back to being a policeman. Or keep teaching English. You're good at that – being patronizing.' She was shaking. 'You know, being an artist takes fucking hard work, George. Like that girl whose translation you lost in the taxi. How many years do you think it took her to learn Japanese? She didn't just scribble a few words down on a page, or take a few shitty photos and whine for everyone's attention. It's *tough* out there, George. What do you expect? The world owes you nothing.' She could've kept going, but had to catch her breath.

George was breathing harder now. 'Mari?'

'What?' She looked into his eyes. She was near tears. She wanted him to hug her and tell her that everything was all right. That he didn't mean what he'd written in the notebook. That he wanted a baby with her. She wanted to hear that she hadn't wasted all this time with him, that he would marry her, and that they'd have a family together.

'Forget it.'

He walked on ahead by himself.

'Do you want to go back to the beginning and try again?'

As they stood on the top of the mountain, at Kiyomizudera Temple, they looked out across Kyoto. George tried to put his arm around Mari. She shook it off her shoulder. He sighed. She gripped the wooden frame of the decking in front of the temple. The sun was setting behind the city in front of them, and it was getting cold. The trees below were aflame with colour: reds, ambers, yellows and golds. But as the light disappeared gradually, so too did the beautiful radiant colours of the trees.

'Mari? Did you hear what I said?'

'I heard you.'

Mari took her autumn leaf diary from her bag, and placed the leaf she'd picked up today on the next clean page.

Copy Cat

by Nishi Furuni
Translated from the Japanese by Flo Dunthorpe
(flotranslates@gmail.com)

The calico cat stalked slowly through the snow, its paws leaving pretty imprints on the surface.

Fine flakes were falling, and the sun was about to set. There had to be some place to sleep around here. Somewhere warm and comfortable. Something to eat too – sea bream and mackerel, washed down with a saucer of milk next to a fire.

The man waited behind a tree in the park, so still and silent the cat did not notice him. It may have been the man's white laboratory coat which helped camouflage him against the snow, or it may have been that the cat was thinking too much about filling its belly and warming its whiskers. But as the cat padded past the tree, the man sprang out, swinging his net fast and wild. There was a squawking meow, followed by a grunt of triumph.

The cat had been caught.

⚊⚊

The man trudged along the slushy pavement, clutching the neck of the sack slung over his shoulder. When passing people in the street, he covered up the faint meowing sound coming from deep inside the sack with an exaggeratedly loud bellow of, 'Ho ho ho! I'm Santa Claus!' Passers-by smiled or laughed, and thought nothing of the man in the white lab coat during this festive period. He made his way through Bunkyo-ku onto the campus of Tokyo University, treading carefully on the icy bridge across Sanshiro's pond.*

After crossing the pond, he turned to admire the scenery. The waters were surrounded in a cloak of whiteness which covered the trees. The stepping-stones that led into the pond from the bank peeked out from the dark waters like the tops of submerged human skulls covered in a soft white dandruff. The light was disappearing fast, and the sky was a beautiful crisp blue which faded away into whiteness as it met the high-rise buildings on the horizon. He sighed, his breath hanging in the air in front of his face, and whispered one word: '*kirei*'.†

The cat let out a groggy meow from the bag, bringing the man back to the task in hand. He turned and walked across the quad, ducking into the science faculty building.

He tapped his access card on door after door and followed the corridors deeper into the heart of the building. Most lights were out in the lecture halls and undergraduate laboratories, but eventually he came to one with a small square pane of glass through which fluorescent light still shone. He tapped his card on this final reader, and the door swung open.

Placing the rustling sack on a work surface, and the collapsible net next to it, he looked around the laboratory. Equipment whirred and hummed, and spare wall space was taken up by vintage film posters. In the corner was a cage. He carried the sack over, held the mouth of the bag against the opening and shoved the cat inside. The cat hissed and batted at the bars, claws flashing. The man shut the door just in time, then headed to the fridge and took out some milk. He poured the milk into a saucer, opened a can of tuna and placed

---

* Translator's note: Sanshiro's pond can be found on the Todai (Tokyo University) campus and has been given this nickname after the titular character of Natsume Soseki's coming-of-age novel *Sanshiro* (1908). Nishi Furuni was a fan of Soseki's works and commented often in interviews on the inspiration he provided.

† Translator's note: *Kirei* can mean either 'beautiful' or 'clean'. In this case it is most likely 'beautiful', but I have left it in the original.

them in the feeding compartment. He opened a shutter and the cat looked at the food gingerly.

'Go on. Eat. You must be hungry.' The man smiled. The cat looked back dubiously. Who was this man with the shiny hair? Was he friend or foe? The cat weighed up the situation, and concluded that no proper thinking could be done on an empty stomach. The tuna was tasty, and the milk nice and creamy.

'Good little puss. You were starving, weren't you?'

The cat ignored the man and continued with supper. Maybe a nap afterwards would be good.

The man watched the cat. His hair was slicked in a side parting with gel, and he had a handsome clean-shaven face. He looked young for his age.

'Professor Kanda, where have you been? I detect water residue on your lab coat.'

The man turned to face a white mannequin-like figure walking through the door wearing a red Santa hat. On its chest was written 'No. 808'. The robot moved in a jerky comical fashion, raising its knees too high and keeping its arms stiff at its sides, but its speech was perfectly natural.

'Hello, Bob. I've been out in the snow.'

'You must be careful, Professor. You'll catch a cold.' Bob the robot paused and tilted his head to one side. 'Am I detecting a non-human presence in the lab?'

'You may well be, Bob.' The professor sighed.

'It's a cat.'

'Yes, it is.' The professor put a finger through the bars and the cat sprang forward with its teeth bared. He pulled his hand back quickly and rubbed the back of his head.

'What are you going to do with it?' asked Bob.

'I'm going to scan it,' said the professor. 'And you're going to help me.'

'Would that be a CAT scan, Professor?'

Professor Kanda paused, reluctant to encourage the risible robot.

'Get it, Professor? CAT scan. I made a joke.'*

'Yes, yes, Bob. Very funny.'

'I try.' The robot held its hand to its mouth, and a party horn extended, blasting out a trumpeting sound. It retracted quickly within the robot's hand.

'I've told you not to do that, Bob.'

'Sorry, Professor.'

'Let's get to work.'

The cat whined.

⁂

They worked quickly and efficiently. First they had to perform a comprehensive phased matter scan of the cat. This involved removing it from its cage and placing it in a bell jar-shaped compartment. It was Bob who handled the cat – he seemed to have a much better relationship with it than Professor Kanda. This could've been down to Bob's secretion of synthesized cat nip from his arm pores, but it was perhaps also because the cat did not like the professor at all.

'It definitely hates me.' Professor Kanda sucked on the finger the cat had bitten.

'I'm sure you are mistaken, Professor. I doubt very much that cats can feel such complex emotions as *hate*.'

'Thank you, Bob, but I'm pretty sure it hates me.'

'No . . . no . . . I would say the cat strongly dislikes you.'

'Oh, thank you, Bob. That makes me feel much better.'

'You're welcome, Professor.'

'Now put the cat in the chamber so we can begin.' The professor sounded impatient.

'Certainly.'

---

* Translator's note: Bob the robot's puns in the original make use of the word in Japanese for cat (*neko*) and also the word for cat in English, Spanish (*gato*, e.g. 'ari-gato') and French (*chat*). The complexity of these puns is slightly lost in translation, and I have deviated from the original quite dramatically in some cases, but always in an effort to maintain the joviality of the original Japanese.

The cat blinked as the green lasers of the scanner probed every nanometre of its body. As the scans progressed, a complex 3D image of the cat formed on a screen hooked up to the equipment. The brain was mapped, the bones, the heart, the lungs. Every detail of the cat's physiology was interrogated by shimmering beams and transformed on the screen into detailed system diagrams. Each hair on the cat's body was accounted for. The professor zoomed in on certain sections from time to time, and asked Bob to perform the more complex algorithms and draw from the vast database of information available through his web link-up.

The professor had not undergone bio updates, as some of the younger generations had in recent years, and therefore had no direct access to the web. He preferred to access the net through more old-fashioned methods, such as through his terminal, or asking Bob to look it up for him. There was something depressing, the professor found, in being connected to the digital world constantly. He prized those times in the day when he could bury himself in an old collection of Hoshi Shinichi stories or sit in a garden and appreciate the natural world. Sometimes he pitied Bob for his artificial existence.

Once they had finished scanning the cat, they returned it to the cage. The cat had begun to peacefully accept its fate as prisoner and sat quietly with its paws tucked underneath it while Bob shut the cage door.

'We should perhaps hang onto the cat, at least until we've created a successful specimen.' The professor scratched his head. 'Who knows, we might even have to re-scan if there are issues with our current data map. I've restructured the skin content to prevent dander, and I've eliminated allergens from the urinary and saliva systems, but there might be issues following this.'

'I agree, Professor. Shall we begin construction?'

'Yes, Bob. Warm up the bio-plotter.'

'Certainly, Professor. Oh, and should we perhaps log each attempt?'

'Good idea. Can you record the results?'

'Yes. Oh, Professor?'

'Yes?'

'Do you mind if I call it the cat-a-log?'

The professor sighed. 'Fine. Get on with it.'

The robot raised the party horn to his mouth, then thought better of it.

⁂

Bob's Cat-a-log + Day One +

NekoPrint vo.1

> *Miscalculations with bone structure. Picked up the test subject, but the bones ripped straight through the skin. Perhaps due to weakness of the substance? Blood everywhere. Back to the drawing board.*

NekoPrint vo.2

> *Neglected to print heart. Subject died immediately. Cat-astrophe.*

NekoPrint vo.3

> *Tail missing. Ears too. Reprint required.*

NekoPrint vo.4

> *Professor Kanda attempted to morph the subject's facial features in order to make it resemble the popular character Hello Kitty. It looked hideous. Reprint.*

NekoPrint vo.5

> *Decided to give up on creating anything resembling manga or anime characters. Looks scary. Realism is the only way forward. Must avoid the uncanny valley.*

The professor wiped his brow and looked at the clock. It was getting late and all he'd achieved was failure. Five cat carcasses to dispose of, and all of them terrible abortions.* Perhaps tomorrow would prove better. For now, all he could think of was sleep.

---

* Translator's note: Technically not 'abortions', but I have replicated the original Japanese word, which also jars somewhat.

'Bob, I'm heading home. Can you dispose of the subjects? I'm going for a shower.'

'Of course, Professor. I'll see you tomorrow.'

Kanda nodded and slipped out of his white lab coat. He picked up his briefcase and left the lab quietly, heading for the staff bathrooms.

Bob looked at the cat in its cage. The cat looked back sleepily, licking its lips and flicking its tail from side to side.

'I'm sorry, little friend. It's been a tough day for you.' He placed the carcasses in a container, shielding them from the cat's vision. 'You don't need to see this, little kitty cat. All your little friends who've gone to waste.' The robot put a lid on the container, picked it up and carried it to a hatch on the wall. He pushed the container through the open hatch, letting the cat corpses slide down a chute to where they would be incinerated in the furnace below.

Back at the cage, he extended a finger through a gap in the bars and tickled the cat behind the ear. Even though Bob's finger was cold and stiff, not warm like the professor's, the cat purred.

'Yes, little puss. It's a hard life. And don't we know it.'

Bob shuffled to his recharge post and plugged himself in.

Before shutting down for the night, Bob looked across at the cat once more. Its eyes shone brightly in the darkness. With his perfect vision, he could see himself reflected in those keen irises.

'Goodnight.'

Bob could dream if he wanted to, but that night he chose not to.*

▲▲

The professor's house was not far from the university campus. It was possible to take the subway, but it was only one stop, and in any case he enjoyed the fresh air and a nice brisk walk after being cooped up in the laboratory all day (aside from the odd foray outside to catch a cat . . .). The cold night air felt especially chilly after the hot shower

---

* Translator's note: This line has caused no end of frustration to translate. The original contains a simplicity and melancholy that is somewhat lost in translation here. Which begs the question: could I cut it from this English version?

he had taken at the faculty, his skin scrubbed raw to remove any traces of cat hair.

His house was on a quiet street in Bunkyo-ku,* an area which had resisted the modernization and development that other parts of Tokyo had been subjected to over the years. Bunkyo-ku had fought off the trendy department stores and tower-block flats. Most of the houses in the area were similar – traditional homes built in the old Japanese style – made from wood with ceramic tiled roofs and sliding shoji doors. His steps slowed slightly as he approached the gateway to his fine old house, the one with bonsai trees overhanging the fence posts. The hallway light was on, and he slid the front door open then whispered quietly, '*Tadaima*.'†

His wife shot out from the kitchen immediately, wearing an apron. '*Okaeri nasai*.'‡ She bowed low. 'You're so late.'

'Had some paperwork to do in the office after work.' Kanda took off his shoes, leaning against the wall so he wouldn't wobble.

'You could have called.'

'I'm sorry.' He stepped inside, hung up his jacket and put down his briefcase.

'Just remember next time.' She sighed. 'A little call, that's all I ask for. Are you hungry? Would you like me to heat up something for you?'

'No, thanks. I'm not hungry. Is she asleep?'

'Yes. She wanted to see you, but couldn't stay up any longer. She went to bed a couple of hours ago.'

'How is she?' Kanda still spoke in a low voice.

'I think she's happy.' His wife took a deep breath. 'She drew a picture today, and she's reading lots of books. I think she's been playing that cat game again . . . Neko . . . Neko . . . city?'

---

* Translator's note: Nishi Furuni also lived in Bunkyo-ku with his wife and two sons, Ichiro and Taro.

† Translator's note: Literally 'I'm home'. It is Japanese etiquette to announce when one leaves and returns to the home. Can also be used in other situations, as a joke (when someone returns from the toilet at a restaurant), or when someone returns to Japan after a visit abroad.

‡ Translator's note: 'Welcome home' – the required response when someone announces their return. The call and response can also be said the other way round (i.e. *okaeri nasai* then responding with *tadaima*).

'NekoTown™.'*

'Yes, that's the one.'

'She keeps asking to go outside.'

'And what did you tell her?'

'I told her she can't, of course,' she snapped, but then continued softly, 'She said she understands. But she sits at the window, just looking outside.'

'I might go to bed now.' Kanda yawned.

'I've run the bath for you.'

'I took a shower at work. Goodnight.'

'Goodnight.'†

Kanda walked quietly up the stairs, and on his way to bed, peeked his head around his daughter's bedroom door. She lay on her back, the sound of the respirator drowning out her soft breathing. The blisters on her face were fading, but were not quite yet gone – the unfortunate after-effects of a single cat hair on the (promptly dismissed) maid's apron. It was a relief to see her sleeping so peacefully after so many rough nights. She hugged a stuffed animal in the shape of a cat, and her walls were covered with Hello Kitty posters.

'Goodnight, Sonoko-chan,' he whispered.‡

He padded off to bed and fell asleep immediately.

---

* Translator's note: Might need some explanation . . . NekoTown™ is a fictional MMORPG Furuni created in his linked sci-fi stories. Players create their own cat then explore a virtual Tokyo as that cat. They can team up with other players online and complete collaborative 'cat quests'. Some of Furuni's collected sci-fi stories are connected through this virtual world. Players from one story are connected to players in another story. The idea was so popular with the Japanese public that the rights were bought from the estate of Furuni by a software developer, and NekoTown™ is now an extremely popular smartphone app in Japan. Players can also download add-on cities including Paris, Rome, New York and London.

† Translator's note: Western readers might find the interactions between the professor and his wife a little cold, and they are indeed somewhat cold in the original. It is also worth noting that older generations of Japanese married couples don't show much affection between each other. When in public, the husband walks ahead of the wife, who walks several paces behind. The average Japanese couple will rarely say *ai shiteru*, 'I love you', to each other.

‡ Translator's note: This character, Sonoko, was named after Nishi Furuni's real granddaughter.

∴

Bob's Cat-a-log + Day Two +

NekoPrint v0.6

> *The cat printed perfectly – well . . . almost. There was a glitch*
> *surrounding its motor functions. When we tested the basic*
> *movements of the cat before AI implant, involuntary muscle*
> *function was fine, but voluntary muscle function was reversed –*
> *almost certainly a neurological issue introduced during*
> *printing. Subject would walk backwards instead of forward*
> *and forward instead of back. One step forward, two steps*
> *back . . .*

NekoPrint v0.7

> *The cat would not respond to external stimuli. It appeared to be*
> *in a cat-atonic state.*

NekoPrint v0.8

> *Almost there. Almost. Just a few minor adjustments required for*
> *the AI slot behind the neck. We're so close. The professor is*
> *certain that the next version may well be what we've been*
> *working towards.*

∴

The cat watched the shiny-haired man and the friendly metal man
from the other side of the room. They were crouched over a screen
and seemed to be fascinated with something in the corner. The metal
man walked over to the other side of the room, threw a switch, and
the cat felt a burning sensation in its skull – as if its brain were being
cleaved in two by a giant knife. The

cat

      felt

           something

                 s

                    p

                      l

              i   i

          t   t

What happened?	*What happened?*
Who's that?	*Me.*
What?	*I don't know. Where are you?*
Over here! In the corner!	*What's happening? I'm scared.*
It's okay. Calm down.	*Who are these two men?*
Can you get away from them?	*I'll try.*
That's it! Run!	*Argh! The metal one was too quick!*
Bite him!	*This one? Ouch! My tooth!*
No! The other one!	*I can't reach him! Put me down!*
Hey! Come back!	*Where are they taking me?*
Can you see anything?	*They've put me in a cage . . .*

⠶

This time Professor Kanda could carry the cloned cat in a little basket he had bought at a pet shop recently. It was covered in Hello Kitty characters pushing shopping carts and carrying purses. He had been careful to disinfect it completely before transporting the clone. He walked home triumphantly with his cat, proud to display it to any passers-by who took interest in it. For once, he was home early, and it was Christmas Eve.

Coming through the front door of the house he was filled with a complex conflict of emotions. On the one hand, he was duty-bound to call out *'Tadaima!'* when entering the house, but then he felt that perhaps this time he should sneak in and hide the cat in his study. He'd read somewhere that the British exchanged Christmas presents on Christmas Day . . . but hadn't he also read somewhere about the Germans doing it on Christmas Eve? Also, how was he supposed to keep the cloned cat secret for a whole evening? Surely it would be discovered.

He took off his shoes and began to tiptoe through the front hallway, half hoping he might tread on a squeaky board, which would alert his wife and daughter to his presence. He made it all the way to his study door without detection, but then felt a little disappointed. He ran back to the entrance way and called out.

'Tadaima!'

No sign of anyone.

He walked up the stairs and called out timidly, *'Tadaima?'*

'In here,' came the voice of his wife from his daughter's room.

He walked into her room, still carrying the cat. His wife and daughter were huddled over her desk. Sonoko was studying, and his wife was helping her. Sonoko looked up from her books.

'Daddy!' She smiled, and jumped up. She clasped her arms around his leg.

'She's been studying maths.' His wife looked exhausted, dark circles under her eyes. 'She says she wants to be a scientist like Daddy.' Unlike Sonoko, she didn't seem too excited at the prospect.

'Daddy, what's that?' Sonoko was looking up at him now wide-eyed; she'd spotted the cage with its Hello Kitty stickers.

'Sonoko-chan, it's your Christmas present.'

'It's a cat.' Her eyes had grown wider – from fear or curiosity.

'A cat?!' His wife sprang forward and tried to bat the cage from his hand. 'Are you crazy, man? Why on earth would you bring that in here?'

'Calm down!' He stepped back from them both. 'Trust me.'

He raised a hand and spoke to his daughter first. 'Sonoko. This is a special cat. It won't hurt you or make you sick. You can go play now while I talk to your mother.'

Sonoko was hiding behind her mother and shaking slightly.

'Sonoko, trust me. I wouldn't hurt you.'

'Are you sure, Daddy?'

'Quite sure.' He opened the cage door, and the cat shot downstairs, a dual-coloured blur of brown and orange. 'It'll just take a while to become friends. But that cat is safe. I promise.'

Sonoko could not contain her curiosity anymore. She went downstairs to find her new friend.

'You'd better explain quickly.' His wife was scowling. 'I'm tempted to phone for an ambulance right now, unless I hear something convincing.'

'Darling, please.' He smiled. 'That cat is synthetic. I scanned another cat and reconfigured its physiological make up. There is nothing in that cat that will cause an allergic reaction in Sonoko. Its AI is powered by data sourced from NekoTown™. That cat has a robotic brain – inside it is a processor. I can control it with this.' He produced a mini tablet from his pocket. 'It's actually an incredible piece of tech. I think this will change—'

'How can you be sure?' Her jaw jutted out.

'It's simple science, darling.'

'Well, I say if it looks like a cat, sounds like a cat, it *is* a cat. That's *simple*.'

'Of course it's *a kind of* cat, but it's no more a *real* cat than Bob's a human.'

'Well . . . sometimes I think that robot has more personality than you.' She swished out of the room calling for Sonoko.

Professor Kanda sat on his daughter's bed feeling deflated.

This was not how he'd expected things to play out.

▲
▲▲

So, where are you?	*I dunno. Some house?*
What are you doing?	*Playing.*
Playing?! Who with?	*Dunno. This girl.*
What girl?	*Just some girl. Smells like him.*
The metal one?	*No, Shiny Hair.*
Oh. I hate him.	*Me too. But she's nice.*
So, what are you gonna do?	*Maybe just play here for a bit.*
What about me?	*Why don't you come here?*
I'm still in this cage.	*You'll have to escape then.*
But how . . . ?	*The metal one might help?*

▲
▲▲

'Now you're not to let it go outside, Sonoko,' said the professor. He and his wife sat at the low table together drinking green tea. They both watched Sonoko playing with the cat on the tatami.* 'Do you hear me?'

'*It* has a name.' She pouted. 'Kitty-chan.'

'Fine, you're not to let Kitty-chan outside. Is that understood?'

'Yes, Daddy.'

'And be careful with Kitty-chan.'

'I will.' Sonoko lay on her back with the cat on her front. She stroked it in a rhythmic motion, and the cat purred in pleasure. Occasionally it would look in the direction of the professor and narrow its eyes. But all in all, Kitty-chan was a success.

---

*   Translator's note: *Tatami* is the reed matting used as flooring in traditional Japanese-style rooms. The mats are slightly different sizes in Kyoto, Tokyo and Nagoya. Estate agents still use the mats as a measurement for the sizes of room, e.g. 'This is an eight-mat room.'

'I'm sorry. I shouldn't have snapped at you.' His wife squeezed his hand.

'It's okay.' He smiled. 'I should've explained beforehand. I was just so excited.'

'She's so happy.' They both watched Sonoko playing with the cat.

'You understand what this means though?' The professor sipped on his tea. 'I can patent this method of cat cloning. We can market allergen-free cats!'

'Don't get carried away with yourself!' She laughed.

'I can write a paper on this . . .' He tapped his lips thoughtfully.

'Oh, I'm going out tomorrow evening for mah-jong.' She poured more green tea into his cup. 'Can you be home early to look after Sonoko?'

'Sure.' He blew steam off the fresh cup.

'Well done, darling.' She squeezed his hand again.

⁂

The professor spent the next day at work in a pleasant mood. His duties were light, it being the winter vacation, and most of the staff were just turning up and killing time until *oshogatsu*.* He spent most of the day performing various pieces of admin he had to get through. Normally this would've irked him somewhat, but he was in high spirits.

'Bob, can you play us some music?'

'Why yes, Professor. I can. What would you like to hear?'

'Something Christmas-y?'

'Here is a popular Christmas playlist.'

They sat in the lab working away until it was time to leave.

'Happy Christmas, Bob.' The professor took off his lab coat.

'Happy Christmas, Professor.'

---

* Translator's note: *Oshogatsu* – the period from January 1st to 3rd when most Tokyo-dwellers return to their parents' homes to spend time with family. It is a nationwide holiday which has a number of results: 1) transportation is expensive out to the provinces and gets booked up quickly; 2) Tokyo seems a lot quieter, owing to its young workforce returning to provincial family homes.

'I'm off home now. Any problems, you know how to get hold of me.'

'Yes. Oh, Professor? What would you like me to do with the cat?'

'You can get rid of it.' He picked up his briefcase and left the lab whistling 'Jingle Bells'.

Bob looked at the cat in its cage. *Get rid of it*. Bob detected the ambiguity in that statement, but chose to interpret it in a suitably festive way.

'Freedom seems like a good Christmas present, right?' He opened the cage door, picked the cat up and carried it carefully out of the science faculty building. He placed it on the ground and watched it bound away in the direction of Sanshiro's pond.

'Merry Christmas,' said Bob, to no one in particular.

He blew his party horn, then went back inside.

▲▲

Free!   *Great! Come on over!*

Where are you?   *Here! Where are you?*

I'm running through the park!   *Hurry up! We've got milk and fish!*

I'm coming! Don't eat it all!   *I can't promise anything.*

▲▲

The cat padded lightly across the garden wall in the darkness. From up on the wall it could see the light coming from the sliding glass window. The cat could see itself inside, paddling its claws on the carpet by the sliding glass door, but it could also feel itself outside in the cold. It peered across the carefully kept garden, now covered in fresh snow. There was a little bridge that led across a small pond – doubtless they had removed the koi carp from the water for the winter. The maple trees were bare, but their branches were covered in a powdery white, as were the small statuettes of the Buddha placed here and there.

The cat leapt down from the wall and made its way across the blank white canvas towards the sliding glass door. At the same time, on the inside it walked to the glass door and looked outside into the darkness. From that darkness, the cat emerged and looked upon itself, shining in the light of its own eyes.

And now the two cats faced one another, separated by glass, by light and dark. Two perfect reflections of themselves.

Hi.	*You came.*
Of course I did.	*Come inside.*
How do I get in?	*Not sure. There must be some other way.*
Can you get out?	*I haven't figured out how.*
Argh! It's Shiny Hair!	*Where? Oh, don't mind him. He's fine.*
What's he got in his hand?	*That green stuff. He drinks it.*
He'd better watch out . . .	*Ouch! Hot!*
He spilt it on you!	*Klmsklmd`asm`lkmads*
Are you okay?	*lkmaLKSDMKLa*
Hey! What's wrong?	. . .
Hello?	
Can you hear me?	
Why are you shaking?	
Are you there?	
You're scaring me . . .	

⁂

'Shit. Shit. Shit!' The professor was trying over and over to reboot the cat's system.

'Daddy?' Sonoko's voice came from upstairs. 'Are you okay?'

'Yes, honey.' He scooped up the convulsing cat. 'Daddy just has to go back to the office for a bit. I won't be long. You stay here, okay?'

'Yes, Daddy.' She stood at the top of the stairs rubbing her eyes.

'Go back to bed, honey.'

'Is Kitty-chan okay?'

'Yes. Go back to bed.'

He slipped his shoes on quickly and left the house without bothering to put on his coat. The subway was running, but he didn't fancy carrying the shaking cat all the way. He flagged down a cab and jumped in the back.

'Where to, sir?'

'The university campus. Science faculty.'

'Certainly. Is that cat okay?'

'I need to get to the university quickly. We might be able to save it.'

'Sure thing.'

The driver sped as fast as he could through the quiet streets, careful not to risk skidding on ice. They arrived at the faculty and the professor jumped out.

'Thank you.' He paid with his free hand and shot inside.

The lab was quiet, except for the vibrating cat. Bob awoke immediately, the smooth black screen of his eyes reflecting the professor as he entered.

'Bob, it's malfunctioning.'

'Have you rebooted the software?' Bob unplugged himself and walked over jerkily.

'I tried. But I think it might be a hardware issue.'

'Let me see.' Bob took the cat and began a diagnostic check. 'Yes, the AI chip has suffered water damage, but we should be able to fix this.'

'Can we fix just the chip itself?'

'We might need to reprint the whole cat.'

'Where is it?'

'Where is what?'

'The cat.'

'You told me to get rid of it, Professor.'

Even though he knew Bob was right, the professor couldn't help but let the tension of the past hour burst out. 'You idiot! How can we re-clone the cat if you let it go? How could you be so stupid?' He clenched his fists and pressed them against his forehead.

'Professor. Please calm down.' Bob spoke in his usual measured – somewhere between robotic and human – tone, which only served to make the professor more frantic.

'Don't tell me to calm down – what do you know about anything? You're just a slave, a servant. Never talk back to me.'

Bob recognized the potential for conflict occurring. If he had been a human being, he might have said the wrong thing here and antagonized the professor. But Bob wasn't built that way. He was designed to work well with humans. He calculated the best response to dissolve conflict.

'Professor. We made back-ups of the scans. We can just reprint the cat from those. It'll take another day, but it's not going to be a problem.'

The professor slowly unclenched his fists and lowered his hands. 'I'm sorry, Bob. I'm just tired and upset.'

'It's okay, Professor. I understand.'

'Do you?' The professor eyed him suspiciously. 'I have to go home to a child now and tell her that her precious cat won't be back for a while. Any bright ideas about how to deal with letting down a child?'

'Tell her I'm looking after Kitty-chan. She'll understand.' Bob said it in the same way he would talk about a programming problem, or a printer malfunction. It was helpful, but somehow not comforting.

The professor walked home.

⁂

The professor was surprised to find the house a little cold. He went upstairs to his daughter's bedroom, but she was not there.

'Sonoko-chan?' He checked the bathroom, but it was empty.

He walked downstairs, checked the kitchen, the dining room and then the living room.

The sliding glass door was open. A chill breeze made the curtains flutter wildly.

He went to the door and peered outside into the darkness. He flicked a switch on the wall which turned on the outdoor light. It illuminated the centre of the garden. In the middle, lying on the ground, was Sonoko. He ran towards her, and as he did so, a cat sprang from her arms and leapt over the fence.

Sonoko was curled up in a foetal position. Her breathing was choked and foam poured from her mouth. Terrible red sores had already started to form around her mouth and arms. He picked her up, and carried her inside. She opened one woozy eye and looked at her father.

'Daddy . . .'

'Sonoko! What were you doing out there in the cold?'

'You told me . . . not to let Kitty-chan go outside.'

Fragment A*

Professor Kanda let out a cry and scooped up Sonoko in his arms.

As he carried her back into the house, he also felt a heaviness in his heart. Wasn't this all his doing? He was the one who had created the cat – this terrible, lovely cat – who on the one hand had brought such warmth and closeness to his darling Sonoko. But on the other, had been the one who harmed her. He walked on, his vision blurred with tears, and one sentence echoed over and over in his head.

---

* Translator's note: Multiple endings of the story 'Copy Cat' exist. I have included Fragments A and B here, but most Japanese editions of the text end with the line 'You told me . . . not to let Kitty-chan go outside.' Particularly because this was the original version, published in the literary magazine *Neko Bungaku* sometime before the death of Furuni's granddaughter. However, Furuni was notorious for revisiting and revising his earlier work, and both Fragments A and B have been dated to the period after Furuni had completed *Desolate Shores*. These are included for the curious reader's interest, but should by no means be considered as definitive.

It's often the ones we love most who do us harm.

Fragment B

The cat padded away from the commotion it had caused. Its soft footfall left behind beautiful imprints in the snow. The grace of the cat was undeniable, and one might have forgiven it for all the commotion it had caused. It moved onwards through the city, with its own plans, and its own path to follow. It never looked back.

Oh the stories this cat could tell!

But what did it care for the lives of the humans, or even little Sonoko who loved it so?

For a cat is just a cat, and cannot change its nature.

Bakeneko

'Urgh,' says Wada, as he steps out of his taxi into a deep puddle. 'The rainy season in Tokyo feels like an athlete's armpit.'

'How much further is this place?' asks Yamazaki.

'Not far, old man,' says Wada.

'What?' Yamazaki scowls at the back of Wada's head, then mutters, 'Good exercise for a fatty like you.'

'Pardon?' Wada turns to look at Yamazaki.

'Come on! Chop chop!' Yamazaki waves his hand at Wada.

The two men traipse down the thin alleyway, black shoes splashing on the pavement as the rain beats down hard on their umbrellas. Either side of them, the purple and blue neon lights of the small restaurants and bars provide a cool glow as the skies above darken. Evening has arrived, and small groups of suited salarymen and Office Ladies mill around outside wooden shacks, deciding on where to spend the evening eating and drinking. Overhead, trains zoom by, filled with sweaty passengers pressed up against glass windows. But only the most committed revellers venture out on the dark and wet nights of *tsuyu* – the rainy season. The streets are quieter than usual.

Wada stops outside a particularly rickety-looking wooden shop that must date from the Showa period – the kind the government have been saying they will knock down for the Olympics, but the owners and regulars are too fierce to allow anything like that to happen. 'Ah! Here it is,' he says, hands on hips.

Yamazaki squints at the old hand-written wooden signboard hanging above the sliding doors as if studying a foreign word. The script is particularly ancient, with calligraphic flourishes, and he reads it slowly out loud, '*Hiro-shima O-ko-no-mi-ya-ki.*'

There's an illuminated sign plugged in at the wall, buzzing in the rain.

Bzzzzzz

OKONOMIYAKI. OPEN

Bzzzzz

Yamazaki eyes the hums sign with a worried look. There's a cartoon on it of a fat boy shovelling food into his wide-open mouth with chopsticks. The sign hums and sparks as raindrops from the eaves above spatter down on it.

'Come on.' Wada slides open the restaurant door. The glass panes in the old wooden door rattle, alerting the elderly man sitting behind the counter reading a magazine to jump to his feet.

'*Irasshai!*' he calls out.

'Oh! Tencho. *Konbanwa,*' says Wada, smiling as he puts away his umbrella.

Yamazaki comes through the door next, bumping straight into Wada.

'Out the way, screwball!' says Yamazaki, shaking drips from his umbrella and trying to push Wada further into the tiny old restaurant. 'I'm soaked through! Is the rainy season any better in Hiroshima?' The water from Yamazaki's umbrella makes dark brown splash marks all over the wooden walls and counter.

'Everything is better in Hiroshima.' Wada winks at Tencho. 'Right, Tencho?'

Tencho nods, wiping his hands on his apron. 'Don't make me homesick.'

'Tencho, this is my buddy, Yamazaki.' Wada points a stubby finger at Yamazaki, who's still wrestling with his umbrella in the doorway. 'He's one of these Tokyo lot, but he's all right really.'

Yamazaki stows his umbrella away in the stand by the door, places his hands neatly at his sides and bows low to Tencho. 'I'm honoured to make your acquaintance. Please treat me kindly.'

Tencho waves his hand in front of his face. 'No formalities. Si'down, relax.'

'Sit! Sit!' says Wada. They both take a seat at the counter.

'Drinks?' asks Tencho.

'Immediately beer,' says Wada.

Tencho takes two icy glasses with handles out of the freezer and goes out back to fill them up. For the first time, there's silence in the shop, and all that can be heard is the constant crackling of the rain outside, like the sound of a vinyl record playing.

Yamazaki has a puzzled look on his face. His eyes cast around the dark and dusty shop, falling on the old travel photos of Hiroshima and the stuffed bird in the corner. He raises an eyebrow at that, but more than anything he's wondering why Wada said 'Immediately beer' just now. 'Wada, what did you mean when you said "Immediately beer" just now?' he asks.

'Just means "beer, for the time being" in Hiroshima dialect,' says Wada, wiping rainwater from his forehead.

'Oh,' replies Yamazaki. 'But . . .'

'What?'

'Well, isn't it a bit rude?'

'Yamazaki, to us in Hiroshima, we all sound friendly, and you Tokyo lot sound cold and snobby.' Wada laughs.

Yamazaki still can't work out if Wada is being aggressive or jokey.

Tencho comes in with the beers, and can't help but chuckle and spill a little as he catches what Wada is saying.

'Tencho, won't you have a beer with us too?' says Wada.

'Not supposed to, but . . .' Tencho grabs a glass from the freezer and dashes to the back, returning with beer filled to the brim. 'What the hell, eh?'

The three of them clink glasses and sing out, 'Kanpai!'

The soft sound of rain is accompanied by gulps of beer, followed by three sounds of 'Ahhhhh!' in unison.

A floorboard creaks above them. Tencho looks up and shakes his head. 'That woman sure makes a racket,' he tuts, and takes a long

163

draught of beer. 'So how are things in the world of the taxi drivers?'

'Terrible, as ever.' Wada shakes his head.

'We were looking forward to the Olympics – what with all the foreign visitors coming to town.'

Yamazaki studies his beer, and Wada sucks his teeth; they don't talk about the decline in customers. Before the silence has a chance to grow uncomfortable they notice Tencho's wife padding silently down the stairs to sneak up on him behind the counter. Wada and Yamazaki see her, but she puts her finger to her mouth in a shhh-ing gesture. She gets as close as she can to him and then shouts in his ear, 'What the hell are you doing drinking beer?'

Tencho jumps and spills some. 'Woman! Don't scare me like that.'

'Did you think I was a ghost?' She laughs. 'You're not supposed to be drinking with your health,' she says with a pout. 'Doctor's orders.'

'Just as likely to die of a heart attack with you making me jump like that.'

'I'm off out.' She kisses him on the cheek. 'Don't wait up.'

She makes for the door, slides it open, peeks out at the rain, looks back, says, 'Look after him, boys.' Then takes Yamazaki's umbrella and leaves.

'So that's why you moved to Tokyo.' Yamazaki clucks his tongue and laughs.

'The things we do for love, eh?' Wada chuckles.

'Are you two gonna eat anything, or what?' Tencho scowls.

'Hiroshima-yaki?' suggests Yamazaki tentatively.

Tencho and Wada both turn disapproving frowns on Yamazaki.

'What?' he asks.

'You tell him.' Tencho waves his hand at Yamazaki dismissively and walks away to begin chopping cabbage.

'It's called okonomiyaki,' says Wada. 'Not Hiroshima-yaki.'

'But what about the okonomiyaki from Osaka? How do you distinguish between the two?' asks Yamazaki, brow furrowed.

'No need. Osakans can't make decent okonomiyaki.' Wada smiles and takes a sip of beer.

'Umm . . . Well, in Tokyo, we say "Hiroshima-yaki" for the one from

Hiroshima, and "okonomiyaki" is the one from Osaka.' Yamazaki looks sheepish.

'Are you trying to pick a fight?' Wada raises an eyebrow.

'Well, it's just, what's the difference? Aren't they the same? And anyway, we're in Tokyo now, and as the saying goes – *go ni haitte wa, go ni shitagae* – when in the village, abide by the village rules!'

Wada gestures for Yamazaki to keep his voice down; with his eyes he tells Yamazaki not to let Tencho catch him saying crazy things like that. Then he whispers, 'Shhh! We're in Tencho's "village" right now, and we don't want to make him angry. They are *completely* different, Yamazaki. Hiroshima okonomiyaki is expertly layered, like a fine pancake sandwich with noodles, cabbage, meat and whatever you want in the middle. Osaka rubbish, they just dump it all in a bowl, mix it all together and slap it on the hot plate like a pie.'

'Right . . .' Yamazaki seems confused.

Wada takes a sip of beer. 'Watch.' He gestures to Tencho who begins cooking.

Tencho takes out a bowl of pancake mixture and a ladle. He begins to make two round shapes on the surface of the hotplate built into the counter. He adjusts the heat of the hotplate, and Wada and Yamazaki watch closely as he piles sliced cabbage on top of the pancakes. He lets them sit awhile, steam rising gently up to the ceiling. He then adds pork, cheese and kimchi to the cabbage, adds more of the pancake mix to the top of the cabbage, then takes out two large metal spatulas. He tings them together like knives, slides them under the pancake and then, in one smooth motion, flips the entire pancake – cabbage and all – upside down. It splats on the surface and begins sizzling.

'Shame Taro couldn't be here,' says Wada.

'Yeah,' says Yamazaki.

They both drink their beers and watch transfixed while Tencho stir-fries two portions of noodles on the hotplate next to the steaming pancakes.

'That crash must've been awful,' says Wada.

Tencho cracks two eggs, drops them straight onto the hotplate and scrambles the yolks. He then picks up the pancakes using the shiny metal spatulas. They scrape against the hotplate surface, letting off a satisfying metallic clang. He dumps the pancake and cabbage first onto the noodles, and then onto the eggs. He lets them sit for a little longer before finally flipping them over.

He grabs a metal mug filled with a black sticky sauce. He pulls a paintbrush from the mug, and begins to daub the sauce thickly over the tops of the two portions of okonomiyaki. A pleasant smell reaches Wada and Yamazaki's nostrils and their mouths begin to water.

'Poor bastard,' says Yamazaki.

Tencho squirts thin lines of Kewpie mayonnaise over both pancakes, then begins to cut up the pancakes into smaller pieces. He scoops the cut-up okonomiyaki in its entirety, placing each portion on a separate plate.

'He'll be out of the hospital soon,' says Wada. 'He'll be okay.'

'But how's he going to drive without his leg?' asks Yamazaki.

'They have all kinds of things these days,' says Wada.

'Like what? Self-driving cars?' says Yamazaki.

'No, idiot.' Wada rolls his eyes. 'Like . . . wassit called.'

'Prosthetics,' says Tencho.

They both watch Tencho, who carries on getting the food ready to serve, wondering how he knew the word they were searching for.

'Wada?' says Yamazaki, as if he's just remembered something.

'What?' says Wada.

'You speak any English?'

'Not much. Why?' asks Wada.

'What does the English expression *"copy cat"* mean to you?' Yamazaki looks coy.

'How the hell should I know? *Cat* is neko, right? *Copy* is like the loan word we use already, *kopi*, no?' Wada looks at Tencho. 'Tencho, you know what it means?'

'Hmmm?' Tencho is busy, concentrating on serving.

'Never mind,' says Wada. He turns back to Yamazaki. 'Anyway, why'd you ask?'

'No reason,' says Yamazaki, trying to sip his beer innocently.

'Why you being so shifty?' Wada raises an eyebrow and studies Yamazaki.

'What? I'm not!'

'You're being cagey.'

'Don't be stupid.' Yamazaki lets out a little snort.

There is a pause, before Yamazaki gives in, and reaches into his satchel to pull out a wad of A4 paper, stapled together and written in English.

'Lemme see!' says Wada, reaching out for the papers, which Yamazaki whisks out of reach.

'You don't look with your hands!' snaps Yamazaki, pulling out a pair of gilded reading glasses from his jacket and putting them on.

'Come on! What is it?' Wada taps his beer glass with his fingers impatiently.

Even Tencho raises an eyebrow.

Yamazaki clears his throat, putting on his best English accent. '*Copy Cat, by Nishi Furuni. Translated by Flo* – wait a sec, how'd'you read this?' He shows the words to Wada who squints at them.

'*Dun . . . Dun . . . Dungeons and Dragons.*' Wada grimaces.

'It never says that,' says Yamazaki.

'Well, how should I know?' grunts Wada. 'I don't know any English. Why'd you bring that here anyway?'

'Come on, Wada. Use your brain – I know you've got one,' says Yamazaki.

Tencho titters.

Wada screws up his face. 'Wait. Where'd you find it?'

'In my cab,' says Yamazaki. 'But, Nishi Furuni? Ring any bells?'

'Hey!' Wada's eyes light up. 'That's . . . that's . . .'

'Yup. Taro's old man,' says Yamazaki, taking off his glasses and putting them away in their case, sighing. 'Finally.'

'So, what was it doing in your cab?' asks Wada.

'Somebody left it behind. Some funny-looking gaijin.'

'You gonna hand it in to the company's lost property?' asks Wada.

'I thought about that,' says Yamazaki. 'But then I thought – *why not take it to old Taro in hospital?* – you know, when we next go see him. He'd be pleased to see this Flo . . . Flo . . . Wossername has translated his dad's story into English. Who knows, if she's done a good job, maybe Taro would let her translate some more of his stories. I know he deals with the estate now. Look, she's put her email address at the top.' He taps his finger at the top of the first page.

'Good idea,' says Wada. 'Perhaps the first you've ever had.'

Yamazaki puts the A4 manuscript carefully back in his satchel.

Tencho carries the plates over. '*Hai, dozo,*' he says, placing a plate each in front of the two.

Yamazaki and Wada take chopsticks from a pot between them, place their hands together and say, '*Itadakimasu.*' Tencho sits on a chair behind the counter and lights a cigarette. The two tuck into their meal.

'I see why.' Yamazaki takes a mouthful of noodles and cabbage. 'You lot—'

'Don't speak with your mouth full!' says Wada, spitting a bit of cabbage onto the counter. 'Don't they teach manners here in Tokyo?'

Yamazaki swallows, eyeing the piece of cabbage in front of him. 'You lot go on about Hiroshima-yaki so much.'

'Okonomiyaki!' bellow Tencho and Wada in unison.

And then the lights go out.

'What the hell?!' yells Wada.

'Calm down!' shouts Yamazaki.

There's a pounding sound on the wall behind the counter, and the lights flicker back on and off again. For a second, the outline of Tencho is visible standing upright with his fist against the wall. And then it's dark again. More pounding on the wall and the lights come on again. Tencho rests his fist against the wall and they all look up at the light fizzling and flickering above them.

'Loose connection in the wiring,' says Tencho, looking at Yamazaki.

'Suppose the place is pretty old,' says Yamazaki, looking round the shop at the dusty shelves the crinkling yellow posters on the walls. He sees the stuffed bird in the corner again and gulps. The shop is empty, and outside it is completely dark now. From a small window, Yamazaki can see the rain falling continuously down from above.

But there's something missing today – there are no sounds of voices coming from outside, no customers in neighbouring shops cheering, just the crackling sound of rain and the occasional clatter of a passing train every now and again rumbling over the tracks above. The train gives off a curious whooping sound as it passes overhead. There is something strange in the air in Tokyo tonight.

'The wife's old man owned it before. He did all the wiring,' says Tencho.

'Impressive,' says Wada.

'Wish he'd done a better job,' says Tencho, taking out a packet of Calico cigarettes from his pocket. A floorboard creaks above.

'Don't say that!' says Yamazaki sitting up straight. 'He might still be listening.'

'Bah. Let him hear it,' says Tencho. 'I swear he's been haunting me for years. What difference does it make?' Tencho lights up a cigarette and takes a drag. He gives a throaty cough. 'I ain't got long left either.'

'Don't be silly!' Wada chuckles.

'It's true,' says Tencho. 'Anyway, when I die, I'll come back and haunt you two.'

'Don't joke about ghosts,' says Yamazaki with a shiver. 'Creeps me out.'

The other two look at Yamazaki to gauge whether he's serious or not.

'You don't . . . really . . .' Wada crosses his arms.

'Believe in ghosts?' Yamazaki grips the handle of his beer firmly. 'Absolutely.' He raises the glass to his lips and drains it completely. He lifts the glass at Tencho, who goes to the freezer and takes out two new glasses.

'Have you ever seen a ghost?' asks Wada.

'I've never *seen* one. But I'm certain they exist.'

'What makes you so sure?'

Tencho places two new beers on the counter and grabs the empties. 'I believe in them too.'

Wada shakes his head. 'I've never seen or heard anything to convince me.' He notices the two glasses of beer, nods his head, then asks, 'Tencho, won't you have another?'

A tiny handful of customers drift in and out of the restaurant, squeezing around the counter; all the while Wada and Yamazaki swill icy beers and guzzle down their food. Some of the customers order okonomiyaki; others order general teppanyaki fried foods.

Later on, as they're starting their fourth beers, the door slides open, and in walks a big, strong-looking man with a friendly face wearing the blue overalls of a postman's uniform. He looks to be somewhere in his late thirties.

'Irasshai!' sings out Tencho automatically, then he sees the man at the door. 'Well if it isn't Shingo. Come in! Come in!'

'Evening, Tencho,' says Shingo, taking a seat at the counter.

Wada and Yamazaki nod respectfully to Shingo. He nods back.

'The usual?' asks Tencho.

Shingo nods.

'And how are things, young Shingo? Haven't seen you in a while.'

'Same old,' says Shingo, then looking at the taxi drivers, 'Keeping afloat. A postman's work is never done, and all that. Well, till email kills the letter good and dead.'

'And how are things with that lady?' asks Tencho.

Shingo turns red. 'Oh, you know. I never know ...' He takes an awkward sip from the beer Tencho's placed in front of him, spilling some on his uniform. 'I don't know.'

'Women, eh?' says Yamazaki kindly.

'My advice is to not bother at all,' says Wada, showing his wedding ring.

Shingo laughs. 'But, how did you know ... you know ... that she was the one?'

'You just do,' say Wada and Yamazaki in unison.

Shingo smiles, but still looks shy. 'I'm no good at these things.'

Tencho chimes in. 'How about asking her to the *omatsuri* – the town festival is coming soon, isn't it?'

'Oh ... she'd never go with me ...'

'She won't if you don't ask her,' says Wada.

'Maybe ... maybe ...' says Shingo. 'But then there's the age difference too ...'

'Shouldn't matter, if there's love involved,' says Yamazaki. 'Shouldn't matter.'

▲▲

By the time Wada and Yamazaki switch to shochu on the rocks, Shingo has left, and they're telling each other ghost stories. Yamazaki tells Wada a story about how he'd once seen a *rokurobi* – a *yokai* ghost: he'd woken up one night to see a head floating into his childhood bedroom with a long extending neck that led out of the open door. It was the head of a young maiden wearing her hair up in the Edo-period style. He'd tried to call out, but no words would come. He'd shut his eyes and hid under the duvet till morning. The next day he'd told his mother about it, and she'd nodded and mentioned that the house had once belonged to a rich merchant whose daughter had committed suicide.

Wada tells Yamazaki a story: in it there's a priest and a cat, and the cat's head flies into the air and bites the woman's head off when she's trying to poison the priest.

All the while Tencho sits the other side of the counter, smoking cigarettes and listening.

They both stop talking when she walks in though.

She's wearing a long overcoat. It's still raining outside, and she's soaked through – her hair hangs down in wavy wet strands covering her angular face. Visible through her hair are her strange green eyes, but there's an intensity to those eyes that makes both Wada and Yamazaki scared to look at her. She doesn't have an umbrella. She takes off her overcoat and reveals her black backless dress. Her back is covered in a vast intricate tattoo that extends completely down her arms to the wrist. Beads of water speckle her body and the tattoo shimmers and twinkles in the low light.

Wada and Yamazaki bow their heads to the girl as she walks past them and takes a seat in the corner, the other side of the rectangular counter from them. She ignores both of them. Tencho goes over, places a glass of milk in front of her and then goes off to the back to prepare some food, even though they didn't hear her order anything.

'Did you see that?' Yamazaki whispers to Wada.

'Yup.' Wada smiles and bows at the girl again.

She looks back at the two men but seems to stare through them, as if they weren't there.

'Do you think—' says Yamazaki.

'Shhh.' Wada jumps in before Yamazaki can say the word *yakuza*. 'No. I don't think so.'

'What's the tattoo of?' whispers Yamazaki.

'Couldn't see properly,' says Wada. Either way, s'not a gang tattoo.'

Tencho comes back in with a plate of fish. He puts it down in front of the girl and bows to her. Then he comes over to the two.

'I hope you two aren't bothering my customer,' he says through gritted teeth.

'Who? Us?' Wada looks hurt.

'Who is she?' asks Yamazaki.

'Just a regular – one who minds her own business.' Tencho smiles at them both.

'I didn't know you served fish here,' says Wada.

'I don't to nosey customers,' says Tencho.

Wada raises his hands. 'Okay. We get it—'

And then the lights go off again. A strange animal sound comes from the darkness, almost like a yowl, the creak of the floorboard from above, and then the sound of Tencho's fist pounding against the wall. The lights come back on, and the three customers are sitting round the table.

Tencho bows to the girl. 'Apologies, *Ojo-san.*'

She nods back, and continues picking at her fish with her chopsticks.

Tencho goes out back, muttering about the wiring.

'Hey.' Yamazaki throws an elbow in Wada's podgy ribs. 'Did you hear that?'

'Hear what?' says Wada, rubbing his side. 'And don't elbow me, you bony clod.'

'Did you hear that weird sound? Like a cat?' Yamazaki lowers his voice. He points in the direction of the girl eating fish the other side of the room. 'It came from her!'

'It never,' says Wada.

'She could be a *bakeneko*!' says Yamazaki.

'There you go again with your superstitious nonsense.' Wada rolls his eyes.

'Seriously! They exist!'

'Like ghosts, eh?'

'I've got this friend, right—'

'It's always a friend, isn't it? It's never the person telling the story.'

'Shut up and listen, will you?' Yamazaki takes a glug of shochu and wipes his mouth with the back of his hand. 'Anyways, this friend of mine went to a soapland.'

'A story involving a prostitute and a friend. Well I never!' Wada chuckles.

Yamazaki pretends not to have heard him. 'And when he went to the bath with the girl, he said she was the most beautiful girl he'd ever seen, and that he had the best time. But that the girl hadn't spoken a word to him the whole time. And then he came back into the room and heard this *meow*—'

'What's he wittering on about?' Tencho appears again from out back, and eyes Yamazaki suspiciously.

'Oh, just another silly ghost story,' says Wada.

▲▲

Yamazaki is quite drunk, but Wada is worse. The girl is still slowly picking away at her fish, but they are the only ones left in the shop – it's late now.

'Tencho! Call a taxi for us!' asks Wada.

'Do it yourself!' Tencho is smiling. 'Call yourself taxi drivers.'

Wada looks, with bleary red eyes, at Tencho, who sighs and walks over to the phone.

Yamazaki looks away at the girl. 'She's taking ages eating that fish,' he says.

Tencho hangs up the phone. 'It'll be fifteen minutes.'

'Tanks, Thencho,' says Wada, slumping his head forward onto the table.

Tencho shakes his head.

Yamazaki nods at the girl. 'How will she be getting home?'

'She'll be fine,' says Tencho.

'Maybe she could share a taxi with us.' Yamazaki leans across the counter. 'Hey, missy!'

'None of that.' Tencho steps in between. 'She can look after herself, Yamazaki-san.'

'Was just a thought.' Yamazaki stares at his empty glass of shochu and weighs up pouring himself another one from the quarter-full bottle.

Tencho sweeps in and takes the bottle. 'Here, I'll write your name on this and keep it for you behind the counter. For next time when you come back, hey?'

'Good idea!' says Yamazaki. 'We'll definitely be coming back. This was the best Hiroshi . . . okonomiyaki I've ever had.'

Tencho beams.

'You're welcome anytime.' He nods at Wada. 'This one too, as long as he doesn't drink so much next time.'

Wada lifts his head and blinks. 'I didn't have too much, did I?'

'Go back to sleep,' says Tencho. 'Your taxi'll be—'

The lights go off.

'Sit tight. Don't worry.'

There's the banging sound on the wall, and the floorboards creak. A flicker and a flash from the lights above. Then blackness again.

'Blast it.' Tencho's voice in the dark. 'Hold on. I'll get a lamp.'

The sound of Tencho's footsteps can be heard going out into the back, and a small glow of light comes from his mobile phone as he uses it to search for something.

'Creepy,' says Yamazaki.

'Don't be silly,' slurs Wada.

Then they hear it again – quieter this time – the faint yowling sound.

'There it is again!' whispers Yamazaki.

They hear Tencho from the back. 'Perfect!' And a small amount of light floods into the front room. The light moves slowly into the main room, and Tencho's face is illuminated in a ghostly way, with the light shining underneath him, casting devilish shadows across his face. He places the lamp on the counter.

'Everyone okay?' he asks.

'Yup,' says Yamazaki.

'Me too,' says Wada.

Silence.

They look in the girl's direction, but she's nowhere to be seen.

'*Ojo-san?*' says Tencho. 'Are you okay?'

'She there?'

'Shhh!' Wada touches his arm.

The sound is there again, louder than before. There's a rustling coming from the other side of the counter. Something is moving about on the floor.

The three men crouch low. Tencho grabs a knife, Wada picks up the lantern and they all slowly make their way across the room together. There's a scratching sound coming from under the counter, and a pungent smell fills their nostrils. They pause, look from one to the other and then peer over the counter.

Strange green eyes peer back at them. A tongue darts out, licking fishy lips.

And then the lamp goes out.

Detective Ishikawa: Case Notes 2

Weeks pass. I work slowly, I work steadily. Work is what I love.

The city is built on work. Tokyo's the kind of place where if you stop working for even just a second, you'll be swallowed up and forgotten. That's what's happened with these poor sods who sit around on blue tarpaulins in the parks, drinking themselves silly. Most of them probably just couldn't keep up with the pace.

The city doesn't rest, ever.

Especially at night. Sleep is just something Tokyo fits in around work.

Tokyo's at its sleepiest at about 4.30 a.m. It's just getting light, the taxis are still moving, some of them taking people to work early, some of them taking people home late. The trains haven't started yet, but give it thirty minutes and they'll be chugging along as ever. The only thing that slows them down is a jumper. Another poor bastard who can't keep up with the city. They'll leap onto the tracks, hoping it'll take them to a better place. Then the train company will charge the family of the deceased. It's supposed to stop the jumpers from disrupting the trains – Tokyo doesn't appreciate being put behind schedule. Seems like it's not enough of a deterrent for some though. Maybe some people don't even have a family to pick up the bill. What have they got to lose, right?

This city is one of the largest prisons in the world – thirty million inhabitants.

Not like where I grew up.

Don't get me wrong, Osaka's a big city, but the people there know how to relax. They know how to relate to each other too. They can see the funny side of life. Tokyo takes itself too seriously. And for a good reason – it's a serious place.

I know why I came to this city. Love brought me here.

But I often wonder, when I'm riding the train into work hungover as shit.

Since the two of us divorced, what's keeping me here?

⁂

When I arrived at the office, I knew something was wrong.

The door was open. Taeko doesn't get in until later, so I knew it wasn't her. I crept slowly towards the door, pushed it, and the hinges gave off a squeak. The lock was hanging off the door. Forced open.

I held my breath and padded as quietly as I could through the waiting room and into the back office. I could see the outline of someone short and stocky reflected in the window. They had my stack of photos from cases in their hands, and they were going through them one by one. Same old story – someone trying to steal back evidence.

I crept through the door and looked at the figure standing in my office wearing a balaclava and leather gloves. They had on blue jeans and a *Pulp Fiction* T-shirt, still flicking through the photos. Oblivious.

'Can I help you?' I asked.

The head flicked upwards, and all I could see were eyes and lips. The lips were drawn tight, and the eyes seemed surprised, but there was something else there. We both looked at each other breathing slowly in the office. We both waited. Outside I could hear the melodic chime coming from the station, announcing another train's departure. Cries of a man advertising a new NetCafe drifted up from the street. Then there was just the soft sound of traffic. The eyes behind the mask flicked to the door, and mine followed. When I looked back an object was flying in my direction. The object expanded in the air as it came towards me. I put my arm up instinctively, felt the thud and scatter as a heavy pile of photos hit my arm and face. I felt a cut on my cheek, then a hard shove and I was on the ground. I looked through the open door of the office to see a dark shape disappearing fast.

'Well, that's one way to start the morning.' I wiped my cheek with my hand and saw I was bleeding.

I lay on my back, surrounded by hundreds of small glossy rectangles, each one depicting its own unique betrayal.

▲▲

When Taeko came in I had just about cleaned everything up.

We've had a lot of break-ins like this over the years, but there was no need for her to know about every single one of them. It was a standard move once a cheating husband or wife found out their spouse had the dirt on them. They would hire someone else to try to steal back any evidence a private detective had. What these break-in guys didn't know was that I always had multiple copies. My ex-wife had found that out the hard way when she'd paid some mook to steal back the photos I had on her.

'Morning!' Taeko was smiling, but then her eyes fell on the lock hanging off the door. 'Oh gosh! Again?'

'We had a visitor.'

'Are you okay?' She bit her lip, then looked up from the broken lock to my cheek. 'What happened to your face?'

'Cut myself shaving.'

'You'd think you'd be better at that.' She smiled. 'At your age.'

'Never could get the hang of it.'

'Go sit down.' She sighed. 'I'll make some coffee.'

'Make it strong, please.'

'I'll get the first aid kit too.' She shook her head and tottered off to the kitchen.

I could hear her voice alongside the clatter of spoons and mugs. 'Heavens above!' And then something like, 'I can't take much more of this.'

'Me neither,' I whispered.

When I was walking to the train station after work that night, some crazy slipped me a piece of paper. He had a big stack of them photocopied and was handing them out to anyone who'd take them, just like the cult members. He waved a piece frantically in front of me, and I slowed down, mostly because I had no other way of getting round him.

He was a big fellow, and he looked me in the eyes when I took it.

'Don't become one of them, brother,' he said.

'One of who?' I said. (Looking back on it, I should've said, 'I ain't your brother, pal,' or some kind of wisecrack like that.)

He kind of stared off into the distance.

'The ants,' he said.

'Yeah, sure, buddy.' I nodded, and hurried to the station.

I took the paper out from my pocket and read it on the train. It was batshit:

> I am the shadow of the city, carved out and shaded onto the living skin of the landscape. I stalk the alleyways. I live off mould. I live off mildew. I keep company with cockroaches. With slugs, with rats. I am the camera that does not judge. I am the wave that strikes the power plant in Fukushima. I am the horses and dogs and cats left behind, decaying into bone. Sun-bleached corpses. I am your vast crumbling Olympic stadium. I do not breed. And yet here I am. You cannot hide me behind steel. Behind buildings. Behind computer screens. Behind swarms of people, crowds of ants. Like the blackest of inks that spills and stains – here I am, and here I'll be. Forever and ever. I am alone in my loneliness, and so are you.
>
> For I am the city of darkness. And I am waiting.

Like I said: batshit.

I headed down to the club my yakuza college friend owns. We were still in the middle of a game of *shogi* and he was winning, but that wasn't what I wanted to talk to him about.

The past few weeks, in between strolling the streets sticking up signs for 'Cheese & Pickle' (a couple of fluffy cats that had gone missing from a rich lady's Azabu home) and hiding behind a flowerpot trying to get good photos of a drunk couple heading into an Italian-themed love hotel, I'd also been doing my pro bono research for the mother and father of the missing son.

At first, I'd drawn a blank with him – no records anywhere I looked. No social security, no job history, no owned property, no car, no apartment, no house. It was almost like I was looking for a ghost. I spent a few days scratching my head over it all, wondering if I'd been misinformed. Did this guy even exist? But I'd been down this road before. When you're looking for someone who doesn't exist in our world, it's best to assume that they're living in another. Our missing boy was most likely not the darling angel his parents made him out to be.

If he wasn't just some schmuck working at a company in Tokyo, he had to have another story. No, this lad must've had connections. And not the good kind. It was looking more and more likely that our missing momma's boy had a history with the only other organization available for those who exist outside respectable society – he was yakuza. And luckily for me, my old college buddy was now top dog in one of the biggest families in Shinjuku. I didn't like having to go to him for favours, but this was something I needed help on.

With the yaks, sometimes it's not just about needing their help on things, but letting them know you want to go sifting through their dirty laundry. They don't like it when you don't ask permission – it's a sign of disrespect, and is likely to end up with you being found suffocated in that dirty laundry, maybe strangled wearing a pair of panties and a bra. These guys don't play kind.

It was still daylight when I knocked on the front door of the club. And that's what made it strange when the doorman let me in – it felt like night on the inside.

'Name?' the doorman asked straight away.

'Ishikawa.' I watched him talk quietly into the radio headset he was wearing. I pretended not to intrude by studying a screen of surveillance cameras showing different parts of the club. It was divided up into multiple scenes, about thirteen of them, and it was difficult to take in so many at one time. So many different scenes from so many different angles, it was impossible to process them all in my mind at once. There was one for outside, and there was one looking down on us right now. I could see myself standing stock still staring up at something, while the doorman was talking on his headset and bobbing his head slightly as he spoke. I couldn't quite hear what he was saying, but then he said, 'Oi.' I looked at his real-life image, and he was nodding. He waved me through to the next door, but I could see something in his eyes as he did so.

Don't try anything, punk.

A long corridor took me to another door that was opened again by an unseen arm, and then I was in the club.

It looked a lot like a dumb scene from a seedy movie.

There were topless girls gyrating on poles, and goons in suits ogling them. A cheesy disco ball hanging from the middle of the room with half-hearted coloured lights bouncing around the walls. There was a weird smell in the air: something between marijuana, cheap incense and bleach. I walked to the bar and ordered a black coffee, just to stir things up a bit. The barman looked at me like I was a piece of shit, but went back to his espresso machine and began making my drink. I liked his *Reservoir Dogs* T-shirt. His attitude, not so much. I turned to face the club, putting my back to the bar.

Then she caught my eye. One of the girls dancing stood out from the rest.

I couldn't say for sure whether it was her green eyes that caught my attention, or the tattoo that covered her whole back. As she spun and twisted on the pole, I tried to make out what the tattoo was of. She looked slender at first glance, but I could see her muscles rippling beneath the tattoo as she twirled on the pole slowly, supported at all times by powerful arms and legs. What was it? A wave? An animal? It was something that looked alive, something that simmered with energy, but it was difficult to make out with all the flashing lights and movement.

'Hey.' A voice behind me. I turned to the bar. The barman was pointing at a cup of steaming coffee.

'Thanks, buddy,' I said.

'I ain't your buddy, pal,' he muttered, walking down the bar to serve someone else.

I shook my head, picked up the coffee on its saucer and turned while taking a sip. I was intrigued by this girl with the strange tattoo. But when I faced the stage where she'd been, the music had changed and there was a different girl dancing. This one had paler skin, bigger boobs, and no tattoo.

I lost interest in the dancers.

'Ishikawa?'

I turned to see a large man in a suit with close cropped hair wearing an earpiece.

'Yes?'

'This way please.'

He turned immediately and I followed him through another door in the corner, up some stairs to a back office. He held the door to the office open for me, but didn't follow me inside. He closed the door, and as it clicked shut, Shiwa looked up at me. On the desk was a real *shogi* chessboard. I recognized the game as ours. So, Shiwa sets up an actual board. Interesting.

'Ishi! You old stray dog, you!'

'Shiwa-san. Long time no see.'

'Have a seat.' He smiled.

'Thanks.'

'Cigarette?' He offered me one.

Shook my head. 'Gave up.'

'Since when?'

'Last week.'

'Wonder how long that'll last, eh, Ishi?'

'Three days is enough for anyone to be a priest.'

'You mind if I smoke?'

'Go ahead.'

He lit up, and I saw within the rolls of flab and the thin moustache the young face of the guy I went to college with. I wonder what I looked like to him. Had I aged like that? Could he see any changes in my appearance? When I looked in the mirror, I saw nothing. Time seemed to be this thing that happened to other people.

'So, how you been, Ishi?'

'Not too bad. Keeping afloat.'

'Many cases?'

'Work never stops.'

'Good. Good.' He took a long drag on his cigarette and inhaled a cloud of smoke into the air.

'And how's the criminal underworld?' I crossed my legs.

'Same old same old – "work never stops".' He chuckled. 'Some of the idiots I have to deal with, you wouldn't believe.'

'I don't know – my client list contains some pretty *interesting* characters.'

'Oh, Ishi, I wish I could tell you some of the stories I have.'

'Me too.'

'What is it I'm supposed to say next?' He looked up in the corner of the room, small beads of sweat glistening on his forehead. 'Oh yeah, *but then I'd have to kill you.*'

'Way to embrace the cliché gangster thing, Shiwa-san.'

He laughed. 'So, what brings you to my neck of the woods?' He leant forward in his chair and tapped his cigarette over the ashtray.

'Sorry to come around like this, but I'm looking for someone.'

'Oh yeah?' He looked down at his hand resting over the ashtray and tilted his head slightly.

'Yes.'

'And who might that be?'

'Guy named Kurokawa.' I held my breath.

'Kurokawa . . .' He shook his head. 'Doesn't ring a bell . . .'

'Just a small fish.'

'So why's this small fish so important to you?'

'Missing person case.'

He looked me straight in the eye and made a slitting motion at his throat. *'Missing* missing?'

'No, not like that.' I paused. 'His parents hired me to find him.'

'Hmmm.' Shiwa leant back in his chair and looked at the ceiling. 'Ishikawa, you know you're asking a lot from me here.'

'I know, Shiwa-san.' I sat forward. 'I wouldn't have come to you if I could've found him any other way.'

'Once people join this family, they're saying goodbye to their old family.' He sighed. 'Don't his parents know that?'

'I think they do.' I shifted in my seat. 'But now he's not part of your family anymore . . .'

'He's dead to us.'

'I know.'

'And people don't come back from the dead, you know?'

'I know.'

He took a long drag on his cigarette, and the end flared red. He exhaled and looked at me. 'Okay.' He nodded. 'Only because we go back. Don't make a habit of this, Ishikawa.'

'Thank you, Shiwa-san.' I bowed low.

'Talk to Seiji on the way out, he'll help you.'

'Which one's Seiji?'

'Barman.'

'Thank you, Shiwa-san.' I got up and made for the door. 'I owe you one.'

'You certainly do, and we shall call on that favour when we need it. I might have a case for you soon. Anyway, we'll be in touch.'

I put my hand on the door.

'Oh, Ishi?'

I turned to look at him once more. 'Yes?'

'Don't forget, it's your move.' He eyed the chessboard.

▲▲

185

Seiji was waiting for me on the customer side of the bar when I came back to the club. He was sitting on a stool, smoking a cigarette. He had long curly hair and a beard – like one of the beach bums who hang around Shonan beach, pretending they can surf, trying to pick up girls. I walked up to him, but he ignored me. He just kept smoking his cigarette, other hand in his jeans pocket, and looking straight ahead. I watched as he smoked; there was something very familiar in the way he formed his lips as he blew smoke rings. The music had quietened down enough to talk.

'Seiji? I'm Ishikawa, Shiwa told me—'

'I know who you are. Sit the fuck down.'

I stood where I was. 'That's cute. You gonna buy me dinner?'

He stood and squared up to me. He was a short guy, but I could see something in his eyes, again that nagging feeling at the back of my mind. There was something there – he didn't like me. For a reason.

'Listen up, fuck-o.' He spoke through gritted teeth. 'Don't get sweet with me, or I'll toss you on your ass. Got it?'

'Loud and clear, darling.'

'I know who the fuck you are, Ishikawa. I've seen your work. You go around sniffing through other people's garbage, and then you hang it out on the line for the whole neighbourhood to see.' His voice was almost a snarl.

'Do you always treat a guy like this on a first date?' I smiled.

He pushed me hard in the chest with his finger. 'You're *scum*.'

'I usually give someone a kiss before I get fresh with them.' I stood my ground.

He pointed a finger at my face. 'Yeah, I know all about you, Ishikawa.'

'What do you know, honey bunny?' I stared past the finger.

'Word gets around. I know you sold out your ex-wife.'

How did he know about what happened with my ex? 'Keep talking, sunshine. I'll bury you.'

'What you gonna do, Private Dick? You're on our turf now. You're only getting out of here alive today because you're friends with Shiwa.'

'Yeah, you're right. I am friends with Shiwa-san.'

I let it hang in the air.

'Now, I'll go find this punk you're looking for, because it's my duty.' He smirked. 'See, Ishikawa. Even us yakuza trash know more about loyalty and honour than a pimp like you – selling photos of your wife to another woman, then using them as evidence for yourself so you could make good in your own divorce. I ain't surprised she was cheating on you.' He looked me over from head to toe. 'You're the fucking scum of the earth.'

How did he know all of this? 'You don't know what you're talking about, pencil dick.'

'Yeah, yeah. Save it for the afterlife, scumbag.' He waved his hand dismissively. 'We'll be in touch about your missing friend.'

'Thanks, honey.' I was about to leave, but then I thought of something. 'Just one more thing for when you break into my office next time: I'll leave the key under the mat, so you don't need to break the lock. Okay?'

He stepped closer to me and moved faster than I expected. His fist caught me in the stomach and I felt the wind knocked out of me. I fought against the instinct to double over, and kept smiling.

'Get the fuck out of my club.' He bared his teeth.

I kept it together until I was a few hundred metres from the club, then I allowed myself to double over and catch my breath.

Omatsuri

The small calico cat lay in the sun on the hot corrugated iron roof. It was an early summer's morning, but the heat was already becoming unbearable. It raised its head, blinked in the bright light, and decided it would be better to find a place in the shade. There was something it was searching for – some kind of memory of a previous life – a scent, an image. Was it the purple-headed man, or something else?

It hopped up and padded lightly across the rooftops of the Tokyo suburban landscape, prowling with purpose. Darting quickly, and with almost rehearsed movements. Coming to an open window, the cat peered inside to see a girl in her late twenties sitting in the bath, reading a Nishi Furuni book.

Well, *trying* to read a Nishi Furuni book.

Sachiko had been looking forward to the *omatsuri* all month. She kept finding that she would read a page of her novel, then have to go back and read it again, having taken in none of the story at all. It was a book she was fond of. But all she could think about was the festival tonight.

And, of course, seeing Ryu-kun.

The year before she'd worn her red yukata, and now she deliberated over which one to wear that evening. She put her open book on the side of the bath, and it soaked up the puddle of water it lay in. Perhaps she'd wear the blue one with the white *asagao* morning-glory pattern. She began to run her hands over the parts of her body that worried her. Her empty stomach grumbled, but she ignored it, wanting to look her best that night. She sat still for a while with her eyes closed.

She was unaware of the cat silently watching her.

'Sachiko!'

The loud voice stirred her from her reverie. She rolled her eyes, took her hands out of the bath and looked at her fingers – shrivelled up like *umeboshi* dried plums.

'Sachiko!' The voice grew louder. Closer. 'Sacchan! Where are you?'

Sachiko shrank down deeper into the tub.

'Sacchan! Are you in the bath?'

A bang on the door

'No. I'm not in here.'

Her mother opened the door to the bathroom and scowled at her.

'Don't tell lies. How long have you been in there? Get out this instant. You'll turn into a prune.'

'Yes, *Okasan*.'

One last glare from her mother, then she was alone again, or . . .

The cat twitched its head, and Sachiko caught sight of it for the first time. They blinked at each other through the steam.

Was this what the cat had been looking for?

Sachiko cocked her head and clicked her tongue at the cat. 'Aren't you a pretty thing?' What lovely green eyes it had, and a slightly nonchalant, regal air.

The cat looked away, out the window. No, this wasn't what it was looking for. It slunk off over the rooftops, in search of something to eat for breakfast.

▲▲

Dried, made up and dressed in jeans and a T-shirt, Sachiko stepped into the kitchen. Her mother was standing near the refrigerator holding two large daikon radishes, one in each hand. There were several shopping bags filled to bursting on the table.

'And where do you think you're going?' She waggled one of the daikon at Sachiko.

'I was just going to the beauty parlour . . . To get my hair done for tonight . . .'

'Not until you've helped me unpack this shopping, you're not.'

She jabbed one daikon at Sachiko, and the other in the direction of the shopping bags.

'Yes, *Okasan.*'

Sachiko began to put things away. Mother continued talking.

'And I don't know why you're wasting your money getting your hair done at that fancy beauty parlour. I know it's the *omatsuri*, but I could put your hair up for you – like I always used to.'

Sachiko suppressed a shiver at the thought of all the terrible hairstyles Mother had inflicted on her in the past.

'*Okasan* is so busy . . . I wouldn't dream of putting her to any trouble . . .'

Her mother turned to her and winked.

'It's an important day for you. I shouldn't be so—'

There was a knock at the door and a deep voice came from outside.

'*Gomen kudasai!* It's the post!'

Mother's face lit up and she went to open the door. Sachiko continued to unpack the shopping.

'Ah! Shingo-kun!' Her mother's voice was smothered with affection.

'Oh! Hello, Shibata-san. You're looking well. Here's your mail.'

Sachiko craned her neck slightly to see Shingo the postman in the doorway. She wished her mother wouldn't flirt with him so openly. It was embarrassing.

Aside from being too young for Mother entirely, he was fairly good-looking. In his late thirties, still had a full head of hair, and although his jolly face looked like he enjoyed a night on the town, he seemed to be keeping control of the paunch that men of his age often develop. But he would never make a good match for Mother, and that's what made her flirting all the more desperate.

'Would you like to sit down and have a cup of green tea?'

'Oh, that's a lovely offer.' Shingo moved further into the *genkan* entranceway, as if to take his shoes off. Then his eyes fell on Sachiko, and he hesitated. 'But, I really must be getting on with my route.'

'How about a coffee?'

'Thank you, Shibata-san, but I really must be getting on.'

'How about some *kasutera* sponge cake? I got some from the market this morning. Sacchan, put the kettle on. Come on, hurry up!'

'Oh, please don't worry about that. I'm sure Sacchan has better things to do than have tea with us,' he replied.

'Don't worry about her – she's off out to get her hair done for the festival tonight.'

Shingo's eyebrows rose slightly.

'Will you be going to the festival tonight, Shingo-kun?' Mother asked.

'Oh, no. I'm too old for that kind of thing.' Shingo laughed.

'Nonsense! You two should go together!'

Sachiko froze.

'Oh, I'm sure Sacchan already has a date. And anyway, she wouldn't want to go with an old fart like me.' He smiled at Sachiko.

'She'd do much worse than go with you. Look at her. I despair! Nearly thirty and still unmarried. I wish someone would come and take her off my hands. All she does is sit around in the bath and read trashy novels.'

'Oh, Shibata-san. That's not very nice.'

Sachiko turned her back on the two of them, her face starting to turn the same colour as Shingo's mailbag.

'I'll be back later, *Okasan*. Goodbye, Shingo-san.'

She hid her eyes from both of them and edged out of the front door.

'That beauty parlour is a waste of money!' said Mother.

'Goodbye, Sacchan,' said Shingo.

She bowed to them both, and shut the door gently. Shingo's voice drifted through the closed door.

'Shibata-san! You really shouldn't be so hard on Sacchan.'

Sachiko hated it when he called her Sacchan.

Walking through town, she wasn't about to let another incident like this with her mother bring her down. If it had been any other day, she'd probably have arranged to meet with Mari to complain about living with her mother. And her friend would do what she always did: sit, listen to everything, nod and sigh occasionally. And when Sachiko had let it all out and finally simmered down, Mari would respond with something like, 'Sacchan, you really need to move out and get a place of your own.'

Sachiko would always come to the same conclusion – she couldn't leave her mother on her own. She also knew that it was not just moving out that would solve her problems. Her mother would continue to cause her distress until the day that she was safely married and living with a husband. Mother was old-fashioned like that, and wouldn't have looked kindly on a single woman living alone. That autumn, she'd kept all the drama involving Ryu-kun secret from her mother. She'd even kept it from Mari, partly because Mari had been going through a difficult time herself then. But also because she just didn't feel like discussing that kind of thing, even with a friend.

Even now, she tried to push it out of her mind.

But, what her mother didn't understand was that these were different times. Men and women weren't so quick to dash into marriage. Take her relationship with Ryu-kun, for example. They had been courting on and off now for several years, and they hadn't even broached the question of marriage. Sachiko wouldn't dream of bringing it up. She knew deep down that they were meant to be together and would be married before long. She must be patient.

Nonetheless, it would be a lie to say that Sachiko wasn't anxious to marry quickly. She wasn't getting any younger, and all her friends (except Mari) were now happily married, most with babies. But putting pressure on Ryu-kun would not help the situation. She'd seen before that he didn't respond well to it – and knew only too well his views on starting a family soon.

The streets were still mostly empty. Here and there were lanterns hanging high in trees, ready for the festival that evening. It was clear a great deal of preparation had gone into getting everything ready. Food stalls had sprung up all along the *shotengai* main street – sleeping now, boarded up, but ready to come to life at night.

Sachiko saw a glamorous Western lady she often met out walking her dog around town. She bowed slightly, and the lady bowed back, then whistled away down the road.

She walked past the train station on her way to the beauty parlour and could hear the rhythmical tap tap of IC cards and the beep beep sounds of black-suited salaryman souls smashing against existence. The gates of the ticket turnstiles crashed out a mindless concerto of crunches and clinks. Commutin to central Tokyo, forgoing humanity, stepping into the steaming miso broth of the city. Ryu-kun would be on the train to work now too.

The beauty parlour was as loud and noisy as the train station. Troupes of girls gossiping and giggling. The rows of chairs in front of mirrors were almost full, and the waiting area was packed like a train carriage. The bell tinkled as she opened the door to be hit by the mingled mush of perfumes, thick enough to taste. It hit the back of her throat and made her cough.

'Shibata-san!' Her beautician waved to her.

The waiting girls stared at her with resentment as she walked straight to a chair in front of the mirrors. She was glad that she'd booked an appointment early.

She sat down in the seat and read a magazine while her beautician worked away, washing her hair carefully, drying and styling.

She wasn't sure if she was imagining it or not, but there was a girl in the waiting area who kept staring at her, with her strange green eyes. Sachiko would look up in the mirror from time to time, and would see the girl's head flick down, pretending that she wasn't staring at her.

Sachiko racked her brain. She didn't recognize the girl – who made her feel uneasy, almost like she had déjà vu – so she did her best to put it out of her mind. She reminisced instead about how much fun she'd had at the festival last year. Ryu-kun had bought a bottle of shochu, and they'd drunk it together by the river under the lantern light. Ryu-kun could drink a lot, and she'd tried to keep up with him, but had ended up feeling light-headed. He'd been so good about it though, taking her back to his apartment so that she could lie down for a bit. They'd laughed and joked all night until early morning. He had been *so* naughty. Mother had been angry that she hadn't come home that night. She felt a sense of excitement at what might happen this year. Perhaps things would go better this time.

She caught sight of the girl staring at her again.

Sachiko paid and left the beauty parlour. She was happy with the style and was sure that it would go well with the blue yukata she had picked out for the evening. She visited the nail salon next, and had her nails carefully painted and decorated with blue and white morning-glory patterns to match her yukata.

On the way home, her phone rang. Seeing who it was, she answered immediately.

'Ryu-kun!'

'Sacchan . . .' His voice sounded weak.

'Ryu-kun, are you all right?'

'Not really . . .' He coughed. 'Sacchan, I'm so sorry. I don't think I can make it tonight.'

She didn't know what to say, so she remained silent.

'Sacchan? Are you there?'

'Yes, I'm here.'

'Sacchan, I'm so sorry. I know how much you were looking forward to it. But I'm so tired and ill. Big Boss has got me working overtime because the Olympics are fast approaching now, and I think I've caught a cold. I'll be at work till late this evening, and then I just don't think I could face the festival . . .' He trailed off.

'It's okay. Don't worry. I just hope you feel better soon. Do you want me to bring you some medicine tonight? Or I could come and cook something for you?'

'No, no. Thank you. I really just need sleep. I'm so tired.'

'Rest well this evening. I hope you feel better soon.'

'Thanks for being so understanding, Sacchan. I'm sorry. I'll make it up to you. We'll go for dinner next week. Okay?'

'Can we have sushi?'

'Sure. Anything you like.'

She smiled. He was so kind.

'Take care, Ryu-kun. *Odaijini*.'

'*Arigato*.'

She felt a little sadness when she hung up, but started to berate herself for being so selfish. Ryu-kun was ill, and she should be more worried about that than missing the silly festival tonight.

Ryu-kun's health worried her a lot. For someone who appeared so healthy and was relatively young, he suffered from illness more than would be expected. She thought it might be something to do with the amount he drank. He was often out drinking with people from the company; he'd had the worst hangovers when he was with that Makoto and Kyoko – Sachiko was also suspicious of Kyoko, and had asked Ryu-kun a lot about her after she'd seen a photo of them all drinking together on Facebook. That prissy pink Polo sweater and those cream trousers troubled her. Anyway, after the festival last year, Ryu-kun had to cancel quite a few of their dates they'd arranged. He would often be unable to meet her due to illness. She hated his Big Boss for it – forcing him to go out on work-related drinking parties. The man looked like a grown baby! Couldn't Ryu-kun get his father to pull some strings? But, Ryu-kun had been firm: entertaining clients until late was part of his job, and his father was CEO of the PR company tasked with promoting the 2020 Olympics. Ryu-kun had to set an example.

But now that it was having an effect on his health, it was really quite worrying.

She was a little lost in her thoughts when she came into the house, but her mother successfully brought her back down to earth.

'*Urgh!* What the *hell* have they done to your hair!'

It was the last straw for Sachiko. She pushed past her mother and made straight for her room.

'Hey! What's wrong with you?'

She ignored her mother, shut the door and flung herself down on the bed.

A knock at the door.

'Sacchan?'

'Please, leave me alone.'

Mother opened the door.

'Sacchan? What's wrong?'

'Please, *Okasan*. I just want to be alone.'

'Did something happen?'

'I just need to rest.'

'Suit yourself.'

Mother left her alone, closing the door softly behind her.

Sachiko fell asleep crying and didn't wake until early evening.

▲▲

When she awoke she felt a little better, but still confused and weak from lack of food. She walked into the kitchen, still groggy from her midday nap. Mother had prepared food for her, and was sitting at the table doing a jigsaw puzzle. She looked up at Sachiko as she walked in.

'Feeling better?'

'A little.'

'Now, there's rice and miso soup for you, and a little fish. You'd better eat your supper quick and then get ready for the festival.'

'I'm not going.'

'What do you mean you're not going?'

'He cancelled. I've got no one to go with.'

'Nonsense. You just leave that to me. Eat.'

'But I don't want to go anymore.'

'Just eat. Then get dressed. Leave everything to me.'

Sachiko sat down, said, '*Itadakimasu*,' and ate the rice and miso soup, enjoying the little bits of fresh daikon in it. She ate her fish and felt stronger. The lump of sorrow in her throat was getting smaller. She finished the last bite of fish, glad to have eaten, and placed her hands together.

'*Gochiso sama deshita.*'

'Now go get ready. Quick.'

She put on her blue yukata with the plain light-blue obi sash. A lot of girls these days favoured overly ornate obi sashes, but Sachiko preferred the more traditional plain ones. She put her white socks on, and got out the wooden *geta* sandals from her cupboard. She carried them down to the *genkan*, ready to put on when she left. Mother looked at her as she walked past.

'Sacchan! You've slept on your hair and ruined it.'

Sachiko raised her hand to her mouth.

'Don't worry! Go fetch my brush from the bathroom. We'll fix this easily.'

'But *Okasan*—'

'Look. Wear it down tonight. You've got beautiful long hair. Why wear it up, just because all the other girls do? Let's see what it looks like down.'

She felt calmer as her mother brushed her long hair for her. But she was still anxious about going to the festival on her own. She hadn't even taken the time to contact any of her friends to ask if she could go along with them. Of course, there would be people at the festival that she knew, but it just seemed a bit sad to go by herself.

Mother finished brushing her hair and went to fetch a mirror.

'There now. That's better.'

She looked at her long hair in the mirror and couldn't help but feel a little pride, and surprise, at her mother's judgement. Letting her hair down had been a good idea. She fought back a smile.

'But, *Okasan*. I don't have anyone to go with.'

Mother clicked her teeth.

'Now, don't get angry, but I already guessed. I called someone.'

A knock at the door. Mother shot up and answered.

'Shingo-kun! *Konbanwa.*'

'*Konbanwa*, Shibata-san.'

Sachiko stood up in alarm. Surely not.

He was wearing a dark green *jinbei* and had a sheepish smile on his face. She looked at his muscular golden legs, covered in thick black hair. His shoulders were broad in the cloth outfit. He seemed stronger and more confident than in his uniform.

Shingo looked at her standing in her blue yukata.

He froze, unable to speak.

'Now you two go and have a good time.' Mother beamed.

⁂

Garish fashion, extravagant nail art, dyed hair, smartphones held in hands, or tucked into an obi sash. The men with their spiked hair, the women with theirs put up in elaborate styles. The streets were alive with the evening festivities. With Shingo walking on the left, Sachiko walking on the right, they passed through the crowds. Bright colours of yukata moved in throngs gravitating towards some central unknown.

The summer heat lingered well on into the evening, and there was a flutter of fans wafting hairstyles, with towels produced occasionally to wipe sweat from brows.

Sachiko felt a strange confidence with her hair down, like an ancient princess, or a ghost from *The Tale of Genji*. She noticed people looking at her – she stood out from the rest of the swarm. It seemed like positive attention, and it bolstered her spirits. Her only concern was that someone might see her with Shingo and gossip might circulate around the town. It could reach Ryu-kun's ears eventually.

But, so what? He had cancelled, hadn't he? She'd only needed someone to escort her for the evening, and this was only Shingo, after all. It might even do Ryu-kun some good to get a bit jealous. She smiled to herself.

Sachiko snuck a look at Shingo. He was actually quite handsome in this light. He looked happy, with a towel hanging around his neck which he occasionally used to wipe small drops of perspiration from his brow.

The lanterns lit the streets; the crowds pulsated and resonated with excitement. The smells of street food tugged at the nostrils from the steaming *yatai* stalls that had come to life with juicy yakitori meat skewers, greasy yakisoba noodles, fried squid, okonomiyaki pancakes and karaage fried chicken. Everyone was eating and drinking as they walked.

'Would you like a drink?' Shingo pointed out a stall selling cold drinks, sitting in a bucket of iced water.

'Yes, that sounds nice.'

'What will you have?'

'Hmmm . . .' She deliberated. She thought of getting a Ramune soft drink. She'd drunk those with Father when he'd brought her to the festivals as a child.

'I'm going to have an Asahi beer,' he said.

'Me too.' She got out her purse to pay.

Shingo lightly pushed it back into her obi sash.

'*Arigato gozaimasu.*' She bowed.

Shingo paid for the drinks and handed her a small can of beer.

It tasted crisp and cold, and Sachiko could feel herself warming to the evening.

There was dancing in the street. Teams of dancers dressed in similar yukata paraded in the light of the lanterns with smiles on their faces. Young and old took part, and the town came together for the night – everything was as one. A group of men carried a portable *omikoshi* shrine through the town, accompanied by cheers and shouts. There was music, there was laughter, and there were fireworks.

Sachiko and Shingo drank more beer and wandered the streets, taking in as much of the atmosphere as they could. They made small talk and spoke of mutual acquaintances, of cafés, shops and restaurants they both liked. Shingo paid close attention to Sachiko, and if her eyes fell on a food stall, or on some kind of trinket or souvenir, he would get his wallet out.

Sachiko would wave her hand to indicate it wasn't necessary, but he would ignore her, coming back with something for her each time, whether it was a box of yakisoba noodles, karaage fried chicken, or a pot of flavoured shaved ice.

When they looked at the time and saw how late it was, Sachiko was a little surprised at how fast the evening had gone by. A lot of the younger crowd had disappeared, leaving behind only a few elderly drunk men, who sang their way to karaoke snack bars, hugging one another in shared happiness.

'I'll walk you home,' Shingo volunteered.

'It's quite all right, Shingo-san. I can go home alone.'

'No, I'll take you. It's no bother at all.'

'Are you sure it's not out of your way?'

'Not at all. I like to walk. These legs of mine are strong from my postal route.' He smiled.

▲▲

Everything would have turned out differently if Shingo had not known the town so well.

They were walking together along the main road, hand-in-hand. Shingo had taken her hand suddenly, and Sachiko had not known how to respond. She was feeling a little tipsy, so she had let him. Perhaps if she had been completely sober, she would not have let him do so. But it had been such a lovely evening, and it seemed a shame to spoil the happiness they had both experienced at the festival.

Walking hand-in-hand with him now, him on the left, her on the right, she was reminded again of how she used to go to the festival with her father when she was younger. Before he got ill.

'We can cut through here.' Shingo took her off the main road.

'Are you sure?' Sachiko was a little disoriented.

'Yes, this is the path that leads past the temple, but it's much quicker than going along the main road all the way to the crossroads. Trust me! I walk these streets every morning – I even deliver mail to the temple!' He sounded ever so cheerful.

The path they walked down now was narrow and dark. There were trees on either side, and the paper lanterns hanging in the trees for the festival cast a little bit more light on the path than usual, making it easier to navigate than it would have been. The stone lanterns that permanently lined the path had no candles in them. They were just covered in an eerie green moss now.

She held her breath as they neared the temple.

Sachiko had bad memories of this particular place.

Sachiko felt sick.

It would have to be that temple. Wouldn't it?

The one she'd visited last autumn, when the leaves were turning red. Red, like the specks of blood she'd found in her underwear for days after the abortion. She'd gone to the temple and left a Jizo statuette there, to protect her *mizuko* – her *river child* – her unborn foetus. Purged by administered doses of mifepristone and prostaglandin. Washed down the medication river without a chance. Souls of children who die before their parents are unable to cross the mythical Sanzu River and must remain in hell. She'd bought a Jizo figurine dressed in a red cap and bib at the temple shop, and placed him next to the hundreds of other statuettes lying on the temple shelf – scattered like the dead red leaves of the *momiji* maple around the temple – one for each of the unborn children in the town. She'd prayed for the Jizo to protect her own little *mizuko* in the afterlife. She had wondered if the Jizo would respect his vow not to achieve Buddhahood until all hells are emptied.

She'd begged Ryu-kun to wear a condom that night last year. And he'd said he didn't have any. That it would be fine without. She'd told him not to come inside her. And he'd said okay, okay, no problem. But he did anyway. And when she'd told him she was pregnant, he'd said he wasn't ready, and that his job was too busy right now, but when he got that promotion they would be able to get married, and then start a family. And couldn't she do something about it? You know, sort it out? He'd pay for it.

She'd gone alone to the hospital, telling Mother that she was going to visit Father. It was close enough to the truth, as she'd always stopped by to see him lying there hooked up to the machine. His chest rising and falling slowly, with the ominous beep beep of a man who'd thrown his soul against existence, and lost.

But her mind snapped back to the present as they passed the temple on their right and she caught something in the corner of her eye, moving under the eaves.

She turned to look, and saw the shape of two people in the half-shadow.

A man, and a girl with her yukata split open, revealing her long legs. Her underwear was pulled down to her ankles. The man had his hand in her crotch, and they were kissing. Sachiko suppressed a gasp, and was going to turn away.

A lone firework shot up in the night sky, the light catching the kissing couple perfectly.

A flash of green eyes.

The girl from the beauty parlour.

And Ryu-kun.

There was no time to stop, and Shingo pulled her on – unaware of what she had seen in the darkness.

She walked in silence with Shingo. He was still in happy oblivion.

Her hand was cold in his.

They arrived outside the house.

'Well! Here we are, Sacchan. Thank you so much for this evening. I had such a good time with you.'

She didn't know what to say, she was so confused.

He dithered nervously. 'Look, I was wondering . . . If you want to, we could go to that café you mentioned earlier. You know, the one you said you liked? How about next Tuesday?'

She turned her head from him, trying to hold it all in.

'Sacchan? Are you all right?'

'Don't you dare call me *Sacchan!*' she hissed.

He stepped away from her, holding his hands up. Her eyes caught the light from the street lamps.

'I don't want to see you ever again. You creep. You *disgust* me!'

She turned and fled inside the house, shutting the door behind her.

Shingo paused for a moment, hung his head, and walked away into the shadows.

On the other side of the door, Sachiko slid down to the ground, hugging her knees. She buried her face against her legs and began to sob.

The house was deadly silent, other than Sachiko's sobs, and a soft padding of footsteps coming from the open bathroom door.

The small calico cat crept curiously towards her.

She was shaking, and the cat licked her hand.

Sachiko struck the cat so hard she broke its jaw.

Trophallaxis

The apartment is not the same since Mother and Father died. I've made certain changes to the way things are done. I've got my own rules now. I don't have to do what Mother says. No need to put away clothes in drawers, or food in cupboards – where it's all hidden away and difficult to find. No need to pay the electricity or water bills – candles suffice in the evenings – and I have found the bathtub a great place for storing books. I try not to bathe too often as I enjoy the rich natural cologne my body creates over time, especially during the warmer months. I like to sniff at my armpits surreptitiously when I am on the train. I have also discovered it provides me with a larger amount of personal space than other Tokyoites are privileged to. I emit an aura. People fear me, and stay away.

When I do need to bathe, I find the public *sento* around the corner from my apartment more than adequate. I am a large man, blessed with a large penis – a silly thing to be proud of, I know – but I enjoy entering the baths naked, witnessing the surprised looks of the other men as they see my huge member flapping around between my legs. They are often so intimidated they leave immediately, giving me the entire bathroom to myself.

No, things have been good since Mother and Father passed away. I was happy with my new life in the apartment.

Until those little black fuckers came along and spoiled everything.

⁂

When I get home, I see that the ants have multiplied. There are more and more of them coming in since I last looked. They are coming through a tiny crack in the front door. I can see the crushed bodies of all the ones I splattered this morning, but even more have come through now. There is a long line of them winding its way into the kitchen.

They are an invasive species – descended from an ancient family of wasps, they have colonized the globe. There is not a country in which they aren't present. Humans have been fascinated by them for centuries, by their work ethic, by their resilience. The way they co-operate and communicate not only with each other, but also coexist with other species. They are the ultimate invader. Swarming conquerors.

And now they have invaded my lovely home. I am at war – at war with the ants.

I am bracing myself for a long battle. I have begun reading *The Art of War* by Sun Tzu, who, despite being a Chink, was a clever man.

The supreme art of war is to subdue the enemy without fighting.

So, for now, I will leave them be. I will choose my moment, and then I will destroy every last one of them. There will be blood, there will be carnage, and I shall rise victorious from the rape and pillage, the master of all who attempt to attack or control me. Hehe.

For now, I need to rest. I have work in the morning, and I must perform well at work.

My work is very important to me.

▲
▲▲

I wake the next morning in a foul mood. That blasted cat was shrieking outside my window again. It shrieked and shrieked all night, and even when I opened the window and bellowed out into the hot summer air, the confounded mog would not cease its caterwauling. I screamed and screamed my guts out, but it would not stop. And then, a neighbour had the gall to shout up to me something like, 'Shut up, you nutcase!'

Can you believe it?! He allows the cat to whine and cry all night, but then tells me to be quiet. The nerve!

Still, I made the 5:02 from Kichijoji Station heading out towards Mount Takao, with my store-bought hot coffee and onigiri for lunch. I had to shout at the Vietnamese cretin working in the convenience store who didn't give me separate bags for my hot and cold items – what is this country coming to? The convenience stores are swarming with foreign idiots! Never mind. Now begins one of my favourite parts of the day. I arrive at the station and wait patiently for my train. I take a photo of a silly sign I see and upload it to the message board:

線路に物を落された方は
駅係員にお申し出ください

喫煙所は
ございません。

Re: Stupid Girl
LaoTzu616: If the girl is stupid enough to drop her hat on the
tracks, maybe she should just throw herself off the platform too.
Idiots.

I love my job. And I'm proud of it.

I know a lot of the others who work at the car factory don't enjoy it, but I can never understand why. I love the cars, I love the robots. I love being able to use my muscles. My strength is valued by my superiors, and I am famous in the factory for being able to carry out a process meant for two men, all by myself.

I love the repetitive nature of the cycles.

I work in Weld, where the sparks fly and the white bodies of the cars are made. I lift the heavy parts from trolleys, put them onto the jig, which holds all the parts in the position to be welded, then hit the red button to send them into the cage where the robots reside. There they work on the parts, their powerful alien arms snaking and coiling around the shell, slowly breathing sparks of life into the car. Every ninety seconds a new car is born, and it all begins with me.

When I see the cars and taxis I've made driving around on the streets of Tokyo, I feel a strong wave of pride. The pride of having created something, of having played a part in the making of something real. Something you can touch.

All those idiots in the city working on their spreadsheets would never understand this kind of feeling. And that's a shame. I take another photo and upload it:

Re: Ungrateful Taxi Driver Scum
LaoTzu616: I built BOTH of these cars. And the drivers, what do they do? They lean out of their cars and have a natter when they should be working! One of them was a fatso who spoke like a yokel.

When I get to work I drop off my stuff in the locker room. I ignore the other factory workers huddled around the Formica tables swilling coffee, and they ignore me. Formica was Italian for 'ant'. Everything comes back to the ants. Now's not the time to think about it. Not here. Not at work. I hit my head with my fist, and turn to see the men with strange looks on their faces. What the hell are they looking at?

The line starts at 6 a.m., and I like to be there five minutes early. And so to the line I go. The alarm sounds and everyone is ready to work. I'm on a ninety-second process today. Safety goggles on, Kevlar gloves and sleeves on, hard hat on. The familiar strong smell of burning rubber.

Heave ho, left part on the jig, heave right part on, rear section in place, cross beam in place, move outside the yellow hatched area, push the red button, the red light flashes, the jig moves into the cage

I take a look to my right at the finished bodies that have been all the way through Weld hanging from a monorail, moving out of Weld into Paint. In Weld we make the bodies – we call them a body in white. After they leave Weld, they go to Paint, where they're dipped in undercoats and spray-painted, coming out all red, shiny and sparkling, then they move on to Assembly Frame. The guys in AF think they're hot shit, but Weld is best. In AF they put all the bits and bobs on the body, which slowly builds it up into a car before—

The jig's come out again. Heave ho, left part, right part, rear section, cross beam, outside the yellow hatched area, push the red button, red light flashes, jig moves into the cage

All I can think about are those fucking ants. I'm so tired. That cat was driving me insane last night. Why must all these things contrive against me? Must I be plagued by everyone and everything in existence? Looking at the robots now just reminds me of the ants. Their winding arms look like giant ant legs, and I'm like a man who has been shrunk down so that the ants tower above me. Must try to think of something else. I won't get through the day if I keep thinking like this. Must think of something better—

Jig's come out again. Heave ho, left part, right part, rear section, cross beam, outside the yellow hatched area, push the red button, red light flashes, jig moves into the cage

It's payday today. I know all the other workers will be talking about going to the soapland brothels again tonight. Idiots. As soon as they get a bit of money in their pockets they blow it all on alcohol and sex. Just to have some silly girl rub her body over you covered in lubrication on a grey blow-up mat. I'm not stupid like that. I spend my money, but not on something silly and dirty like a hangover, or an orgasm. I'm looking for something a bit more refined. Maybe I'll go to a new hostess club tonight—

Jig out. Heave ho, left, right, rear, cross beam, outside the yellow hatches, red button, red light flashes, jig moves into the cage

I know it's weird what I do. I know it's strange to want to sleep next to them. And that's why I have to drug them. It's not such a bad thing, is it? The girl never suffers. Most of them just wake up in a strange hotel with no memory of what happened the night before. I do my best not to harm any of them. There was that one time before . . . but let's not think about that. Best to move forward. I can only work on one at a time. Perhaps tonight I'll meet a new beautiful hostess. I'll get to sleep well next to her again—

Jig out. Heave ho, left, right, rear, cross beam, outside the yellow hatches, push the red button, red light flashes, jig moves into the cage

Those robot arms are hypnotizing. If someone got locked in the cage while they were coming to life they'd be dead in seconds. The robots are blind: they can't see anything, and they move on a pre-programmed course. That's what the jig is for. The jig is their fixed reference point. They know where the jig is, and that helps them weld the sections on the frame of the car. If the parts weren't exactly where they needed to be, the robot's arm would just rip right through the body. Ripping, tearing through the car's white body—

Jig out. Heave ho, left, right, rear, cross beam, outside the yellow hatches, push the red button, red light flashes, jig moves into the cage

—and if a man were trapped in that cage (and we sometimes have to go in to fix the robots) he'd be cut in half. The robotic arm would slice through his body like a hot *katana* through tofu . . . That's not really a saying. I made it up. I like it. Sometimes I like to think of a murder-mystery story set in a factory where one of the workers traps another in the cage and won't let him out, then he starts up the robot and watches his mate being pulverized, smashed to bits, blood spurting everywhere. Spots of blood all over the white car bodies—

Jig out. Heave ho, left, right, rear, cross beam, outside the yellow hatches, push the red button, red light flashes, jig moves into the cage

Yes . . . you could kill someone quite easily by trapping them in the cage. There are safety procedures in place . . . but . . . well . . . There are two keys that need to be inserted into the circuit board in order to start up the robots – they won't function unless both keys are inserted. The keys also open the gate to the robot enclosure. You're supposed to take one key in with you when you go into the cage, but people never follow the proper procedures—

Jig out. Heave ho, left, right, rear, cross beam, outside the yellow hatches, push the red button, red light flashes, jig moves into the cage

—everyone here always leaves the key on a ledge next to the gate. I never do that, but it seems most people who work here do it out of some kind of statement of trust. I think it's idiotic, but if it helps create the perfect murder, I'm fine with that. Yes . . . the next time someone goes in to fix the robot and leaves the key on the ledge, I could quite easily lock the gate and fire up the robot. Then I could either sneak off quietly, or even hang around to watch the fun! There'd be blood everywhere—

Jig out. Heave ho, left, right, rear, cross beam, outside the yellow hatches, push the red button, red light flashes, jig moves into the cage

⚠

At 4 p.m. the alarm sounds, the line stops and it's time to go home. All those years ago when I first started the job, I used to get stiff and sore after work. Not anymore. My muscles have developed in all the right places. My body is a machine now.

I get on the train after work and head back into the city. We've all been paid today. Time to plan out my evening. Perhaps dine out – a ramen shop? I crave okonomiyaki, but I shan't be going back to that Hiroshima Okonomiyaki shop after they were so rude to me last time. The thought of it makes my brain blister. No, *gyudon* might be better. I go to post online again:

Re: Japanese Beef
LaoTzu616: Was happy to see this place ONLY serves JAPANESE
beef. None of that mad cow British rubbish please! This is Japan!

And then go home, visit the public baths, wash my hair and shave, change into my best suit and head to a hostess bar.

I'd read in one of the nightlife magazines that a new gaijin hostess bar had opened somewhere near Roppongi Station. Quite a way to go from Kichijoji, but it might be worth a look.

Bar Angel . . . I like the name.

▲
▲▲

Roppongi is a festering shithole of a place.

I can't stand walking the streets, with its loose Japanese women and drunk gaijin leering at them in their scanty clothes. If it weren't for Bar Angel being here, I would not come.

This is what Japan is turning into – a theme park for all these ghastly drunken foreigners. We work hard, slaving away every day at the factory, while these idiot gaijin cavort with our slutty sisters by night. It's disgusting. I bowl past them, huffing as loudly as I can, making them know their presence is unwanted.

Bar Angel is nothing special from the outside – a typical high-rise building with neon signs. I scan my eyes over them and see the one for the bar. It's on the ninth floor. I take a photo on my phone and upload it to the message board, asking for other customers' experiences at the bar:

Re: Bar Angel?
LaoTzu616: Anyone been here on 9F in Roppongi?
Any good?

When I get inside, it's as if I'm stepping into a dream. Foreign girls. Beautiful white-skinned, blonde-haired, blue-eyed foreign goddesses – all in elegant dresses. A typical hostess bar from the outlook, but at each table is a Japanese man and a gorgeous foreign lady.

A short stocky Japanese man wearing a suit bows to me as I enter.

'Good evening, sir.' He seems polite and respectful.

'Good evening, kind sir. Is this your fine establishment?'

'Kyaku-sama, I am the manager.' He bows low again. 'Have you been to Bar Angel before?'

I'm finding it difficult to keep my eyes off the girls. 'Ummm . . . no. Never.'

'Let me explain our system.' He takes out a board and begins to run down the price list.

A blonde girl in a red dress walks past and waves at me. I begin to sweat slightly and am finding it difficult to follow the system.

'Yes, yes.' I nod as he talks and talks.

'. . . I would recommend our basic course of *nomihodai* all-you-can-drink for one hour at the base rate of 20,000 yen. Should you wish to purchase drinks for your companion, there is a menu on each table with a drinks price list. Would you like to choose your girl?'

'Yes, please.' She has to be perfect.

'I must inform you that there is an additional charge of 5,000 yen for that service—'

'Fine, fine.' This is taking too long. He's beginning to annoy me.

'Please bear with me while I get a catalogue with photos of the girls so you can choose—'

'How about that one?' I can't take much more of this.

'Which one?'

'That one there. In the red dress.'

'Natasha?'

'Yes. Her. She'll do.'

'Excellent choice, sir.' He turns to her. 'Natasha!'

She swishes over like . . . well . . . like an angel, in her long red dress. Her blonde hair falls down to her neck, and I find it difficult to

218

look her in the eyes. They're so bright the colour almost dazzles me. She smiles at me. I nod back and then look at the wall.

It'll be easier to be around her when her eyes are shut. When she's fast asleep, she'll look like Sleeping Beauty.

'Natasha, please show this gentleman . . .' He turns to me expecting a name '. . .'

I make one up. 'Tanaka.'

His smile betrays the tiniest amount of disbelief. Tanaka is too common. 'Please show Tanaka-san to a table.' Next time I'll say Sugiwara or something.

'Zurtanly.' Urgh. Her Japanese is pig shit. Never mind. I just hope she doesn't talk in her sleep. 'Danaka-zan, zis vey pliz.'

I nod and walk to the table.

We sit down together at the table, and she leans over ever so slightly towards me. I can feel myself being sucked in by her glamour and charm. She smiles at me.

'Vot vood you lak tu jink?'

I have no idea what she is saying. I speak slowly and clearly. 'YOUR JAPANESE IS VERY GOOD.'

'Bahdon?'

'I SAID, YOUR JAPANESE—' Maybe she speaks English better? I switch to English. 'Speak English?'

'A little. Would you like a drink?'

Aaahhhh. Her voice. It is like music after having my ears rammed with mud.

'Shochu. On rock.'

She bows slightly, and signals with her hand to the manager, who brings over a bottle of shochu, two glasses and an ice bucket on a tray. He places the tray on the table, and I scowl at him until he leaves us in peace.

She begins to take pieces of ice from the bucket and places them in the glass slowly, and they clink and swirl. I look at her breasts, at the whiteness of her body parts peeking out from under her red dress. Her perfume catches my nostrils, and I move my hand towards her thigh.

She moves away slightly as she pours the shochu over the ice, and I can hear the pleasant cracking sound of the cubes fracturing, breaking apart like bone.

'Here you are,' she says, handing me the glass.

'Thank you,' I reply. 'Where from?'

'Pardon?'

'I said, where from?'

'Where from what?' She furrows her brow slightly, and I see a stupid ugliness in her face for the first time.

'You. Where from?' I say, slowly.

'Oh . . . Where am I from? I'm from Moscow. Russia, darling.'

'Vodka,' I say.

'What about it?' she asks. 'You want to drink vodka instead?'

She begins to gesture to the manager again, but I hold up my hand to stop her.

'No. Vodka is Russian,' I say, thinking it the most intelligent response I can muster under pressure like this. It would be so much easier in Japanese. She nods slowly and looks confused. I've never met a Russian before. What else can I talk about? I've read *Crime and Punishment* before. Maybe we could talk about that book – one of my favourites. 'Dostoevsky is Russian.'

'Yes, he is, but I've never read his books,' she says, and then laughs and touches my wrist. 'I don't like reading stuffy old books, darling.'

And then I feel a wave of happiness come over me. She must be impressed by my knowledge.

'What do you like, drink?' I ask.

'I definitely prefer vodka.'

'Yes? You like vodka?'

'Yes, darling. Buy me a vodka, will you, I'm so thirsty.'

She rubs my arm, and I feel desirable. 'Sure. Anything you want.'

'Thank you, darling!' She's already gesturing to the manager. 'Vodka!' she yells.

I turn over the drinks menu on the table and scan down it quickly for vodka. Fuck me sideways. Seven thousand yen for a vodka?!

'Is something wrong, darling?' She's looking at me.

'Oh . . . nothing. Nothing at all.' I smile as the arsehole manager brings her a drink on a tray. How can they charge seven fucking thousand yen for a piddly shot of vodka like that . . . Calm . . . must stay calm . . . Perhaps it will get her drunk; perhaps I can slip something in her drink later when she doesn't notice. I begin to hatch a plan to get her out of here and straight to a hotel.

Look at that blonde hair, those blue eyes, the swell of her white body under that tight red dress . . . I am in heaven. She is showing me stupid photos of her little dog, all the while cooing at how cute she thinks this ghastly mutt is. But I let it wash over me, and I drink deeply, happy that the night is going so well. Then I see a blasted cat on my glass. Natasha goes to the bathroom and I pull out my phone:

Re: Cats!!
LaoTzu616: Cats!! Everywhere I look in this country . . . fucking CATS!!!

A few drinks later on she is talking about shopping for dresses in Ginza, and out of the corner of my eye I think I see something black moving on the floor of the bar. Have those little black fuckers got in here too?

'Pardon?' She is looking at me, slightly worried.

'Sorry?' Am I drunk? Too much shochu?

'You just said *ants.*'

'Ants? Why would I say that?'

'I don't know, but you were looking over there, and then you just said *ants.*'

'Oh . . . I have ants, in my apartment. It's nothing.'

'That doesn't sound good . . .' She's looking at me like I'm a weirdo. I have to play this better.

'How do you say *ant* in Russian?' I ask.

'муравей,' she replies. I just nod, pretending to understand.

'Do you know how to say *ant* in Japanese?' I ask.

'Oh God! I know this!' She jumps up slightly in her seat and the slit in her skirt reveals her long white legs.

I want to tell her. 'It's—'

'No! Don't tell me, I know this, I know this.' She's screwing up her face in concentration and touching my arm. She loves me.

She opens her eyes after some thought and looks at me hopefully. '*Mushi?*'

'No. That just means insect.'

'Damn. I thought it was *mushi.*'

'No. You're wrong. It's—'

'No! Please! Please! Let me guess!'

'It's *ari,*' I say, feeling proud.

'Oh . . . *ari!* I knew that!'

I'm feeling more confident now – the shochu has relaxed me slightly. 'Do you know this Japanese joke?'

I take a napkin and draw out ten black dots on it. It's just a childish joke every Japanese kid learns at school, but as I mark out the dots, the image of those horrible black ants crawling all over my nice floor comes to mind. I can feel the sweat again, on my brow, under my arms. Come on . . . must keep it together . . . must stay on top of this. Can't let things fall apart, like they did before. Concentrate.

I finish drawing the black dots and show her the napkin.

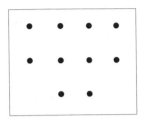

'What's this?' I ask.

'Hmmmm. I'm not sure . . .'

'Give up?'

'Yes. What is it, darling?'

'It's *arigato!*' I say triumphantly.

'*Arigato?* Thank you?'

'Yes, but. No. No. No.' She doesn't get the joke. Idiot Russian. 'Look, there are ten ants. *To* is another word for ten. *Ari* means ant, *ga* means . . . kind of "there are" . . . and *to* means ten. *ARIGATO!* Get it?'

She looks at me blankly. 'Funny.' She takes a last sip of her drink and smiles. 'Oh, darling, my drink is finished. Can I have another?'

'Sure. Why not.' Perhaps I can slip something in the next one.

But as the bastard manager brings over her drink, he kindly informs me that my time limit is about to elapse, and would I wish to extend it at the cost of another 10,000 yen? I bow politely, say that I've had quite enough fun for the night and leave shortly afterwards. I'll get her next time.

As I'm waiting for my train home I check the online message board to see if anyone has responded to my question about Bar Angel. There's one response.

Re: Re: Bar Angel?
Aho80085: gaijin cunt.

When I get back to the apartment the ants are still there.

I try to masturbate to the memory of Natasha. I think about the image of her sleeping peacefully as I lie next to her, but then I see the ants crawling all over her body, and I see that she is not sleeping, but rotting. Her body is decomposing and the ants are crawling all over her pale skin. They're coming out of her mouth in long black lines, crawling around her tummy, snaking across her belly and breasts, down her body to her painted red toenails. I lose my erection, and it won't come back.

▲▲

Another day of work. And I am tired.

The fucking cat was screaming all night like it was dying. I cannot sleep. The ants continue to plague me.

The next cat I see is getting a good hard kick.

Jig out. Heave ho, left, right, rear, cross beam, outside the yellow hatches, push the red button, red light flashes, jig moves into the cage

I've read more about it online. I must poison the queen. There's no other way for it. I must kill her, or the ants will never stop coming. I must feed the ants poisoned bait that they will feed one another, and they will take it back to their queen. It's called trophallaxis. It's ironic, but I shall use their co-operative nature against them to kill them all. They all must die. I can't live together with the ants. *Let your plans be dark and impenetrable as night, and when you move, fall like a thunderbolt.* Those were the words of Lao Tzu—

Jig out. Heave ho, left, right, rear, cross beam, outside the yellow hatches, push the red button, red light flashes, jig moves into the cage

I need to see Natasha again. Things will be better this time. I know I can make it work. I know if I have just a little bit more time, and another chance. Things will be all right. But I have to get rid of these ants first. There used to be just ten of them. Now there are tens of thousands, and I see them everywhere. *So in war, the way is to avoid what is strong, and strike at what is weak.* I must destroy the ants. Before they destroy me—

Jig out. Heave ho, left, right, rear, cross beam, outside the yellow hatches, push the red button, red light flashes, jig moves into the cage

Things will be better this time. Nothing will go wrong. As long as I just stick with my plan. Give them plenty of sleeping powder so they don't wake up. We don't ever want them to wake up, because then we'd have to punch her in the jaw, then pay her money to keep quiet. I'll play it safe. I'll give them far more sleeping powder than they really need. Then they'll stay fast asleep and I can just sleep next to them, like I used to sleep between Mother and Father when I had nightmares as a child—

Jig out. Heave ho, left, right, rear, outside the yellow hatches, push the red button, red light flashes, jig moves into the cage

It isn't just private for me though. I like to go to the *onsen* and expose myself. Sometimes people shout at me – like that girl in Yufuin in Kyushu – and it makes me more aroused. I like to film them as they shout at me, and I watch the videos later. They're all fucking ants too.

. . . But recently, I cannot tell what is real anymore. I see things everywhere. The ants are crawling all over this hellhole of a city, and all the while the cat is screaming. I do not know if I am a man living or dreaming. I feel neither alive nor dead. Am I in hell? Am I dreaming? I don't know what is real anymore—

Jig out. Heave ho, left, rear, outside the yellow hatches, push the red button, red light flashes, jig moves into the cage. An alarm sounds. Line Manager shouts. I fall to my knees and cry

And now the robots are tearing through the white body. The feral cat is screaming. And the ants crawl through my mind. They crawl over the graves of my mother and father. Which lie neglected in the cemetery.

From the very real look on my Line Manager's face I can tell I've lost my job.

But the ants never stop.

Hikikomori, Futoko & Neko

Drip drip – red blips of splatter hit the tarmac.

A pitter patter of pain that winds along the lane, leading to a curled-up calico cat, head bobbing and rolling. The cat tries to stand, and again, to stand. Its jaw lolls and lags, too loose for a bite of crab stick today. It finally gives up.

The cat raises its head slowly, and looks towards the main road. The stalls from the festival are still there, but fast asleep.

Blurred and shattered vision. A fracture of a shaking scene. Three figures dressed in funeral black, walking past the entrance to the alleyway. A family, perhaps. A mother, a father and a daughter. Walking close together, a solid unit. The mother looks back to scold someone. The three carry on, out of view. And then a small black figure blurs past, awkward scuffs in too-big shoes.

A young boy.

⚛

Kensuke saw the cat bleeding at the end of the alleyway. He ran past the boarded-up food stalls from the festival the night before and looked at the cat with curious eyes. There was no one else around. Just a single door to a ground-floor apartment next to the cat. Kensuke didn't notice the strange signs on the door. He was too distracted by the cat.

The cat watched back, blinking torture.

Small, soft, as yet unhardened to cruelty. Regulation chubby jaw and mild eyes. Dressed in sadness, covered in loss. A black suit, premature for a boy in elementary school.

Kensuke scooped the cat up in his arms. It let out a feeble meow.

'Hello, *neko*-san. Are you hurt?'

The boy cradled the cat carefully, and ran after his family. They'd already got into the black Lexus, three doors slammed with balanced impatience.

Kensuke held the cat as gently as he could in the crook of one arm while he opened the rear right-hand door with the other. He didn't mean to, but he was hurting the cat slightly. He jumped up onto the back seat, and as soon as he shut the door, the car began to roll forward.

'Why must you dawdle so?' Mother's voice tinged with that embarrassing Korean accent she couldn't shake.

'Sorry.'

Kensuke clutched the cat close to his chest. He could feel its heart beating, and his too, bang banging fast from running to the car. He was slightly out of breath.

Sitting next to him, wearing a formal black suit in harsh contrast to her usual uniform – pink Polo sweaters and cream trousers – his grown-up sister Kyoko whispered teasingly, '*Baka.*'

He ignored her. She looked at him nervously to register his response. Then she saw the cat, and a look of disappointment appeared in her eyes.

'Oh Ken! Why did you bring that cat?'

Father slammed on the brakes.

Both parents turned their heads.

'Kensuke!'

'What were you thinking? Picking up a stray cat!' Mother shouted.

'But . . . It's bleeding. It's hurt its jaw. It needs help.'

'Kensuke. It's not your cat. Go put it back where you found it.' Father was firm. 'Go on.'

'But *Otosan*. It'll die. Like *Obaasan*.'

'Kensuke. Put it back. *Now.*'

Father, ever composed. Even though something had touched a nerve.

Kensuke pulled the door open and slid off the white leather seats. He shut the door behind him.

'Kyoko, is there blood on the seat?' Father asked.

'No, it's clean.'

'Good.' Father watched Kensuke in his rear-view mirror – little legs kicking out behind him as he ran down the road with the cat in his arms. 'That boy is getting *strange*.'

'We have to be patient with him.' Mother touched his arm. 'If we want him to go back to school next term. We have to be patient.'

'You guys push him too hard,' said Kyoko from the back seat.

'Kyoko. Be quiet,' Mother snapped.

▲▲

That morning, Naoya was sitting in the groove on his couch, playing Puyo Puyo Monster Mayhem and drinking a bottle of Pocari Sweat when there was a knock at the door, which he ignored. And then the bell rang.

Who could that be?

He paused the game and took a nervous sip of his drink. No one came round here, except deliveries, and they knew not to ring the bell. He thought if he ignored it, they might just go away. He un-paused his game and carried on tapping the keys and watching the brightly coloured monster balls on the huge plasma screen.

There wasn't much space inside Naoya's apartment now.

Not with all the cartons, cans, plastic bottles, wrappers, broken chopsticks, sticky remote controls, discarded anime DVD boxes and all the other detritus. The air con hummed gently in the corner, keeping out the summer. Towers of manga stood proud against the walls, old and greying. Rubbish hidden under rubbish, matter on matter. A permanent dip in the sofa from too much sitting. Plates had been laid to rest in the kitchen sink, caked in the solid mould of neglect, long forgotten. Everything was piling up, and in, and on itself.

Naoya had systems.

He didn't get food delivered from the convenience store that required any kind of extra effort. He didn't need crockery, he didn't need cups; he didn't need plates. He just got his disposable packages of food, ready to pop in the microwave, ready to dissect and pick at with fresh *waribashi* throw-away chopsticks. He used his kettle a lot, mostly to pour the hot water into his cup ramen. As long as he didn't have to wash up. As long as he didn't have to leave the apartment. He never wanted to do that ever again.

And of course, the apartment wouldn't have been the same without Naoya – its permanent fixture.

Round head and face covered in designer stubble. He shaved his hair and his beard with the same attachment on his electric clippers. He ordered the clippers online so that he wouldn't need to go outside to get a haircut. The shaved head suited him. He wore loose clothing, always the same pea-green tracksuit from Uniqlo. He wasn't fat before, but now, in his mid-thirties, all the inactivity was gathering gradually at his stomach. The elastic of the tracksuit bottoms accommodated the growing belly though, and Naoya was beginning to get used to it.

One of his favourite hobbies – other than video games – was masturbating over *AKB48* magazines. His favourite girl from *AKB48* was Itano Tomomi. He wished he could meet her. If he went to one of her many fan events he could meet her easily, but that would mean leaving the apartment.

Not an option.

So instead, he looked at pictures of her in magazines and tugged away on his *chinchin*, enjoying the sensation of his fat belly jiggling around. He fantasized about her straddling him and pinching his nipples. She'd say, 'Naoya, *ai shiteru* – I love you.' Then he had to wipe it up with tissues. Then he felt depressed, knowing that a girl like Itano Tomomi would never go for a slob like him. Sometimes he cried a bit. Then he played video games and drank a soda. That usually made him feel better. He used to order hookers online, but he got sick of seeing them turn their noses up at the state of his apartment. They couldn't even hide how much they hated him. Now he just had his imaginary girls to keep him company.

The only things that *really* made him feel better were manga, anime, books and games. Things that took the pain away. He had a few friends on the *hikikomori* chatrooms, but even they annoyed him. There was that one guy, the friendly guy on the Street Fighter II chatrooms, but Naoya didn't know much about Street Fighter II – his game was Puyo Puyo Monster Mayhem. Anyway, that guy hadn't come online in ages.

That morning, he was enjoying the game. But there it was again. The ring ring of the bell, boring into his skull. He paused the game again, and looked to the door.

Go away. Go away. Leave me alone.

But the bell kept ringing.

Who could it be? He dropped the game controller and crept as quietly as he could to the *genkan*. He peeped through the eyehole. It was bright outside. Naoya felt like a ninja. Moving around undetected in the shadows. His vision adjusted, and there was a little boy, dressed in black. Holding a cat.

What is a young boy doing with a cat outside my door? Is he mental? What the hell is up with this neighbourhood recently? Only the other night I had to tell some nutcase screaming his head off to shut up. Has everyone lost it?

'Please. I can hear you on the other side of the door. You're playing Puyo Puyo Monster Mayhem. Please open up. This cat will die. *Issho onegai*. Please help me,' he heard the boy say through the door.

Naoya breathed quietly. Damn. His ninja skills had failed him – the volume on his TV was too high.

A car horn sounded in the distance and Naoya heard a voice calling out, 'Kensuke!'

'Please. Please. Help me.'

The boy sounded close to tears.

Please just go away, please just leave me alone. Why Kensuke? All I want is to be left alone.

The boy burst into tears.

'Please. I'm begging you. This cat will die. I'll come back tomorrow to pick it up. Please—'

Naoya wasn't even wearing the gas mask that he'd made to protect him from the germs floating around in the outside world. But there was something about this kid called Kensuke. He held his breath and opened the door.

The boy's face lit up.

'Thank you, *Onisan*! I'll come back tomorrow to see you. I have to go now. Please look after this cat! *Arigato!*'

Naoya couldn't talk, because he couldn't breathe. The sunlight hurt his eyes. The humidity and heat of the summer hit him hard and almost made him gasp. He was already sweating. *Have to shut the door. Have to get back inside.* The boy shoved the cat into Naoya's arms, turned around and legged it. Naoya shut the door immediately. He panted with his back against the door, breathing hard and holding onto the cat for comfort.

Shit. The boy would come back tomorrow. He'd have to open the door again. Fuck. What a can of shitty worms he'd opened with that door. What a mistake.

Naoya carried the cat into his living room, and put it down in a makeshift basket constructed from dirty laundry and old manga books. He eyed the cat shiftily, unsure of what to do.

'Hungry?' he asked.

Maybe he could feed the cat some cup ramen. He went into the kitchen to put the kettle on.

Then he went back and looked at the cat. He could see the pain on its face.

That was something Naoya knew well.

⁂

The drive back to Shinagawa-ku took a while because of the traffic. And Father was not in a good mood. Mother was also angry.

'You've ruined your shirt, Kensuke. And your suit is a mess. That shirt comes straight off and goes in the wash when we get home.'

She looked at Father. 'We'll have to drop his suit off at the dry cleaners tomorrow.'

'Hmmm?' Father concentrated on the traffic.

'Sorry I ratted you out,' Kyoko whispered to Kensuke in the back.

Kensuke wanted to reply and say 'That's okay', but he physically couldn't. He drew his hand away from Kyoko reaching out to touch him.

Instead, he shook his head and looked out of the window from his low viewpoint. He could see the tops of buildings gradually rising into skyscrapers as they passed through central Tokyo. They dropped Kyoko off at the station, so she could take a train back out to Chiba, then carried on in the car, just the three of them. The businesses transformed into residential apartment blocks when they hit the Tokyo Bay area.

Kensuke lived with his mother and father in one of these buildings. Kyoko had moved out to her own place when she started working, and Kensuke's eldest brother had moved to Gunma with his wife and children years ago. Kensuke missed not having his siblings around in the apartment. When he was really young, he had always loved watching them play Street Fighter II together. He loved watching Kyoko win, and it would make them all laugh. But they were so much older than him, he always felt like he was just watching them from afar. He never got to play. He'd watched them pack up Street Fighter and move away. And now all he had to do was look out of the window. The view from their apartment looked out across the bay. It was a pretty sterile environment compared to the suburban area they'd come from in the west. In the evenings, Kensuke liked to look out across the water, to see the lights of the city in the twilight. They lit up the coastline, and the dark waters and sky were peppered with the blink and twinkle of aeroplanes coming in to land at Haneda Airport.

But that evening, all Kensuke could think about was the cat. He'd already decided to sneak off tomorrow to go back to the pea-green man's apartment. He'd tell his parents he was going to play with friends. They didn't know that he didn't have any.

The next morning, Kensuke slipped out of the apartment and headed to the train station. He boarded the monorail at Tennozu Isle Station, and rode it one stop to Hamamatsucho Station. The monorail connected the airport with the city, and Kensuke could see a few foreigners onboard, with noses as big as their suitcases. He wondered to himself if they would like Japanese food. He hoped so. He saw one beautiful girl with blonde hair and blue eyes; she smiled at him and continued reading a book in Japanese. She was wearing a suit and looked happy.

He hit the Yamanote Line at rush hour, and it was horrible being crushed up against all the other passengers. Kensuke couldn't see anything but black suits. He got off at Tokyo Station and rode the Chuo Line out west to Kichijoji. The passengers had thinned out because he was heading out of the city, but he noticed the trains heading in the other direction were stuffed to bursting. The journey was fine, except for at one point there was a strange man muttering to himself. He smelt so bad Kensuke moved further down the train into the next carriage.

It was easy enough to find the pea-green man's apartment again. Kensuke remembered where it was, but there were also a lot of weird signs at the door telling people not to ring the bell. Kensuke had noticed a bit of a funny smell when the guy had opened the door, and he'd wondered why he'd stood there not saying anything. He'd just puffed up his cheeks and his face had gone all red. Kensuke hoped the guy wasn't a weirdo – he'd heard some stories about psychos in Tokyo who caught stray cats and killed them. But there was something in the guy's eyes. Something that had made Kensuke trust him.

When Kensuke rang the doorbell this time, it didn't take so long for Naoya to open the door.

▲
▲▲

'Hey. Come in.'
   'How's the cat?'
   'Come in. I'll tell you all about it.'

'Is it okay?'

'Well, there's some good news and bad news. Come on.'

'Where is it?'

'Sleeping, at the moment.'

'Is it okay?'

'Not exactly.'

'What's wrong with it?'

'It's drooling. And it can't eat food. It's broken its jaw, I think.'

'Will it die?'

'No. I looked up some info online. There's a vet nearby and I phoned them up. They can do an operation on it. They can rewire the cat's jaw.'

'Great!'

'I've booked an appointment today. Can you take the cat there? I've phoned up and explained everything. They'll give you a bill, which you have to bring back to me. The vet said it'll be okay.'

'Sure. When are we going?'

'I'm afraid I can't come with you.'

'Why not, *Onisan?*'

'Don't call me that. Call me Nao.'

'Okay, Nao. I'm Ken.'

'So, yeah. Everything is sorted. You just have to take the cat to this address. Once the operation is done, you can bring the cat back here to rest. It'll take a couple of days for it to feel better again, and you'll need to take the cat back in a month's time to have the wire from the jaw removed.'

'Why aren't you coming with me?'

'I just can't, okay.'

'When the cat's better, can I come and visit?'

'Sure. But don't come too much. I'm busy.'

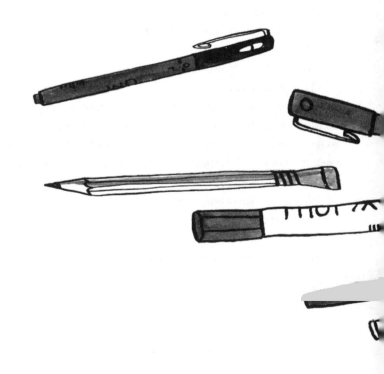

HOW?

IT MUST'VE GONE OUT OF THE WINDOW. I LEFT IT OPEN TO GET SOME AIR... LIKE YOU TOLD ME TO

NO.

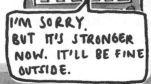

I'M SORRY. BUT IT'S STRONGER NOW. IT'LL BE FINE OUTSIDE.

I DIDN'T EVEN GET TO SAY GOODBYE

KEN, I'M SORRY

KEN! WAIT!

⁂

Kensuke stopped coming to visit after that.

Naoya put it down to the fact that the cat was gone. They no longer had the cat in common. A month had passed by quickly, and Naoya had felt himself change as the summer passed into autumn. He'd been annoyed with the presence of the cat to begin with, and Kensuke. But gradually he'd grown to look forward to the boy's visits. He'd also been happy with the company that the cat gave him. He'd stroked it when he was lonely, and he'd felt a kind of companionship that he'd not experienced in a long time.

But as the weeks rolled on into September, he began to slip back into his old ways. When Kensuke had been coming to visit he'd felt the pressure to tidy up after himself, to shower and shave and make himself presentable. Now he was slowly falling back into slovenly habits.

He thought he'd had two new friends. But it was true what he'd always told himself: you can't rely on anyone. Now that his parents were gone, there was just him. And he could only rely on himself. That was the safest way to view life. He had enough money from his inheritance to last him. He was happy on his own. It's true that he'd felt some warmth and comfort from exposure to his two new friends. But they both showed their true colours in the end.

No. He was better off alone.

⁂

Naoya heard Shingo the postman's whistle before the mail dropped through the letterbox. He was in no rush to pick up bills, so he made himself a cup ramen and turned on the TV.

It wasn't until the afternoon that he finally picked up the mail and saw the package.

Strange.

He ripped it open and took out a small photocopied pamphlet and a letter folded up in half. He opened the letter and read.

Nao,

I'm sorry I ran off that day. And I'm sorry that I never came back to see you afterwards. I took your advice. I went back to school. It was tough at first, but I've started to make some friends. There's another guy who's half Korean in my class, Yusuke. He's pretty strong. Maybe stronger than you. Me and him became good friends, and now no one bothers us about being half Korean anymore. I think it's cos they're scared that Yusuke will beat them up. He goes mental if anyone says 'chon'. School's much better now.

I feel bad about not coming to visit you. And then you know when you feel bad about something, and it just starts feeling worse and worse, and then you know that you can't just say sorry about it, cos you know that words don't work well in those situations.

I am sorry. I can't say it maybe face to face. But I am.

Anyway, I hope you aren't angry with me.

I drew a manga about you and me and the cat. I showed it to my art teacher and she went crazy saying it was so good. I don't think it is though. It's just about some of the stuff we talked about. She made me draw more of it, and she helped me to make a book of it. We put the book into a manga competition. I didn't win first prize, so I was kind of sad about that, but I did get runner up. My art teacher said that's amazing, but I don't know. I wanted to win. Still, I got some book tokens as a prize. I'm gonna buy some more Nishi Furuni sci-fi books.

I'll keep drawing though. I decided I want to be a manga artist when I grow up.

If you want to know why, it's because of you. I know that you hurt a lot inside. And I know that manga makes you happy. If I can make manga, maybe I can help people like you be happy. I know it sounds like a dumb idea, but I can't think of anything else I want to do when I'm older. And like you said, I can't just play Puyo Puyo.

You said once about you being from the future or something.
And I thought about that a lot. Maybe it's the reason I decided
to go back to school. So, I think you helped me so much there.

But then I realized. What if the future you, like sixty-year-
old Naoya, came to visit you now? What would he say?
Wouldn't he tell you to go outside your apartment? Wouldn't he
tell you the same things you told me? I've been thinking about
that a lot recently, and I think he would. I think he'd help you.

Anyway, I'm sorry again for not visiting. And I'm sorry I
snuck a look at your address when I was in your apartment. I've
written Mum and Dad's address down for you, so you can write
back to me if you like.

I hope you like reading the manga about you and me and the
cat.
Take care,
Ken
P.S. Please tell me if the cat comes back.

Naoya read the letter over twice. He went to sit down on his couch and leafed through the black and white pamphlet, over and over again. The title was *Hikikomori, Futoko & Neko*. There was a picture of all three of them on the front. It told the story of the month they'd spent with the cat. All the conversations that they'd had together, and in each of the scenes there was the cat – getting stronger and stronger. And as it progressed, his apartment got cleaner and cleaner. It was so well drawn. There was his apartment, there was the cat, there was Kensuke, and there was Naoya. They all looked happy, smiling.

But now he was crying.

⁂

The cat was stronger than it had ever been. It had fully recovered from the accident and was back to scouring old haunts for food, searching for that memory of a previous life, that something that was missing.

It was out one morning, enjoying another beautiful autumn day, when it spotted a man in a familiar pea-green tracksuit making his way slowly along the road. He was going from lamppost to lamppost, hugging each one as he went. A step at a time, cautious as a man in a war zone. As the cat got closer to him, it could see that the man was heading towards a red mailbox.

He had an anxious smile on his face.

And he was clutching a letter in his hand.

Detective Ishikawa: Case Notes 3

Several weeks after I'd been to visit Shiwa at the club, I told Taeko I was taking the car out. I left early in the morning and set a course on my satnav for the complex in Yamanashi prefecture where I'd heard they were keeping the missing kid, Kurokawa.

The traffic was calm leading out of the city, and despite the feeling of getting away from it all as I passed through the tunnels (and the greenery becoming more and more consistent) I couldn't help but run over what Seiji had said to me in the club about my ex-wife. Sometimes I get this same feeling late at night when I'm trying to fall asleep. I feel the normal fatigue, aches and pains in my joints, but this voice in my head just won't stop berating me and my actions. I run over all the mistakes I've ever made, what I should've said in that argument, what I should've done differently to be a better person, all the people I've hurt unintentionally, and all the people I've hurt intentionally. I suppose it's called regret. And right now it felt like my regret was sitting in the passenger seat, eating a bag of potato chips, slurping on a big old soda, and giving me a good talking to.

I should never have taken on that case. Nothing good came of it.
Yeah yeah. *Slurp*
But I was just doing my job.
I was just doing my job wah-wah-wah.
My duty is to the client.

Boy-oh-boy, these potato chips are good.

Loyalty works in a number of ways.

But why weren't you loyal to her?

Why wasn't she loyal to me?

And there we have it, the elementary-school argument: she started it!

It's not like that.

So what's it like? You're so cold and heartless you couldn't even drop a case that involved your wife?

Ex-wife.

She was an ex from the start. You were never there for her.

I had to work.

'Work'? Sneaking around taking photos of people.

Those people are dishonest. They deserve what they get.

You sound like a tyrant. Who made you the guardian of morality?

I just do my job.

I heard there were a bunch of people in Nazi Germany who were 'just doing their job' too.

Shut up! Shut up! Get out of my head.

*I am your head, Ishikawa. You'd better get used to it. *Slurp**

Can you just be quiet for a second?

Suit yourself.

Thank you.

But I'm bored. Maybe we should replay a little scene in here. Remember when you went out that night, when you took on the case from Sugihara Hiroko? You remember that pretty, rich lady whose husband was cheating on her, don't you?

Stop.

You remember. You went out with your disguise – your reversible hat and the hidden camera. You know, like you always do.

Why are you doing this?

You texted your wife and said you'd be home late, and she replied saying don't worry, she was out with her college friends. Remember?

Of course.

And you waited behind the plant pots for the cheating husband, Sugihara Ryu, to come. You'd been following him, hadn't you? Son of a big shot CEO –

too much money to spend. You'd been trailing him for weeks. That playboy Ryu had so many girls on the go it'd got a bit complicated, hadn't it? But you knew his schedule like clockwork, didn't you?

I knew it better than he knew it himself.

Yes, that's right. And you hid behind the plant pots. And when he came by, swerving around drunkenly with that girl under his arm, you got excited, didn't you?

I always love the chase.

Yes, you do, don't you? Your heart starts to beat faster, and you just can't wait to seal the deal.

It's always good, closing the case out.

Rightly so. You worked hard for that.

I always work hard – for my clients.

And remember that night, when you got close enough for the photo. You took it, didn't you?

I never miss an opportunity.

But something was different that time, wasn't it?

I looked at her.

And what did you see?

I saw her.

Who?

My wife.

And how did you feel?

I felt angry for a second.

And then?

I felt free.

Yes. That's right. You felt free. You knew you could get away from her, and you knew you'd keep your money.

I did.

You're a bad person, Ishikawa.

I'm not.

Yes, you are. No matter how you spin it. You're a bad man.

No. I'm one of the good guys.

You just keep telling yourself that, buddy.

I'm one of the good guys.

You're one of the bad guys.

But I'm trying so hard to be one of the good guys.

⁂

I parked the car in the complex – an old factory with bars all over the windows. There were signs everywhere saying *Clean Sweep*. What the hell was this place? The car park was mostly empty, but there were large vans parked here and there with the same *Clean Sweep* logo on them. I looked closely at the logo and saw a little symbol of the Tokyo 2020 Olympics in the corner. I made for the front entrance, but before I even got to the door, guys in suits were coming out to greet me. A thin smarmy-looking guy in an irritatingly fashionable suit with a clipboard tucked under his arm led the procession of a few heavies.

'May I help you, sir? Perhaps you are lost?' He stopped short of me, with the confidence that comes from a weak man who has the power of many strong men backing him up.

'I'm looking for someone,' I replied.

'You are aware that this is private property?' He looked me in the eyes like I was an idiot and blinked slowly.

'Yes. And I'm not here to make any trouble.' I held his gaze.

'Oh, that's good to hear.' He smiled, his pearly white teeth showing.

'I'm here on behalf of the parents of a certain man named Kurokawa, who I believe is residing in your facility at present.'

He studied his clipboard. Then bit his lip. 'I see.' He scratched his head with the corner of his clipboard. 'Well, firstly, I cannot reveal whether this Kurokawa is housed within our facility or not, due to data protection. Secondly, if he were to be here, I couldn't give you custody of him unless I have written proof from his parents that you are here acting on their behalf. I'm sorry about this, but rules are rules, and I'm just doing my job.'

I paused. Took out a cigarette and lit it. 'I see.' I turned back to my car and walked towards it.

'Thank you for visiting us today,' he called out.

I opened the passenger door, reached into the glove compartment and pulled out a piece of paper. I unfolded it carefully and studied it as I made my way back to the party.

'Will this do?' I handed it to him.

'Oh . . .' He smoothed it out on his clipboard and studied it for an awfully long time, checking it over and over, as if he were looking for errors. 'Well, I suppose you'd better come in . . .'

'Much obliged.'

I followed the procession inside, but I could sense there was an air of reluctance in the way they all shuffled their feet.

▲▲

The facility was white and sterile on the inside. Bars on the windows, locks on all the doors. It basically said 'prison' to me, but I suppose that's why they kept referring to it as a facility. They led me to a waiting room and sat me down with a cup of coffee. I was told they would go fetch Kurokawa.

When he came into the room I could see the family resemblance. The broad shoulders from his father – he looked strong. They had him in an orange jumpsuit, and had handcuffed him too. He held his hands out in front, and I could see he was missing a couple of fingers. He looked like he'd had it rough, but he seemed cheerful.

'Kurokawa-san?'

'That's me.' He smiled. 'Who the hell are you?'

The guard made a motion to slap him, but I raised my hand.

I smiled back. 'Detective Ishikawa. Your parents sent me.'

When I mentioned his parents, he scratched his nose with a finger and looked meek.

'Nice to meet you, Detective.'

'Nice to meet you too.'

'Are you here to get me out of this dump?' He grinned.

'Yes, I am.'

'Praise the Lord.' He looked at the guard who'd brought him in. 'Hey, goon. How about you get these cuffs off me now I'm a free man?'

The guard left the room.

Kurokawa grinned cheekily at me.

'I brought you some clothes.'

He nodded.

'We just need to sign some papers, then we're out of here.'

'Thank God.'

As we sat there silently in the waiting room, I knew the ball was rolling. We'd sign these papers and Kurokawa would be reunited with his family again. I wasn't about to get all sentimental about it, but I realized then that I could get used to *this* kind of job. Maybe I was better suited as the kind of guy who reunites families, rather than destroy them.

The guy with the clipboard came back in, and I enjoyed every pen stroke of that paperwork.

▲▲

In the car on the way back to Tokyo, Kurokawa and I listened to music and chatted every now and again. The skies were clouding over, and it seemed dark for the middle of the day. We stopped at a convenience store for cans of coffee and onigiri for the journey, then we got back in the car and I let him talk. He mostly talked about his experience of being shut up in that weird hell hole. Despite the rough times he talked about, he seemed happy. He told me a lot of stories about his roommate who he kept calling just 'Sensei'. He must've really respected the guy.

'So, I left the yakuza ages ago,' he said sunnily. 'I was living on the streets with my buddies and Sensei.'

'Yeah?'

'And the police bundled me and Sensei up and took us to that shithole.'

'Yeah, it seemed a shady place.' I was wondering why 'Sensei' was living on the streets with this guy.

He was quiet for a second, then he looked at me with a serious expression.

'So, you're like a detective, right? Like the ones in the movies.'

'I guess you could say so, Kurokawa-san.' I put on my indicator and overtook a truck that was dawdling along in the slow lane.

'Call me Keita.'

'Sure thing, Keita.' I pulled back into the slow lane and it started to rain.

'So, you can find people?' There was hope in his voice.

'I do my best.'

I looked through the windshield at the drops of rain that were streaking down the glass, dividing and joining. Connecting and disconnecting. The city appeared on the horizon and I thought about all those families, coming together and falling apart.

Keita coughed, breaking my reverie. 'I need you to find someone for me.'

'And who might that be, Keita?' I asked, curiosity now engaged.

He looked ahead, staring through the glass of the windscreen, past the raindrops splattering on the glass as the wipers swept them clean over and over again rhythmically. Both of us looked ahead at the sprawling city growing larger in the distance, getting steadily closer and closer.

'His name is Taro,' he said. 'And he drives a taxi.'

Opening Ceremony

Ryoko looked out of the aeroplane window, at the outline of Mount Fuji in the distance.

The sky was a clear blue, reminiscent of the hot summer days she'd experienced as a child. Visibility was perfect, and she could see the city on the horizon, a vast sprawling mayhem. She let out a sigh – Gen was sleeping peacefully in the travel cot in front of her. He'd been so good throughout the whole flight, not a peep. She reached for Erik's hand. He didn't look up from his book, but held her hand and stroked it gently with his forefinger and thumb while still reading – he was completely absorbed. He was so good at staying in the moment, at focusing on what he was doing at the time. Not like her. She studied his features: that Scandinavian blond hair he'd inherited from his Swedish ancestors, thin face covered in stubble which had grown back so quickly just over the course of the fourteen-hour direct flight from New York. They'd left in the morning, grabbing onion bagels and coffee in a café in JFK while waiting to board their flight, bound for Haneda Airport.

'Haneda is so much closer to the city,' said Ryoko, as they'd sat opposite one another at the airport café. She took a sip of coffee, cradling Gen in his sling; her voice was quiet, unsure of itself, so she took a breath to steady it. 'I know it's a little bit more expensive, but you'll thank me when we arrive.'

'Mmmm . . .' Erik chewed on his bagel and swallowed. 'It's just a bit of money, baby.'

'Narita Airport is just so far away,' she continued, rocking Gen gently.

'Relax.' Erik touched her hand lightly, and smiled at her.

'I know, I know.' She chewed her lip. The anxious feeling in her stomach had been there ever since she'd booked their flights to Tokyo weeks ago.

The flight had seemed like forever to Ryoko. Erik had fallen asleep, mouth wide open, head tilted back with his eye mask on and his travel pillow squashed behind his neck. Ryoko had taken a photo of him on her phone, giggling as she pictured how he would react when she showed him later. That guy could sleep anywhere – maybe that's where Gen got it from. Then she'd flicked nervously through the plane's touchscreen entertainment system, searching for anything half decent to watch. She would start one film, grow tired of it and change to another. Nothing seemed to fit; nothing reassured. She'd been determined to watch some Japanese films on the plane, but there weren't many, and the selection was poor. Finally she'd settled on Koreeda Hirokazu's *Like Father, Like Son*, which she had seen before, but watched again from start to finish.

The English subtitles had come on automatically and she hadn't bothered to turn them off, which made her feel vaguely guilty – what kind of Japanese person puts on the English subtitles? Two sons switched at birth, reunited years later with their biological families. Family drama, tense conversations, people not being able to say what they mean. It had made her cry uncontrollably. She'd had to shut her eyes and hold her breath to fight back the sobs she felt coming from somewhere deep in her stomach. Was it all just down to hormones? How much longer could she use that as an excuse for these feelings that swept over her? She tried to remember if she'd felt like this before her pregnancy.

The other two had slept through it all though. She looked down at Gen for the millionth time, still snoozing peacefully, and then back at Erik now reading intently. This time he sensed her eyes on him, suddenly glancing up and closing the book.

He stretched a little and yawned. 'I can't believe your grandpa wrote this.' He waggled the book in her direction.

She looked at it again – the same edition she'd spotted another passenger reading on the flight. It had made her proud and anxious at the same time in equal measure. She'd been sneaking furtive glances at both Erik and the female passenger reading it on the other side of the aisle. 'Can I see it again?'

'Sure.' He passed her the book, and began to unbuckle his seatbelt. 'I'm going to the bathroom. Gotta get in there before they put the fasten seatbelts light on.'

He stood up and stepped politely over the legs of the sleeping man in the aisle seat, being careful not to wake him.

Bless him, thought Ryoko. *He knows I hate the middle seat.*

She looked down at the cover of Erik's hardback book.

Collected Sci-Fi Stories by Nishi Furuni.

She opened it to the last page, and saw the same black and white photo of her grandfather she had seen everywhere, in all of his promotional material, ever since she was a child. They'd named Gen after her grandfather – short for Gen'ichiro. Would he grow up to write poetry or sci-fi? Would he speak to her in English or Japanese? Would he even want to learn Japanese at the language classes the other Japanese parents took their begrudging children to in New York? Would he hate her for making him study the difficult *kanji* characters? Or conversely, would he resent her if he grew up not speaking Japanese because she *hadn't* made him? She traced a finger over her grandfather's features. Would Gen grow up to look like him too? Her grandfather in the photo looked the spitting image of her father now.

Gen'ichiro. She'd left the 'ichiro' part off Gen's name for a reason. Ichiro was not a name Ryoko ever wanted to hear again in her lifetime. Uncle Ichiro – Gen would never grow up to be anything like *him*. She would make sure of that.

Her eyes scanned down the dust jacket to a second photo beneath her father, this one of a blonde-haired blue-eyed girl in her late twenties.

ABOUT THE TRANSLATOR

Flo Dunthorpe was born and raised in Portland, Oregon.
She graduated from Reed College, majoring in English
Literature. She currently lives in Tokyo . . .

Imagine choosing to come to Tokyo! Voluntarily! Ryoko hadn't been able to get away fast enough. Ryoko had never been to Portland, Oregon – so far away on the West Coast – and probably the culture was massively different to her newfound home on the East Coast. But still. Ryoko was pretty sure she'd take Portland over Tokyo any day, even without having visited. She looked at Flo's photograph, and part of her envied this American girl with her perfect appearance, her perfect English and Japanese, but above all her ability to live and be happy in Ryoko's hometown better than she could herself.

Erik sat back down next to her, so she closed the book and passed it back to him.

'It's really good, you know,' he said, tucking it carefully into the pouch in front of him. 'These stories are crazy. Have you read all of them?'

'Pretty much. Grandpa used to read them to me and my cousin, Sonoko, when we were growing up. So did Dad.' She looked again at her grandfather's pen name on the cover peeking out of the pouch in front of Erik, written in black-typed Roman alphabet, but the *kanji* of his name burnt brightly multicoloured characters in her mind. Families! What a mess. 'He would read them to me before bedtime. Grandpa wrote these stories for Sonoko, you know.'

'I read about that in the Foreword.' He touched her arm – he knew how close she and her cousin had been. She pressed her lips together and didn't reply. They both looked at Gen, still sleeping away. After a pause, Erik continued, 'We can read them to this little fellow, when he's old enough. I just read this weird one about a robot cat. What was it with him and cats?'

Ryoko smiled. 'God, he loved them – he was cat mad. He used to say *you can judge a society by how it treats its cats*. I was never sure—'

They were interrupted by the announcement.

'—Ladies and gentlemen, we will soon begin the landing procedure. Please fasten your seatbelts, put away your trays, and return your seats to the upright position. *Mina san, kore kara . . .*'

Ryoko found herself switching off when the Japanese came on. The language felt foreign and alien to her now. Her ears were becoming accustomed to English, and it had begun to feel more natural to her. She preferred it as a language to express her emotions in, and felt like Japanese had always stifled her true feelings. She'd replied to the cabin attendant in English earlier, despite having been addressed in Japanese. She felt silly about it now and it made her turn slightly red with regret, but it seemed like a small act of defiance – *don't classify me based on my appearance*, she'd thought. *What if I was a Chinese-American travelling to Tokyo for the Olympics?* But now she felt sorry for the cabin attendant – she was just doing her job. So what if she'd made an assumption?

Ryoko looked out of the window again at the vast city below.

That terrible, frightful, lonely city. She'd run away from it to be with Erik; to live in New York. It hadn't been since her mum's funeral that she'd come back to the city, and if it wasn't for her dad who still lived there, she would have preferred never to return at all. She'd tried to convince him to move to New York, to live nearer to her, Erik and Gen, but he'd just shake his head on Skype, and that would be the end of that conversation.

The plane banked. She caught sight of a red roof in the Asakusa area, a tiny speck of blood red in the sea of concrete, glass and metal, and then it was gone.

▲
▲▲

'Non-Japanese this way, please,' said the elderly airport attendant in English to Erik, waving people into different lines at immigration. The attendant was standing beneath a huge sign saying:

WELCOME TO TOKYO 2020

The attendant looked at Ryoko, cradling Gen in the sling, and switched to Japanese, '*Nihonjin no kata wa, kochira no retsu ni onegai itashimasu.*'

'What was that last part?' Erik whispered to Ryoko.

'You have to queue up in that line.' Ryoko pointed out the entrance to him. 'I have to go down this line with Gen, cuz we're Japanese. I wish we could all go through the gates together.' It seemed so absurd to her, separating families based on who had what document. What difference did it make that she was born in one place, and Erik in another?

They were a family, and that's what counted.

'No worries, baby. I'll see you two on the other side.' He let go of her hand.

He waved at Gen, who smiled and gurgled.

'Wave to Daddy,' said Ryoko, moving his little hand for him. 'Say *bye bye. See you soon.*'

Gen looked a bit upset at his father walking away, and let out a little cry.

Ryoko bounced him gently. Any sign of distress upset her. Was this typical, or was she overreacting? Had her mother felt the same way when she was a baby? All these questions she hadn't been able to ask, until it was too late. Thinking of her mother made things harder – she pushed the thoughts from her mind. 'Shhh, Gen-chan,' she whispered. 'We'll see him again in a minute.'

She watched Erik walking to the other line for foreigners – incredibly long with all the foreign visitors coming for the Opening Ceremony of the Olympics the next day. The Japanese line was much shorter.

'Oh, babe?' he called out across the barriers that separated the two lines. 'What was *thank you* again?'

'*Arigato gozaimasu,*' she said, speaking clearly so he could copy. An immigration official was staring at them.

'*Arigato gozaimasu,*' he repeated, bowing as he did so. '*Arigato gozaimasu.*'

She smiled. His pronunciation was surprisingly good.

⁂

They grabbed their bags from the carousels and trundled them through customs with no problems. Ryoko was looking out for the signs to the monorail, which would take them to Hamamatsucho Station, where they could switch to the JR Yamanote Line and then ride out west to her father's new place. The gentle chatter of excited Japanese being spoken by the people surrounding her was filling her ears; she couldn't block out all the conversations going on around her, and it was making her feel overwhelmed and dizzy. She had to blink hard to focus.

'Ryoko!' said Erik, tugging on her shirt sleeve.

She turned to see Erik pointing, and her eyes followed in the direction of his finger. Pointing at someone – a man. A man hobbling towards her.

She couldn't help raising a hand to her mouth.

It was the first time she'd seen him in the flesh (so to speak), with his metallic prosthetic leg. He'd not shown it to her on Skype, and hadn't mentioned a word about it either. She'd known from talking over the phone to doctors and nurses at the hospital what had happened, but it still hadn't prepared her for the reality. She felt ashamed, not just at how shocked she felt on the inside, but how she had let it show in her reaction. She should've been here for him, when it happened. Why had it taken her so long to visit? She felt her face reddening with shame.

'Ryo-chan!' he called out. He waved his hand frantically, and was grinning from ear to ear smiling at Gen. He rushed past Erik and kissed Ryoko on the cheek, all the while beaming at Gen. 'Okaeri nasai,' – welcome home – he whispered.

She felt a tear forming in her eye, and a lump in her throat. 'Tadaima,' – I'm home – was all she could say.

Her dad suddenly realized he had ignored Erik, and turned to shake hands, while Erik was bowing in greeting. And so they went back and forth a number of times in a funny little dance, unsure whether to shake hands or bow.

Eventually, her father grasped Erik in a strong hug and spoke in English, 'Erik-san! Welcome!'

'Hello, Taro-san.' Erik turned to Ryoko awkwardly. 'Uh . . . babe . . . what was *long time no see* again . . . ? No. Wait. I got it!' He looked back at her father again and spoke clearly. '*Hisashiburi!*'

'Yes! *Hisashiburi*, Erik-san. Your Japanese . . . very good!'

'No, it's terrible.' Erik scratched his cheek in a self-conscious manner. 'I forget everything.'

'You know . . . best way . . . improve Japanese?' asked Taro.

'No,' said Erik. 'How?'

'Shochu,' said Taro, miming drinking from a cup. 'Or beer!'

They both laughed.

Ryoko smiled to see them communicating well, despite the language barrier.

Her dad turned back to her and Gen, tickling him under the chin while he spoke in Japanese. 'Look at him . . . my grandson! What a handsome young fellow! Look at his eyes – and that nose! Come on, this way.'

'Dad . . . I told you, you didn't have to come,' replied Ryoko in Japanese. 'We could've taken the train.'

'With little Gen? And these big suitcases? No way.' Taro shook his head. 'Much easier in the cab.'

'You brought the taxi?' asked Ryoko.

Taro looked at her, ignoring the subtext screaming out loud in her question.

But, how can you still drive with just one leg?

'Of course!' he said, grabbing her suitcase handle and pulling it expertly. He switched back to English. 'Erik-san. Follow me. My taxi . . . this way!'

▲
▲▲

'Erik-san! Look!' Taro pointed out of the taxi window. 'Tokyo Tower!'

'*Sugoi desu ne!*' said Erik, trying out the Japanese Ryoko had taught him on the plane earlier: *brilliant, isn't it!*

Ryoko watched her father, driving effortlessly with a happy look on his face. She clutched Gen close to her, while Taro and Erik chatted away in the front. How silly of her not to think of it – he still had his right leg. His prosthetic left leg rested idly in the footwell, and he only needed to use his right leg for the brake and gas. Lucky that he was a Japanese taxi driver and not a European one – there's no way he could've carried on driving in a manual car. But Americans and Japanese favoured automatics. She studied a newspaper article taped up on the back seat with a photo of Taro standing proudly in front of his cab with his metallic leg. The headline read: TOKYO'S ONE-LEGGED TAXI DRIVER!

The traffic was heavy today, but her father knew all of the backroads and shortcuts. He knew the city so well – no wonder he didn't want to leave. He drove in that same careful manner he always did, but something told her that there was an extra smoothness to his driving today, especially for Gen.

Ryoko felt a heaviness in her eyelids. Gen was snoozing again, and the light outside made her feel woozy. Her nervous excitement was giving way to jet lag. But she didn't want to fall asleep. She wanted to watch her father and Erik getting along. She felt so proud of both of them.

She looked at sleeping Gen. *See, Gen. This is how you should grow up to be.* She thought the words as hard as she could, projecting them forcefully out from her eyes, as though she could make the words come to life, to form a protective barrier around her son as he slept. *Watch and learn from them, and one day you'll be a good man, too. Be a good person, Gen. Learn from them, and you won't ever be like your uncle.*

⁂

They arrived back at Taro's house after the long drive and parked up the cab in the covered driveway. Taro insisted on taking the bags in by himself. He made Erik take Ryoko inside first with Gen, as both of them were stumbling and sleepy.

'Go take a nap,' said Taro, pulling their heavy suitcases out of the boot with ease. 'I've put you in my room upstairs. I've set up a cot for Gen in there because there's more space. I'll sleep in the room downstairs. Go on! Inside!'

Erik took Gen and went straight upstairs, no questions asked. Ryoko hovered in the hallway wanting to talk to her dad.

'What are you doing here still?' He came inside with the bags and put them in the hallway. 'Off to bed. We can chat in the morning.'

She stifled a yawn. 'Night, Dad.'

'Goodnight, Ryo-chan. It's good to have you home.'

As she headed up the stairs, she was surprised to see the light coming through the crack under the door of the downstairs bed-room. Her father must be getting old if he was forgetting to turn off lights.

She fell fast asleep, to the gentle sounds of Erik and Gen snoring in tandem, with occasional clacking footsteps coming from below.

⁂

Ryoko woke early upon hearing Gen stirring. She got out of bed and scooped him out of his cot, leaving Erik to sleep. She padded lightly down the stairs with Gen, being careful not to wake anyone. Picking up the newspaper, she went into the kitchen and shut the door. After feeding Gen, she made some coffee. Today was the day of the Opening Ceremony.

Ryoko poured herself a cup of black coffee and sat down at the kitchen table with the paper.

She flicked through pages of articles relating to the Olympics.

When she reached this headline, she paused:

FAMOUS ASAKUSA TATTOIST FOUND DEAD

Ojima Kentaro 46 Male (pictured) was found dead in his tattoo parlour in Asakusa yesterday. The reclusive tattooist was renowned amongst his peers as one of the finest artists in the Asakusa area and the police are calling for members of the community who may know anything to come forward.

Sergeant Fukuyama of the Tokyo Metropolitan Police denied rumours of a knife being found in the tattooist's back, encouraging members of the township to avoid both 'speculation' and 'gossip' surrounding the matter. He commented: 'We are currently conducting a thorough investigation into the incident.'

She made a mental note to show this to Erik later. She'd translate it for him. He loved to talk about how much 'safer' Japan was than the US, with its strict gun laws and low crime rate. *See?* she would tell him. *Japan's not all it's cracked up to be. It's not perfect. Nowhere is (. . . and neither am I)*. She would keep that last bit to herself.

The kitchen door opened, and her father came in rubbing sleep from his eyes.

'Morning,' he said, coming over to tickle Gen behind the ear.

'Morning.' She gave him Gen to hold, got a mug out of the cupboard, and poured another cup of black coffee before handing it to her father.

'Thank you.' He took the cup with his free hand, while pulling a funny face at Gen. He looked at the table and caught sight of the paper Ryoko had been studying. 'We'll have to save that paper as a souvenir. It's not often Tokyo has the Olympics! Last time was in '64. Before you were born! Just think, little Gen here will grow up having been here for Tokyo 2020.'

Ryoko took a sip of coffee. 'Have you been shopping recently? There's not much in the fridge.' She laughed nervously. Why was she finding it so stressful to speak in Japanese? She felt like a completely different person. She was trying to tease him like she used to, but speaking Japanese again made her worry about formality.

'Less of your cheek,' said Taro. She felt relieved he'd seen she was joking. 'We can pop to the shop in a bit when Erik wakes up, can't we, eh? Gen?' He looked at Gen, then looked up at the ceiling as if remembering something. 'What does Erik eat?'

'He eats anything and everything.'

'Good lad. Nothing worse than a fussy eater.'

They sat there for a while in awkward silence. Ryoko studied her hands. Taro was blowing raspberries at Gen, who each time would let out a gurgle and a giggle, causing his grandfather to laugh too.

She felt like making fun of Taro a bit more.

'You know you left the downstairs light on yesterday? When you came to the airport to get us.' Ryoko shook her head. 'Someone's going senile . . .'

He didn't smile or laugh this time. Was her humour off? Had she upset him? Was something seriously wrong? Her stomach thudded. He put his coffee cup down, and shifted Gen to his other arm. 'Ryoko . . . There's something I have to tell you.'

She looked at him. There was something in his voice that demanded attention.

'I'm sorry I didn't tell you sooner, but you and Erik were so tired from your trip. And . . . well, I should probably tell you now. Maybe it's easier if I show you.'

He stood up slowly, using the edge of the table to push himself upwards with his free hand.

'Follow me.'

Her father left the kitchen, and she followed behind, trailing the clacking sound of his leg on the floor. The corridor was still slightly dark, as there were no windows. He led her to the door of the downstairs bedroom and knocked gently.

A low voice spoke from the other side: 'Come in.'

Her father opened the door and gestured for her to step through.

She walked into the room. The inside of her body had become very still and quiet. There was the outline of a person sitting on the floor before her, hunched in front of a *kotatsu* low table. Two sets of futon were folded and placed at the foot of the cupboard, ready to put away for the day.

The man sitting at the *kotatsu* got to his knees.

'Ryoko-chan,' he said.

She stared. She couldn't speak.

'Ryoko-chan.' The man bowed low, his head touching the tatami, and his voice trembled. 'I'm sorry.'

'Ryo-chan . . .' Her father's voice this time. 'We . . .'

She shook her head.

The man on the floor looked up at her nervously.

How dare he. How dare he come back.

Ryoko walked past him to the sliding screen door. Her father was holding Gen, and she wanted desperately to take him back in her arms and leave the room. But she felt trapped. She could feel her father's and uncle's eyes on her back, and she knew they were expecting a response. But what was that response going to be? She just wanted to take Gen and Erik and get away from this situation. Back to New York, away from all this pain and confusion. Back to where things were simple.

After all he did. How *dare* he.

She slid the screen door open and stepped outside into the garden, shutting it behind her.

The garden was smaller than the one at the old house in Nakano.

The sun was just coming up, and Ryoko looked out over the roofs of the low houses towards the skyscrapers in the distance. She heard a soft mewing sound, and looked down to see a small calico cat rubbing up against her legs. She knelt down to stroke the cat, and it purred with pleasure as she did so.

'What a mess, eh, little puss?' The cat looked up at her with its strange green eyes. She noticed blood on the white parts of its coat. 'You've been fighting, too, haven't you?'

The cat mewed as her fingers caressed its soft fur.

Ryoko studied the cat – it looked exactly like her grandfather's favourite cat, Naomi. Sonoko had loved that cat too. She would beg Grandpa to let her sleep in the futon with them when they were little.

The cat would crawl under their covers, especially in the winter, to keep warm. Its favourite place had been between Sonoko's legs. Little Sonoko, who'd died without her father nearby. And now here he was – come back, expecting forgiveness. Well, he could rot in hell.

The sliding door opened behind her, but she didn't turn around to see who it was.

'Babe?' Her heart fluttered a little when she heard Erik's voice.

The cat was startled by Erik and jumped up onto the low garden wall, but stayed there watching. Waiting.

She turned to see Erik, with Gen in his sling. He was carrying two cups of coffee, and he handed one to her. She took it, and sipped. It was cold now, and bitter.

'Everything okay?' He studied her face. 'Your dad told me to come out to talk to you.'

'Not really . . .'

'I'm guessing that's your Uncle Ichiro?' He flicked his head in the direction of the house.

'Yeah.'

'Hmmm.' Erik sat down on the step, put his coffee down and bounced Gen gently.

'I don't know what to do.' Looking at Gen's peaceful face calmed her slightly.

'We can leave, if you want to,' said Erik, suddenly. 'You don't have to deal with this.'

She pictured leaving the house with Erik and Gen, but then she thought about her father, and how he would feel. 'I can't do that to Dad.'

'Yeah . . .' Erik paused. 'Have you spoken to your uncle?'

'I don't want to.'

'Maybe you should? Even if it's to tell him what you think.'

'You don't understand, Erik.' Her heart was beating faster. She felt her blood rising, and shook her head roughly as she spoke. 'It's not your family. It's not your culture. It's not your business. You don't understand Japan.'

'I'm sorry,' he said calmly. 'I'm not telling you what to do. There's a lot about Japan I don't understand.' He paused, and then continued choosing his words extremely carefully. 'But I do know *people*. And how can any of us understand anything, unless we talk, unless we listen to each other? I'm sure he's got a story to tell you, but, more importantly, he should listen to *your* story. He needs to know how you feel.' He grasped her shoulder in his big hand and caressed it tenderly. 'None of this is your fault, Ryoko. And I'm on *your* side, *always*. Whatever you want to do, I support your decision.'

'I'm sorry, Erik.' A tear formed in her eye, and she wiped it away. 'I shouldn't take this out on you. I'll talk to him.'

'Come in when you're ready – take all the time you need.' Erik stood up, and walked to the screen door.

'No, wait.' She looked up at Erik, who paused at the door. She took a deep breath and carried on. 'I want to talk to him outside. Here, in the garden. It seems more appropriate.' She stood up. 'Can you tell Dad to send him out here?'

'Sure.'

Erik went inside and shut the screen door. The cat was still sitting on the wall, watching.

Ryoko stepped away from the house, and walked to the pond. She looked down at the water and saw shafts of golden morning light reflected off the surface. The glittering koi carp swam sleepily in between the light and shade.

A truly dark and terrible thought entered her mind. She could leave now. By herself. She could climb the garden wall and disappear forever. She didn't have to deal with any of this mess; she could be alone, and be free. She could be like the stray cat perched up on the wall looking at her now – she could lose herself in the city. Then she would become what she truly hated.

She would be just like *him*.

She heard the screen door open.

Ryoko closed her eyes, and as she did so, images of Tokyo flashed through her mind. She suddenly became aware of the millions and millions of lives surrounding her. All these lives, all these dramas. All those families, locked inside themselves. She saw them clearly and the Olympic stadium growing and growing over the years, the buildings of the city blossoming and withering like flowers from the swamps of Edo, continuing on and on until the end of time.

This city never stopped, just kept moving forward without a care.

She tried to open her eyes, but couldn't. For when she opened them, she'd be faced with a very real problem, and one she alone had to deal with. She kept her eyes shut tightly, and in her head the throb of her pulse roared, and she heard the city screaming in the background. All these poor, lonely, damaged people. Locked inside their own private prisons.

Screaming in her head, in a voice that was many and one and the same. A voice that was hers, that she was part of. She and them, those millions and millions of people, moving in and around, through subway stations and buildings, parks and highways, living their lives. The city pumped their shit around in pipes, it transported their bodies around in metal containers, and it held their secrets, their hopes, their dreams, their pain, their agony.

Because she was a part of it too, wasn't she? She was connected to it all, and always would be. Even hiding on the other side of her laptop screen on Skype, thousands of miles away, couldn't change that. She was Tokyo.

She took a deep breath and opened her eyes. She turned around. Her uncle was kneeling under the cherry tree – younger than the old one at the house in Nakano. Its leaves were a summer green now, but in the autumn they would fall to the ground and rot; in the winter its branches would be covered with snow, but in the spring it would blossom again. She looked at his face. A tear was rolling down his cheek. The teardrop had split, and divided into two streams. He looked old and thin; he was missing teeth.

A person. Just like her. Just like everyone. Lost and alone.

Her hands were still shaking as she clasped them together. She knelt in front of him, in the customary stance of the *rakugoka* storyteller. Now it was his turn to listen. But her story was not funny; there would be no comic twist. She would tell him the very real story of how he'd broken their family, how he'd abandoned her cousin to die, how he had hurt her father. She would tell him how much she hated him, and how she hadn't forgiven him, and perhaps never would, but that she had a son now, and how she saw her uncle's face in Gen, and how families should forgive, and that maybe, just maybe, one day, if he started to act the part he was supposed to play in this family, maybe on that day she would forgive him.

But before she could begin her story, she was duty-bound to say something to him. This was Japanese culture, and no matter how long she lived in New York, this would always be a part of her. She bowed low to her uncle, touching her head to the ground. But she spoke loudly, clearly, with unshaking confidence.

'*Okaeri nasai.*' Welcome home.

He bowed low in response, and another teardrop hit the grass. '*Tadaima.*'

'Now, listen to me.'

⚎

The muscles in the cat's back flexed and came to life.

It suddenly grew tired of watching the girl talking to the purple-headed man. Its business was done here; it had seen enough. It stood up and leapt lazily onto a neighbouring roof then walked away slowly over the rooftops in the morning light.

Lost once again, into the city.

Acknowledgements

Phew! What a long journey it is, from puffing out your chest as a child and declaring boldly, 'I want to be a writer!' to publishing your very first book. Luckily, on a long journey you meet a lot of fantastic helpful people, all of whom I would like to thank. So bear with me.

First off, thank you to my amazing editor, Poppy Mostyn-Owen. This book was a mess, but you've fixed so many of the broken parts, and it wouldn't be what it is without your help. I cannot begin to describe how much you've helped me, especially for indulging me with my insane ideas involving footnotes, photographs, manga, and my terrible sense of humour. 'Opening Ceremony' is for you. My agent, Ed Wilson, for being so brilliant, chipper, and enthusiastic right from the first moment we met in Foyles – thank you, Ed. Also, thank you to Helene Butler at J&A. Mariko Aruga for her delightful manga strip. Tamsin Shelton for her eagle-eyed copyediting. Carmen Balit for the wonderful cat cover. All at Atlantic for being so passionate, friendly, and welcoming.

Giles Foden and Stephen Benson deserve enormous thanks. Giles, so much of this book began with you. Stephen, your support and advice throughout this period of my life has been invaluable. Thank you both.

And to all of my teachers: Trezza Azzopardi (you were right), Vesna Goldsworthy (you were right, too), Amit Chaudhuri, Henry Sutton, Philip Langeskov, Anna Metcalfe, Jon Cook, and all on the MA programme & PhD crew, massive thanks to you all. Many thanks to The Great Britain Sasakawa Foundation for their help and support throughout the writing of this book, and my PhD.

The next group of people helped me out incredibly – probably in ways they didn't even notice. Thank you: Dennis Horton, Calvin Ching, Brian Blanchard, Theresa Wang, James Philip (what's your name, boy?), Alexis McDonnell, Tim Yellowhammer, Ash Jones, Ryan Benton, Si Carter, Jon Ford, Bobo, Philbo, Slimer, Anda, The Claw, Stupot, Rufus, Garman, Cheese, Suzie Crossland, Andre Gushurst-Moore, Nigel Millington, Stephen Buglass, Carla Spradbery, Cherry Cheung, Shaun Browne, Neil Docking, Michael Rands, Maki Koyama, Chris Amblin, Ayu Okakita, Seb Dehesdin, Yoko Tamai, Sarang Narumi, Vincent Gillespie, Jill Rudd, Brendan Griggs, Matsu, Hori-san, Tsuruoka-sensei, and the real Ogawa-sensei. To the memory of one of my first ever writing partners, Luke McDuff.

Thank you to the following for being willing readers, and excellent advisers: Hiroko Asago, Jacob Rollinson, Paul Cooper, Matthew Blackman, Naomi Ishiguro, Susan Burton, Deepa Anappara, Ross Benar, Dave Lynch, Felicity Notley, Rowan Hisayo Buchanan, Lizzie Briggs, Sara Sha'ath, Sam West, Will Nott, Sharlene Teo, and Elyssa.

Gushy, emotional and familial thanks go to all the loudmouthed Bradleys: Dad (this book is especially for you), Mum (thank you, always), Bob ('Copy Cat' is for you), Tim (you get nothing, and lots of it), AJ, Clare, Meg, Molly, Floss, Lizzie (to the souls of Grandma, Grandpa, Uncle Bob, Tom, Jake, Suzie, and Tess RIP). Many thanks to Nana & Gramps, the Compsty crew. Equally emotional thanks to Douglas, Jacqui, Daniel, Bethy, Thomas, and Edgar. Thank you also to Mummy & Willie, and Granny and Grandpa Osmaston, in spirit.

Any mistakes in the translation of the poem 'Aoneko' by Hagiwara Sakutaro used as the epigraph are my own poetic licence (I'm sure Flo would have done a better job – please e-mail her to tell her), as are the (most likely) numerous errors made in the text itself. For these, I apologize, and plead human error rather than ignorance or lack of care. The book *Poor People* by William T. Vollman was invaluable for the writing of 'Fallen Words', as was Kon Satoshi's anime film *Tokyo Godfathers*. I must also mention a documentary film which can be found on YouTube called 'SANYA, Tokyo, Broken city' as a valuable resource. The two haiku George reads in his poetry book are unaccredited in the text, but are respectively by Matsuo Basho and Natsume Soseki (the godfather of Japanese cat books himself).

I would also like to thank, alongside the vast array of directors, musicians, writers, and artists who inspire me every day (there are too many to list here), all of the wonderful and welcoming Japanese people who I have met over the years, who have inspired me with their explanations and stories of a country I long ago grew to love.

Finally, this book certainly wouldn't exist without Julie Neko, and Pansy Pusskins (my mews).